The Conscience of Love

The Conscience of Love

MARCEL AYMÉ

Translated from the French by
NORMAN DENNY

ATHENEUM

NEW YORK

1962

3549 Atheneum 9-10 (12) Bembo by 17 picas

First published in France in 1960 by Librairie Gallimard as LES TIROIRS DE L' INCONNU; *copyright © 1960 by Librairie Gallimard; all rights reserved. English translation by Norman Denny copyright © 1962 by The Bodley Head Ltd.; all rights reserved. Library of Congress catalog card number 62–9410. Printed in the United States of America by The Murray Printing Company, Forge Village, Massachusetts. Bound by H. Wolff, New York.* FIRST AMERICAN EDITION

The Conscience of Love

II

MY name is Martin. I am twenty-eight. Returning home unexpectedly one afternoon I found my brother and my fiancée asleep together in my bed. For the moment I controlled myself. I left the apartment without waking them and started to walk downstairs, meaning to go out and think the matter over in the street. But on the next landing, the fifth, I encountered Chazard, a quarrelsome man who lived below us and was always complaining of the noise that went on over his head. He did so now, with his usual vehemence, and when I tried to pass on without taking any notice he grabbed me by the lapel of my jacket. Then I went berserk. I turned and punched him on the jaw, and when he kicked me on the shin I heaved him over the banisters so that he fell to the bottom of the stairway. He uttered a scream that must have been heard by everyone in the building and died the instant he reached the ground floor, his skull shattered on the stone flags.

The doctors, inquiring into my mental state, decided that it was a case of diminished responsibility, so I got off with only two years' imprisonment. I came out of prison on a morning in October, and at about six o'clock the same afternoon I ran into Tatiana Bouvillon under the arcade in the Rue de Castiglione. I was walking furtively with my head bowed and my shoulders hunched, feeling that everyone must recognise me at once as a convicted criminal, perhaps even as a murderer. I believe men commonly have this sensation on their first day of release from prison, but women, it seems, are less prone to it. Tatiana saw me first and came running towards me with her arms outstretched, causing my name to echo under the vaulting with her deep, sonorous voice. I panicked and would have run

7

away if I could, but in another instant she was vigorously embracing me.

'So you're really out! When?'

'This morning,' I muttered, not looking at her.

Only then did she become aware of my shrinking posture and the hangdog air which, as she told me afterwards, she thought was due to shame and contrition. She hugged me again, calling me poor darling, and gave me a hefty bang on the back to drive penitence down to my heels. She was extremely beautiful and these effusions attracted the notice of the passers-by. I had no need of an audience to tell me how intriguing this encounter with a young woman like Tatiana must appear in the eyes of an onlooker. On her stiletto-heels she was nearly three inches taller than I, and the sway of her body in her well-cut suit, her red hair twisted with seeming casualness on the nape of her neck, her big laughing mouth and bold eyes—everything about her clashed with my own aspect. Short, thick-set and heavy shouldered, surly of countenance and badly dressed into the bargain, I looked like a chestnut-vendor. I still do and I always will, even dressed in the height of fashion. I said to Tatiana:

'It's nice meeting you, but my brother's waiting for me. I'll be seeing you.'

Yet I would have liked to stay and talk to her. She was two years younger than I and had been born in the house where I had lived all my life, and where she herself had lived until she was thirteen. When I was in custody awaiting trial she had got in touch with my lawyer and had visited me several times. But at the moment my nerves were quivering. Two elderly English ladies, coming out of a shop, glared fiercely at me, as though outraged by my very presence in that fashionable part of the town.

'Martin! Martin!'

I had started to run like a man gone mad, terrified by the

8

eyes and at the same time conscious of the absurdity of my behaviour. I knew perfectly well that there could be no better way of attracting notice than by taking to my heels like this. Simply to run was bad enough, but in addition I was carrying a small suitcase, the one I had brought with me from prison, so that even the most indifferent bystander would be likely to assume that I was a thief caught in the act and bolting with the loot. When this thought occurred to me I stopped dead, afraid even to move. Feeling that the whole world was against me I stood awaiting the *coup de grâce*, Fate's final, lethal blow; and Tatiana caught up with me and slipped her arm through mine.

'I'm on my way home. I was going to buy a brooch that I saw in a window yesterday, but after all I don't think I want it. Martin, I've treated you so badly. I didn't come to see you once in all those two years, although I promised. And I haven't written for ages. Are you angry with me?'

I pressed her hand. She led me towards the Rue de Rivoli without letting go my arm, and to make still more sure that I did not escape she took my suitcase.

'There were reasons. I was working terribly hard and not getting anywhere. I'm going to take you home with me. I'm dining out tonight, but I'll try to get back early, and anyway I'll wake you up so that we can talk. There's so much to say. For instance, I——'

We had reached the edge of the pavement. Tatiana broke off in mid-sentence, pulled off her glove and with two fingers in her mouth blew a blast which caused twenty vehicles to slow and a taxi across the street to pull up sharply. She glanced at me smiling to remind me that the art of whistling with two fingers was one of the things I had taught her. We ran across, and when we were in the cab she went on:

'Of course you don't know that I flunked my honours degree. Two years running. You can't think what it was like, the life I lived during those two years, teaching maths in a

9

private school five hours a day, and private pupils as well, and correcting exercises at night, and then working for my finals till three and four in the morning. I may be as strong as a horse but I almost killed myself. Why are you laughing?'

I had laughed without knowing that I did so. Seated in the small, enclosed box of the taxi, which had about it something of the prison flavour that I still missed, I no longer felt the dizzy sense of insecurity by which I had been tormented during the past few hours of wandering through the streets. The crowd jostling on the pavements was no more than a surrounding surge of movement, hostile and malignant no doubt, but kept securely within bounds and not dangerous to me. There was one moment, however, when I had a return of panic. The cab had been brought to an abrupt stop at a pedestrian crossing. People swarmed across, dodging in front of us and picking their way between the vehicles; and a woman with a face like a lizard stopped for a moment with her nose almost touching the window and proceeded coolly to examine us.

'Maths . . .' said Tatiana. 'I stuffed myself with maths till I almost choked. I so longed to get a good degree because it meant security, a safe, steady job and a pension at the end. Yes, I even thought of the pension. That's the prudent side of me, the money-in-the-bank side. I'm a daughter of the steppes, but also of a little employee with a neat moustache. But the thought of another year like that was more than I could bear. Of course I could have got a teaching job in a girls' school somewhere—thanks very much! So I chucked it up and now I'm fashion modelling for Orsini. I may say that it isn't the most restful of jobs.'

Tatiana went on to discourse at length about the advantages and tribulations of her new calling, talking entirely about herself so as not to have to talk about me. She evidently felt that the time was not yet ripe for ticklish matters, and that the way must be paved and a suitable atmosphere prepared. Finally it was I who changed the subject, when we were held up in a traffic-block on the near side of the Place Clichy and she was clearly beginning to run out of conversation.

'I said my brother was expecting me. It isn't true.'

'You'd no need to tell me that.'

'Have you seen him?'

'Not for about six months. I ran into him one evening in Montparnasse. He said he was trying to get a job as a ticket-collector on the railways.' She paused and then said in a cold voice: 'I was surprised to hear that he hadn't once been to see you or answered any of your letters. He told me so without seeming to care in the least.'

'Well, Michel's like that, thoroughly lazy and neglectful. But really he——'

'Really your brother's nothing but a monster. My poor idiot, don't you know that he's been living with Valérie for the last two years? It's about time someone told you. . . . Well, don't you mind?'

Tatiana did not know that I had found them in bed before I killed Chazard. I had not told anyone of this, not even my lawyer. The traffic-block had now cleared and we were moving on again. It had begun to rain. Turning away from her towards the window I stared out at the raindrops in the lights of the Place Clichy and thought of Michel and the vegetable existence to which he must have condemned himself when he settled down with Valérie. I could feel Tatiana's disapproving gaze on the back of my head—she probably wanted to shake me. The taxi put us down in the Rue Eugène-Carrière and we climbed the six flights of stairs. On the third-floor landing Tatiana made me stop, and taking me by the hand said in a low voice:

'Martin, you're not being silly, are you? You're not still full of remorse for what happened to Chazard?'

11

'Oh, no,' I said.

The reply came so promptly to my lips that I felt slightly embarrassed and was tempted to add something in extenuation. The truth is that I had never felt any real remorse but simply compassion for the victim and extreme regret for the sudden impulse of rage that had had such disastrous results. Neither by day nor by night had the ghost of Chazard come to haunt me. Indeed I had been a good deal troubled by the apathy of my own conscience, which I think I can explain, although the reasons are not an excuse. The way the thing happened was in itself something that relieved my mind, because I am almost certain that I had had no intention of committing murder. The fact that Chazard was fifty-nine was another consolation. However I may struggle against it, I cannot get it out of my head that the place of elderly people, those over fifty, is no longer on this earth, and that they have nothing to offer us but the spectacle of their physical ugliness and cheeseparing morality. Finally, Chazard had done eight months in prison for collaboration with the Germans during the war, and the FFI men who came to arrest him had beaten and spat on him. He was probably innocent, because in the end he was released for lack of evidence, but the beating and spitting, the obscure misfortune that led to his arrest, had, against all justice, rendered him suspect and unclean in my eyes. Both before and after my crime I had tried to see the case impartially, to establish a fair judgement in my own mind, but I was never able to think of Chazard except as a thoroughly unpleasant person. With this Tatiana was in vigorous agreement, and she had rejoiced aloud over what she termed his 'accident'.

'You know he was an old beast. Whenever I met him on the stairs, when I was a child, he'd try to put his hand up my skirt. It was always happening.'

I was most happy to hear this, since it afforded moral substance and warrant for my dislike of the man.

12

When we entered the apartment we found Madame Bouvillon, Tatiana's mother, on her knees on the sitting-room floor reading a book. She was a woman of something over fifty who in no way resembled her daughter. Her face had grown puffy but there was nothing in it to suggest past good looks, and indeed, going back as far as I can recall, I cannot remember that she was ever handsome. She had soft, gentle eyes and talked with a tranquil simplicity, pursuing every digression that entered her head. She got up to welcome us and when Tatiana told her who I was her face lightened, although she clearly did not recognise me and the name of Martin touched no chord in her memory. However, she seemed to find my presence quite natural.

'I'm glad you're home early,' she said to Tatiana. 'Today is the anniversary of your poor father's death.'

'Mother, what are you talking about? I'm always telling you that father died on the seventeenth of July.'

Madame Bouvillon agreed that this was so but went on talking as though it were not.

'The poor man. It's so sad to die in winter with the rain falling. The coffin goes down into the damp earth and it makes you shiver to think of that poor, cold body. It was raining on the day he first spoke to me, in 1919, near the Galeries Lafayette. Adrien. . . . He was wearing a beautiful lieutenant's uniform— or no, I think he was a warrant-officer. Yes, a warrant-officer. He was a hero and he had a row of decorations. There was one medal in particular, a yellow one——'

'The *médaille militaire*.'

'Yes, military. I lost it when we moved into the Rue des Dames or else into the Rue d'Alésia. He came up to me and I thought it was so nice of him to come and speak to a poor refugee girl in the street, but the first thing I told him about myself was a lie. He was astonished at how well I spoke French, and although I was only the daughter of a small linen-draper in

Kharkov, who did a bit of money-lending on the side, I told him that in the great Russian families everybody spoke fluent French and that my father was a count. Perhaps God whispered that fib in my ear, because Adrien had been meaning to take me straight to a hotel, but after that he gave up the idea, when he heard I was the daughter of a count. He was so proud of me always, I never dared tell him the truth.'

'Mother, you mustn't bore Martin with the story of your marriage. Go and get supper.'

When her mother had gone into the kitchen Tatiana led me into her bedroom, which was very small and plainly furnished. There was a photograph on the wall of Katia, her elder sister, who was killed by a machine-gun bullet in 1940, on one of the evacuation roads. My recollection of Katia as a girl was overlaid by the thought of her death, which had left a harsh picture in my mind, that of a figure shadowed from birth by the tragic destiny that overtook her. While I stood staring at the photograph Tatiana began to undress behind my back and I was rather troubled by her nearness. I could see the shadow of her nakedness reflected in the glass, and I thought that if I were to turn suddenly and press my face to her body she would not take it very much amiss.

'You can turn round now, I've got my peignoir on. Did I tell you—Christine's trying to marry me off.'

'Christine?'

'The Comtesse de Rézé—I'm dining with them tonight. She was a model with me at Orsini's, and she married de Rézé in the spring and now she wants to marry me into the same set. It's not my cup of tea. To be part of the decorations in a rich man's house—not bloody likely! All the same, I do want to get married. What I want is a man I can work with, do difficult things with, the sort that need patience and staying-power and may even force you to give up everything else. Of course, *you* can't offer me anything like that, and yet you're exactly the

14

type—hard-working and stubborn, like I am. I'd be ready to marry you if you felt like it.'

'You're joking.'

'Wait a minute. I'm going into the kitchen. There are no washing facilities in this apartment. We have to use the sink.'

I glanced again at the picture of Katia. Between the bed and the window there was another photograph, that of Tatiana herself at the age of thirteen, thin-faced, resolute and almost boyish despite the hair falling over her shoulders. It must have been taken shortly before the death of their father, during the Occupation. Lying in the hospital where he had been taken after the accident which cost him his life, he had said to Tatiana, 'I leave your mother in your care.' She had left school at once and had worked as a packer, as a delivery-girl on a bicycle and later as a typist, while she still went on with her studies at home in the evening. For two years I had helped her with these, and in doing so I had learnt to admire her strength of character and sense of duty towards both her mother and herself. When I was forced to break off my own studies in order to earn a living and look after my younger brother our meetings had become less frequent; I had seen her only at rare intervals, always hard at work, tense with the struggle, never taking time to be pretty. So the news that she was now a fashion model, which I considered a frivolous calling, the complete change in her appearance and above all this apparent emptiness of mind which was so contrary to everything I had known of her, had come as a shock to me, as though it were a renouncement of all that was best in her. She came back from the kitchen and I turned away again while she put on her dress. While she was making up her eyes at a mirror fixed to the window-fastening she proceeded to sum up the problem of marriage as it affected her, letting fall occasional details of her love-life. She was bending forward, too intent upon her lashes to pay much attention to what she was saying, so that she spoke with complete honesty, as though it were an act of self-communion while she looked herself in the eyes.

'I'm not making a song and dance about it, but I'm blessed if I see many women who are as attractive as I am. And yet my experience of love amounts to precious little. When I was working like mad I hadn't time to think about it. Sex seemed just a nonsense to me, a bit of fun that I had now and then. Since I was eighteen I've steered well clear of the sort of young chaps who are always grabbing at your skirts and only want to waste your time. Older men are better. They have their work and their friends, and they don't want anyone clinging round their neck. To them women are like scent, you must only use a little. And I think they're afraid they'll get sick of them if they see them too much. But when I went into modelling my ideas changed. I had more spare time and I began to learn how to dress, and so the men started to take notice. So then I began hoping for a great love-affair, a real romance. I wanted a young man, handsome and hot-blooded, who would live for me alone. Well, I found one. He was as beautiful as a god, and elegant and frantic, steeped in passion and romance. I got rid of him last week, after a furious scene. I couldn't take it any longer. All that wrestling, and the passion and the stickiness, and the tempests and the quiverings, in the end it made me sick. Love and love alone—to me it's like some ghastly piece of machinery spinning in a vacuum. During the Occupation, in the spring of '44, I made a trip to Vendôme, delivering a package of fifty dozen pairs of braces to earn two hundred francs. On the way back the train came to a stop somewhere in the country, and in a field by the track I saw a woman harnessed to a plough. She didn't care who saw her. She was leaning forward with the leather strap digging into her breasts and her mouth twisted with the effort she was making. And the man holding the handles had his head down and was trying to push the plough as well as guide it. He called out, "Jeanne!", and

16

they stopped to rest, and she turned and they looked at one another and at the furrows they had ploughed. The sweat was running down their faces. Then they went on again. I've often thought of those two and envied them. You know, Martin, love, it isn't just getting your knees apart, and the moans and the ecstasies and the thirty-six varieties of rapture. Love, real love—it's that plough!'

I said, 'Yes, surely,' without being sure of anything. Presented in these terms the problem was beyond me, or at least it had found me at a loss. While Tatiana pencilled her eyebrows I thought it over and said:

'Frankly, I don't think I could ever get carried away by this plough-love of yours. Put yourself in my place and think what I'm in for—a third-rate job in an office or factory, long hours and low wages and having to watch every penny, and on top of that the sort of troubles an ex-convict has to expect. I killed a man, remember. You must see that for me love has got to be something separate from everyday life, like a bunch of flowers that you keep hidden away to smell in private, precisely in order to forget the daily round.'

'Dear Martin, the first thing you have to forget is that Chazard business and everything that happened. If you get it into your head that you're a sort of pariah you'll never really escape from prison. So you killed a man! It isn't going to stop you living, and above all it's no reason for being afraid of love. How do you like my dress? The manageress lent it to me for this evening.'

The dress was a black sheath rising up to her chin. I seem to remember that there was some sort of pleating in the shape of a fan, but I don't know if it was at the waist or the hips.

'It suits you wonderfully.'

'The thing I'm worried about is my coat. It's so shabby. Luckily Janick has lent me a stole which isn't quite right for the time of year but at least won't make me look ridiculous. I may

17

say that the matter of a winter coat is very much on my mind. You've no need to tell me that I'm silly and that one ought not to fuss so much about clothes. I know it, and I also know why women marry or become whores. Well, now I'm off. I'll see you later.'

The soup was burnt, the omelette too salty and the wine sour. Madame Bouvillon, still celebrating the memory of the deceased, noticed nothing and ate with a solid appetite.

'. . . Just once, but only once, I went to the Samaritaine and watched Adrien at work without letting him see me. He was head of the laces and ribbons department, always very friendly and polite with the customers but terribly hard on the poor sales-girls I thought, standing on their feet all day long and earning so little that they could scarcely live. When I got home I cried, I was so ashamed of being married to a man who was so hard on poor working-girls. I should have told myself that it was the job that made him like that, and perhaps it wasn't the job he would have chosen. But there was one girl, a pretty little thing called Fernande, that he wasn't hard on because he slept with her. I knew Adrien was often unfaithful to me. And I wasn't ever unfaithful, or scarcely ever, and only to prove that I could be if I tried. . . .'

I had a lively recollection of that laces-and-ribbons floor-walker. Although I had only met him on the stairs or in the concierge's *loge*, I had seen enough of him to be greatly impressed by his dignified manner, the noble carriage of his head, the deep, grave voice and his evident conviction of his superiority to all the other inmates of the house. While I was still a child I had heard it said that he was a member of the Fascist organisation known as the Croix de Feu, and the tragic effulgence of the name, which meant nothing to me, lent him an almost magical prestige in my eyes. And then there was his famous encounter with Chazard on the first-floor landing, in which he had had the last word: 'Monsieur, I have no intention of arguing with a nonentity who did his military service in the supply department, and I give you warning that in the event of any future dispute between us I shall address myself to your bottom in a manner that will at least keep it warm.' Commenting upon those splendid words my father, who also had a taste for fine language, said to my brother and me: 'You can say what you like about Bouvillon, but he's a man with aristocracy in his blood and he holds remarkably deep political views.' Sonia Bouvillon, still tenderly dwelling on the departed, brought him to life for me with an impartial vividness that made me smile despite myself. She said finally:

'When he died I thought I was going to die too, it hurt so terribly. And yet I got over it almost at once, in fact by the day after the funeral I scarcely missed him. But I loved him so dearly, with love and with so much admiration that I felt small and insignificant beside him. He always knew what had to be done and he did it. And above all he had a conscience, while all I ever had was feelings. And feelings are things that come and go, but a conscience is something that lasts. If I'd died first, Adrien wouldn't have forgotten me as quickly as I forgot him. His conscience wouldn't have let him. He would have gone on mourning me for years. He was a true knight and he bored me very much, and I hope he will forgive me if he can hear what I'm saying, but the fact is, I much preferred talking to the shoemaker or the concierge to listening to his conversation.'

Madame Bouvillon had no showmanship in her nature; she sought neither to please nor to amaze. She simply thought aloud, but without forgetting my presence, which might have been that of a lifelong friend; and her lack of inhibitions created so warm an atmosphere of confidence between us that I could not help being equally candid in return. So when we came to the subject of Tatiana and her job of modelling I made no bones about the fact that I was disappointed at this change in her life.

'I know what you mean,' Madame Bouvillon said. 'In a way I'm less proud than I used to be of being her mother. But then again when I think of Adrien I can't help feeling that what made him so dull and obtuse was his courage and his opinions and his conscience, and I think that there may be other things in Tatiana which didn't have a chance to come out while she was working for her mathematics degree. Who can ever say what is best for people? And still I'm afraid when I see her worrying about clothes and longing for a new coat the way she once longed for that degree. If one day she gets some man to keep her I shall be mortified to death, but the worst of it is that I know I shall get over it in no time and shan't mind a bit, just as it was with Adrien. The Russian exiles had so much courage and energy, but I never had any. I don't know how to do anything good or even useful. When Adrien died and Tatiana started keeping us both, although she was still only a child, I tried to work too, but I was never any good at anything and never really ashamed of the fact. And the most dreadful thing of all is that I've always been so happy—always, all my life, so wonderfully happy! About the only thing that really upsets me is my corns.'

After telling me about her corns Sonia went on to ask me what I did in the world. I said that I had just come out of prison and when I mentioned Chazard she suddenly remembered who I was. With exclamations of apology, and self-reproaches for being so scatter-brained—'really I can't keep a thing in my head!'—she got up from her chair and leaning over me put her arms round my neck.

'My dear boy, I was so afraid for you during the trial, so terribly afraid, and now here you are in my home and I didn't even recognise you. And knowing you ever since you were a child, when we lived in the Rue Saint-Martin! I remember your father so well, with his sweet, gentle face, like an animal that has grown tame and resigned.'

She continued to evoke these memories of the past while I felt the weight of her arms on my shoulders, round and a little plump, and my gaze was lost in her full bosom. The thought that she was now an elderly woman did not enter my mind. With a tightness at my temples, my head spinning and my breathing suspended, I had an obscure sense of being abandoned by myself. I got up so abruptly that the chair fell over, but I had already put an arm round Sonia's shoulders and a hand to her breast and was pressing my mouth to hers. I passed a hand fiercely over her body, and for a moment she was greatly dismayed, but then I felt her relax in my arms. It was the sound of footsteps and voices on the landing that brought me to my senses. I felt then that I had been guilty of an unforgivable offence, disloyalty to Tatiana and, still worse, a brutal assault on an unprotected woman. I picked up my valise, which I had left in a corner of the room, but as I turned towards the door Sonia thrust herself in front of me, begging me not to go.

'If you do I shall get into the most dreadful trouble with Tatiana. She'll think I've been stupid and said all the wrong things.'

'You've only got to tell her what happened.'

'But she'll still scold me for not having done everything I ought to have done. Be kind, Martin, and stay. You've let yourself get worked up over such a little thing. Adrien always slept with a pretty girl if he got the chance. He was so handsome with his little stiff moustache and his dignity, like a musketeer, and me, well, there was more than one man that took me in his arms, and now Adrien's gone and it'll be my turn soon, and even today I can scarcely remember the arms that clasped me. Adrien, lying there in hospital, he'd quite forgotten. You mustn't reproach yourself for something that matters so little. Give me your case, and sit down and eat your cheese.'

Tatiana, returning home at about two in the morning, came

and sat beside me on the divan in the living-room where her mother had made a bed for me. Her eyes were shining. She said as she laid a hand on my forehead:

'I hope you'll be pleased. I've found you a job.'

'A job! But did you say who I was?'

'I told the whole story, all about Chazard and what a pig he was and everything.'

'Tatiana, this evening I behaved abominably. I failed to treat your mother with respect. I almost—I tried to——'

I was stammering. At last I managed to explain what had happened.

'Poor lamb!' said Tatiana. 'And then of course you realised that she was too old.'

I gave up attempting to tell her that I was a monster and we returned to the subject of the job.

'I had a vicomte on my left at dinner, about your age, handsome, charming, gay, brilliant—in fact, just the type I can't stand. And on my other side there was a perfectly huge man, enormous, I'm sure he weighs a good two hundred and fifty pounds. He didn't know where to put his stomach. When he tried to look at me his head would only turn a quarter of the way, and you could see the flesh quivering all down his waistcoat. Between fifty and sixty years old. And do you know who he was, the old mastodon? He was Lormier!'

She uttered the name as though it were that of a major prophet. I asked who Lormier might be.

'Why, Lormier, the chairman of S.B.H. and a dozen other companies. Lormier, one of the buttresses of the temple of gold! I talked to him nearly all the evening. I told him all about my life and hard times and failing my degree and having to be a model. We also talked about Algeria and General de Gaulle and the cost of living, and I managed to bring in one or two bits I'd happened to read in the paper. I could see that I was getting to him. Those very rich men, they're always impressed by deserving poverty with diplomas, particularly when it has a nice figure. When I told him about your problem I could see at once that it was in the bag. What's more, I think the old boy was very much taken with my attractive little person.'

'And does that give you ideas?'

Tatiana turned her head away, and with wrinkled eyes and pursed lips took time for thought.

'Yes,' she said at length. 'On the whole it does.'

II

At eleven o'clock I presented myself at the building in the Rue de Monceau which housed the offices of the S.B.H. Corporation. I was shown up to the second floor and ushered almost at once into the office of the chairman, a vast, luxuriously furnished room. Lormier, seated behind a large desk, was just as Tatiana had described him to me. A man stood facing him at some little distance from the desk, his shoulders rounded in subjection.

'You quite understand?' said Lormier.

'Yes, sir.'

'Then get out, you fool, and see that it doesn't happen again.'

As the man turned to go I saw his face; and his distraught look, the tears of mortification gleaming in his eyes, ruled out any possibility that he was putting on an act for my benefit. But I had a feeling that Lormier had caused me to be shown in at that precise moment so that I might witness the conclusion of the interview. He greeted me with a smile and spoke in a friendly tone.

'Mademoiselle Tatiana Bouvillon has told me of your misfortune and that you are looking for work. She assures me that you are intelligent, industrious and of good moral character. I think we may be able to find something suitable for you here. I understand you have a knowledge of accountancy?'

'When my father died, in 1953, I had to go out to work to keep myself and my younger brother. I took my father's place in the firm of Sentier and eventually became chief accountant.'

'Did your employers offer to take you back after you came out of prison?'

'Most decidedly not. My lawyer asked them to appear in court as witnesses to my character, but they refused on the grounds that it would be damaging to the firm's reputation.'

'May I ask how you came to know Mademoiselle Bouvillon?'

'We were born in the same house, in the Rue Saint-Martin. She left there when she was thirteen, but we kept in touch although we didn't see a great deal of one another.'

'Have you any strong political views?'

'I have never belonged to any political party.'

'That is all I need to know about that. I believe you were a student when your father died?'

'I went to the lycée from the communal school after getting my General Certificate, but by the time I had passed my second baccalaureate there were only three months to go before I was due to be called up for the army. I could have applied for a postponement, but I was not happy about entering on a long course of study that would have been a burden to my father. The money I could earn by tutoring in Greek and Latin was not nearly enough to keep me. So I decided to do my military service at once to make matters easier for him and also to give myself time to think things over. But he died suddenly just when I finished my term—in fact, a fortnight after I came back from Germany.'

Lormier had listened to this with intent interest. Despite the shapelessness of his face, bulging with fat, he possessed a remarkable, almost childlike delicacy of feature, and his violet-blue eyes were unusually expressive. My meticulous account of myself had afforded him some insight, at first hand, into the difficulties encountered by the impoverished young who seek to better themselves, and so far as I could judge from his expression this rather gratified him. He said with a twinkle in his eye:

'At least you dodged the war in Algeria.'

'I went with the rest of my class.'

'That was in 1950? But you might have volunteered for Indo-China.'

I smiled, foolishly no doubt. By the time I had collected my wits and was looking for a suitably forthright reply the moment had passed. Lormier asked when I would be ready to start work. I said that I should like to do so at once, and we agreed that I should begin the next day. I badly needed to be fitted in somewhere, not to feel at a loose end both in body and mind. Even the thought of the one day of freedom lying ahead of me caused me great unease.

After leaving the S.B.H. building at about half-past eleven I walked in the direction of the Rue Saint-Martin. I had no idea of visiting my brother. The notion of entering that house where my crime had been committed, of meeting the gaze of its occupants, seemed to me like lunacy. It was about midday when I crossed the Rue Saint-Martin and turned off along the Rue Réaumur.

There were a lot of people about, and to be lost amid the crowd on the pavement was a kind of protection. I walked round the church of Saint-Nicholas-des-Champs, crossed the street again and, as I entered the Rue de Turbigo, came face to face with Valérie, my one-time fiancée. She was a small girl, a natural brunette turned platinum, with a good figure, a pretty face and lively eyes. The meeting took her very much aback, but I had been hoping for it. I had indeed thought about it a great deal while I was in prison.

'Darling,' I cried, 'darling, how wonderful to find you again after two years! Aren't you glad to see me?'

She gazed at me in agitation and bewilderment, murmuring, 'Yes, of course.' I took her by the arm and led her down a side street, and she came meekly, not daring to refuse.

'I thought of you so much while I was in prison, I thought of you day and night. Isn't it marvellous that our love should have survived this long separation? Don't you think it's marvellous?'

She nodded with her lips compressed. I went on to talk rhapsodically about our first meeting in a bar in the Rue Réaumur, when we had sat up at the counter eating sandwiches side by side. A fateful moment for us both!—and Valérie, darting apprehensive, sidelong glances, murmured non-committally, 'Yes, quite. . . .' I stopped suddenly outside a one-night hotel and pushed her towards the door.

'In you go.'

At this a gleam of anger shone in her dark eyes and she made some attempt at resistance, saying that she hadn't time, but in face of the cold and resolute expression which I now assumed sheer panic overwhelmed her. The hotel maid led us up to a dismal room, not very clean, with damp-stains on the wallpaper, and departed after switching on the light and drawing the curtains. Valérie seemed to have decided to make the best of the situation; her face had relaxed, her eyes had grown softer. Taking her hands in mine I talked of our past happiness and of the days that had dragged by so slowly without her. 'When I thought of you in my prison-cell I pictured you most often in that blue dress you used to wear, do you remember, a blue dress with white-embroidered button-holes. Or else you were in that light-coloured raincoat with the belt tight round the waist and your figure looking absolutely divine. Or else—or else you weren't wearing anything at all. . . . Oh, darling, please. . . .' It was decidedly chilly in that unheated room. Without much sign of enthusiasm Valérie took off her jacket of blue plastic lined with felt, and then removed her dress. To occupy my mind and preserve my detachment while this was going on I diverted myself by considering the evolution of cheap feminine attire which had taken place during my imprisonment. This enriched aspect of Paris had already struck me in the course of my wanderings on the previous day and that morning. Valérie by now was reduced to her pants and brassière. After making her take these off I screwed up my eyes and frowned.

'Good Lord,' I said, 'what has happened to you? Really it's—well. . . .'

Valérie in dismay crossed her bare arms over her bosom, which had not changed in the least. Letting my gaze travel slowly down over her belly and thighs I managed to produce a suppressed chuckle which sounded genuine. She flushed to the roots of her hair.

'Would you mind turning round?'

She did so, moving awkwardly, greatly distressed by the thought of her physical imperfections, and I studied her rear view, which was charming, the slender legs, the rounded thighs and firm buttocks, and the well-shaped hips beneath the pure, flowing curve at her waist.

'Oh, dear,' I murmured.

'Why, what's wrong?'

'Oh—nothing, nothing.' I crossed to the other side of the room for safety's sake, and said over my shoulder, 'Well, it can't be helped. You might as well get dressed.'

Although it is said of revenge that it is a dish best eaten cold, I can truly affirm that my own gave me little satisfaction. Indeed, I was only pursuing a line of conduct which I had long ago decided upon, during my first days in prison; and even then the desire for revenge had not been my chief motive. I had decided, since I did not want to part company with my brother, that my best course would be to stage an incident between Valérie and myself which would save us both from the danger of a relapse. This was the true reason for my performance in that squalid room. Tears were now running down the cheeks of the mortified young woman whom I still affected to consider my fiancée, perhaps not only of humiliation but of remorse as well. I waited with my back turned while she put on her clothes and then came and sat on the bed beside her.

'I need hardly say, now that I've seen you again, that I release you from your promise.'

Valérie uttered a scornful laugh. Fortitude had returned to her with the covering of her nakedness, the more so now she knew that all was over between us, since she no longer needed to worry about my intentions. Her black eyes—dark chestnut, to be exact—still shining with tears, began to sparkle with fury.

'My promise? You poor fool, I broke it ages ago, and if you want the truth, it never meant a thing to me.'

'Valérie, I can't believe it!'

'Well, you might as well try. I had a lover even before you killed Chazard. Yes, I did!'

'You're just saying this to hurt me, because I don't find you attractive any more.'

She laughed again, a shrill, spiteful laugh. For an instant fear made her hesitate and her angry gaze wavered beneath my own, but the sheer longing for revenge, sheer destructiveness, carried her away.

'I hate to shock you, dear Martin, but as a matter of fact my lover was your brother—Michel!'

'I just don't believe it.'

This display of innocence evoked a further burst of laughter. The position was reversed, and now it was she who was looking me over, in evident amusement at my thick-set form, my heavy-featured, ravaged countenance with small eyes half-buried under dark, thick eyebrows. I began to feel genuinely uncomfortable, and this delighted her.

'Incidentally,' I said, 'do you see anything of Michel these days?'

'Well naturally, seeing that I live with him. Don't you believe me even now? I can show you my identity-card if you

29

like, and you'll see that I live in the Rue Saint-Martin—with Michel.'

She opened her plastic bag and got out her wallet, but I waved it away.

'All right. I believe you. But if you were Michel's mistress before I went to prison why didn't you tell me that you'd made a mistake and that you loved someone else? It wasn't such an impossible thing to say.'

'You might have quarrelled with Michel.'

'But suppose I had?'

'If you'd turned him out I'd have had him on my hands. It's what happened in any case after you went to prison. Michel doesn't do a stroke. We're both living on what I earn as a typist. He gets up at one o'clock in the afternoon after I've brought him a meal in bed. He spends the rest of the day reading or day-dreaming, and in the evening, after supper, he goes off by himself and comes home at two or three in the morning. That's his life—or rather, our life.'

'Do you still love him?'

Valérie answered the question merely with a shrug of her shoulders. Bonds more solid than those of love united her to the indolent, indifferent youth who was my brother Michel. Without ever meaning to do so, and simply because of my imprisonment, she had taken over my responsibilities as head of the family, and now she was past the stage where she might have asked herself if Michel was worth the keeping. More or less unconsciously she had come to accept the fact that his very indolence gave him a claim on her, and perhaps if he had earned his living she would have been less attached to him. I was beginning to feel rather contrite for the way I had treated her.

'You've been very brave, but if you'd left him to look after himself he'd have been forced to earn a living.'

'The same applies to you. It was while he was living with

you that he got into the habit of doing nothing. And now I'm off. I've got to get our lunch.'

'Tell Michel I'll meet him at three o'clock in the little café near the house.'

'All right.'

'There's no need to say anything about me bringing you here.'

'There's no reason why I should hide it. In any case, he doesn't give a damn.'

Valérie went off, giving me a glance in which I now seemed to detect more mockery than resentment, and I stayed a little longer in the room, thinking of that strange youth, my brother Michel.

He had been a pretty boy when I last saw him, agreeably nonchalant in manner, with a singularly lucid intelligence and a kind of elasticity, a fluid quality of mind and heart, which had always made me feel that he would never devote himself to anything or anyone. After leaving school he had started to read for a history degree, had grown tired of it and, regardless of the cost to me, accepting everything as his due, had taken a course in acting and for three months had played a small part in a piece adapted from the English. Presumably he had now given up the theatre, since Valérie said he was doing nothing.

At three that afternoon I took a seat in the café where I had said I would meet him. I waited in growing anxiety for nearly an hour, half-rising every time the door opened, but not able to blame him since I could not be sure that Valérie had given him my message. Finally, unable to bear the uncertainty any longer, I got up abruptly and ran to our house in the Rue Saint-Martin. I had a moment of panic as I reached the door, but I did not stop. The concierge, mercifully, was not in her *loge*. Averting my eyes from the spot where Chazard had died I went up the five flights of the big stone stairway, running most of the way to lessen the risk of meeting anyone. The

31

sixth floor, that of the attic apartments, was reached by a narrower flight of wooden stairs which I climbed more slowly while I got my breath. Michel—unless it was Valérie—had left the key in the door of the apartment. I knocked and opened as I did so. In the small lobby I found myself confronting a girl of about twenty, quite pretty, clad in a skirt and brassière. She darted into the living-room, from which Michel emerged wearing trousers and a dressing-gown. He came towards me smiling, and I clasped him to me without being able to speak, my throat constricted and my lips trembling. For a moment he bore gracefully with this display of emotion, then withdrew from my embrace and called towards the open door:

'You can come out, Lena. It's my brother.'

Lena returned to the lobby and Michel introduced us. He then pulled up her skirt to show me her legs and said, 'Would you like her?'

Lena was gazing at me with a kind and gentle smile. I stammered that it was Michel I had come to see.

'Well then, Lena, you'd better be off. Perhaps I'll see you tonight. Take care of yourself.'

When she had gone we went into the living-room, which he had turned into a sort of study. The table was loaded with piles of books and sheets of paper covered with his handwriting.

Now that we were alone I could look at him more closely. He was handsome, and his face, which had retained the soft features of adolescence despite his twenty-four years, had at that moment an expression of serene detachment or indifference which caused me sharp distress. He had always been my superior in intelligence, with a mind quicker, broader and more imaginative than my own; but the life we shared, and my anxious care for his health and his studies, had brought us very close together. It hurt me to feel that none of this was left, and I became clumsy in consequence. I asked him what he was

32

doing these days. 'Nothing', he said simply, with no particular emphasis or apparent desire to shock me. He was gazing absently at the table, and he did not trouble to raise his eyes to see what I made of his reply. He seemed to think it perfectly natural that he should be doing nothing. I scarcely knew what to say.

'But what about the stage? You'd made a beginning. You had a part.'

'Yes, a small one. Afterwards I got a better one, but I gave it up, I couldn't stand it any longer. Acting came too easily to me, it was too natural to be interesting. I had the audience with me from the start, you see, and that close contact was just what I disliked. Some nights I really hated it. I'd always thought that the opposite ought to be the case, and that the footlights should create a gulf between the actors and the audience. As a matter of fact, I still think so. Well, tell me about prison.'

He listened while I talked and then said:

'It sounds as though it would suit me rather well—to see the world through prison-walls.'

This view of the matter, which sounded to me like a literary affectation, was scarcely calculated to appeal to anyone just out of prison; but I did not pursue the point. Looking at the sheets scattered over the table I remarked that he didn't seem to be entirely idle.

'No, but I don't do anything to earn a living,' he said. 'That's what I meant. At the moment I'm writing a play—that's to say, I'm trying to write one.' He smiled. 'So what do you think of that?'

I didn't think anything of it, except that as a pastime it was no doubt as good as any other. For politeness' sake I asked what the subject was.

'Love', said Michel. 'I've never been in love. So I conclude, or I'm pretending to conclude, that I'm particularly well qualified to write about it in the detached spirit that the subject

33

calls for. But the real truth is that I've always resented the existence of this emotion of love which apparently I'm unable to feel. I started by writing a sort of essay, but I gave that up.'

He had fished out a blue exercise book from the pile while he was speaking. He held it in his hand, leaving me uncertain whether he meant me to take it or not. I did so, but I did not open it at once.

'I felt that the drama was a better mode of expression, not necessarily more clear but more able to suggest ideas in concrete terms, even when they were still hazy in my own mind.'

At this point Michel bent over the table, ran his eye over one of his sheets of dialogue, and crossed out a sentence. He then sat down to look into the matter more closely. I took a chair opposite him and opened the blue exercise book. It contained about forty handwritten pages with a great many corrections, but the writing was neat and very legible. Michel, now absorbedly crossing out and re-writing, had forgotten that I was there.

III

THE illustrated Petit Larousse, which I hold in great respect, gives us the following definition of love: 'The feeling whereby the heart goes out towards that which strongly attracts it.'

I pause at the word 'heart', which is used figuratively and must therefore be regarded as suspect. Larousse also tells us that love is a 'disposition of the soul' and in conclusion it defines the soul as 'the principle of life'. From this we may gather that love, although one might not suspect it, is to be defined in metaphysical terms. The Petit Larousse is among the most solid institutions of our country. If it falls into error, or into vagary, it is because it cannot help itself.

Let us suppose that Romeo, having married Juliet and lived six months with her, is visited by a Martian who addresses him as follows:

'You must understand, Monsieur Romeo, that for us Martians sex does not exist. Four or five times in our lifetime a single hair grows on our head which we pluck out and plant in the garden. We water it three times a week for a year, by which time it has grown into a little Martian. All we then have to do is dig it up and let it run about. I know that you earth-dwellers employ other methods, and I have heard the word 'love' much used among you. I gather that the love existing between yourself and Madame Juliet is of an exemplary nature. Would you be so kind as to explain to me what this love is?'

'Gladly, Monsieur. Love is a state of ecstasy in which the mere mention of the adorable name of Juliet causes my heart to melt and my body to feel lighter than a bird.'

'So then you fly away?'

'Oh, not at all. That was just a figure of speech.'

'I see. But tell me, this melting of your heart, which must be of rather frequent occurrence, is it not prejudicial to your health?'

'I must apologise. When I said that my heart melted, that was another figure of speech.'

'Monsieur Romeo, I beg you to be serious. Can you not express yourself in more concrete terms?'

'It is extremely difficult, Monsieur. Love, for me, is the irresistible attraction which I experience with my whole being for the being of Juliet.'

'That is precisely the definition I was looking for, plain, lucid and concise. So, then, your liver, your spleen and your bowels are all irresistibly attracted to Juliet.'

'Your interpretation, my dear sir, verges on coarseness, but I will excuse you on the score of ignorance. It goes without saying that my liver, my spleen and my bowels have nothing to do with the case.'

'And the skin on your buttocks?'

'Sir!'

'But if your liver, your spleen, your bowels and the skin on your buttocks, all of which are integral parts of your being, play no part in the attraction which you experience for Madame Juliet, it seems to me you must look for another definition.'

'When I say my whole being, Monsieur, I naturally refer to my soul. That is the underlying sense of the words.'

'What sense, Monsieur Romeo . . . ?'

It is, as you see, not easy to make oneself intelligible on the subject of love, even to a person as little versed in such matters as a sexless Martian. Romeo and Petit Larousse, both of whom possess wordly knowledge and charm, talk of heart and sentiment, but there are also persons who maintain that love does not exist, that it is simply a matter of the reproductive instinct finding a particular object suitable for its purpose; imagination, verbal delirium and the possessive instinct being responsible for what ensues. 'My dearest girl,' they say, 'when you gaze deep into the eyes of your Gontran you feel your twenty-year-old flesh melt while sighs of rapture rise to your lips; but we who are knowing old codgers, coldly materialist in our outlook, we who therefore chuckle at so many things, we too know what it is to feel our old bones turn to water while our lips stammer in delight—not for the eyes of any Manon or Héloïse, but at the beauty of a daffodil in the dew of an April morning. No, my love, your reproductive instinct has not been sublimated, as your letters to your dearest girl friend might lead one to suppose; but you have a charming fancy and a taste for prettiness, and you have cultivated the art of clothing the nakedness of your desire with agreeable imagery. This, however,' they conclude, 'does not alter the fact that your exalted passion for Gontran is simply the desire of the female for the male, differing from that of a cow only in point of its more frequent occurrence.' One blushes to have to record such words. Let it be said at once that the reproductive instinct is a simplified view of the spirit, or better, a hollow expression having no precise significance. As for the 'desire' to which these iconoclasts seek to reduce love, everyone knows that it is merely one of love's ingredients and, at that, not indispensable. More than a quarter of all women are frigid. This represents, in France alone, several million women lacking all physical desire, who nevertheless fall in love with a man, or with several, and experience physical love.

To define anything is to set aside all the countless shades of meaning which in our ignorance we may have attached to it; it is, where the thing is concerned, to exclude infinity. I find it useful and intellectually sufficient to define such words as cassock, hair-curler and saddle-girth, because it would cause me some dismay if, for lack of a precise definition, a cassock should come to assume abnormal dimensions in our minds, and expand to infinity. The same applies to hair-curlers and saddle-girths. On the other hand, there are words whose meaning cannot be circumscribed and which outrun all definition. They are the most beautiful and dangerous words in our language, they enlarge our world, but they may easily lead us astray if we do not take pains to ensure that their content is left as vague as possible. To employ them in argument in the way one uses such words as cassock and saddle-girth is to introduce not merely a source of error but error itself. It seems to me that 'love' is one of these words, and if I were Larousse, instead of compromising my authority by attempting an impossible definition, I would catalogue it as follows: 'A magical but also bromidic word of which the meaning is variable almost to infinity. Commonly used in the following contexts: He placed his love and fortune at the feet of the Baroness. He loved her deeply. His love was born of the highest sentiments. Marceline knew she could rely upon a solid love. They knew four years of great love. He loved her, but with a tepid love. He loved her with a burning love. Unfortunately the love of Alcide was not reciprocated. Léonie did not respond to his love. The rich old man's love was odious to Léonie. Love is blind. Love is singularly clear-sighted. The young man was hungry for love. She could only accept an honourable love. It was no more than a holiday love-affair. The perverse love of Maximus, the unnatural love of Francesca, the bestial love of Balthazar, revolted the poor girl. Pierre and Paulette cherished a perfect love. I am dying of love. One does not die of love. In contrast with the furious love of Auguste, that of Ernest was pale indeed. You are the love of my life. She knew love one 14th of July under a *porte cochère*. Love presented itself to Hermeline in the form of a coloured man. A murderer for love, he knelt sobbing beside

38

the corpse. It was Andrea's first love. On the ashes of that first dead love a new love was to be born and soon to flower. Melchior's love rapidly declined. The spectacle by which Alfred was confronted swiftly clipped the wings of his love. Love makes the world go round. Love knows no impediments. Even the truest love grows weary in the end of its own trammels. Love is indulgent. Love is exigent. Love is a dancing thing. Love cannot be forced. Love cannot be gainsaid. Love and a cough can't be hid. When he learned that Edmonde was his own daughter, Flaminius banished that incestuous love from his heart.'

Of the countless writers who have written about love the wisest are those who have refrained from discoursing on the subject (as I am doing now) and have been content to write novels, tales, plays or poems of which love is the theme. The best of them teach us nothing. Shakespeare teaches us nothing, neither does Racine, who is said to be the greatest portrayer of love. It will be argued that their only purpose was to touch our hearts. No doubt, but it is nevertheless surprising that minds of such penetration and precision, endowed with the highest poetic genius, should have made no new discovery in the sphere of love. There have been fortunate novelists who have known how to move us with their chronicles of love, but they too have taught us nothing.

Stendhal, who spent his life studying himself in the mirror with an almost obscene passion for his own person, and who so sighed for women and adventures, believed that he had much to say and even to teach his readers on the subject of love. Accordingly he wrote an essay entitled *De l'Amour* wherein he embarks upon the first chapter of the first book as follows:

'I seek to give some account of that passion of which every true manifestation is a thing of beauty. There are four different orders of love: 1. Passionate love; 2. Love born of affinity; 3. Physical love; 4. Love born of vanity.' Stendhal refrains from defining the object of his study and he has the added adroitness to treat it as a matter of universal knowledge and comprehension. Knowing that in the mind of every individual the word corresponds to a set of personal sensations, feelings or speculations, he talks of it without fearing to generalise. Having, so to speak, carved love into four and numbered the pieces, this admirable word-spinner, who was also a painstaking observer, explains what is to be understood by his various labels. Speaking of love born of vanity he says: 'The immense majority of men, particularly in France, desire and possess a fashionable wife as a luxury, like a handsome horse, necessary to the equipment of any young man.' Thus we are informed at the outset that to Stendhal the love which is the subject of his treatise belongs exclusively to the upper-class, the world of aristocracy, of the very rich bourgeois or, in the case of military men possessing neither family nor fortune, of high-ranking officers. I am loath to say that he regarded the common people, shop-keepers and others of no social standing, merely as cattle whose sighs and effusions were not worthy of the name of love; or that his approach to the subject was that of any young lout of good family; but the fact remains. His 'immense majority' of men possessing fashionable wives must evidently belong to an aristocracy, and one not of the spirit; but this small, glittering and inflated world is the only one which Stendhal finds worthy of his psychological probings. We are told at the outset just what we may expect of what is nevertheless an ambitious attempt. But it is surely self-evident that if I set out to enlighten posterity regarding the intelligence of my contemporaries and confine myself to studying the minds of drum-majors I run the risk, not only of rapidly exhausting the subject, but of arriving at somewhat baroque conclusions. Stendhal, who claimed to be a writer of the left, and indeed was one within the limits of what was permitted to a well-to-do citizen under the *ancien régime*, and who prided himself on his advanced views, believed that he might apprehend the universe and penetrate its secrets by observing it wherever duchesses had romantic natures and well-shaped bottoms. Having said which, let us consider that if he was wrong about love, he was not more or less so than other writers. What he writes on the subject is what had already been written by all the members of that honourable brotherhood. I read, for example, in his fifth chapter: 'Man is not free not to do that which gives him more pleasure than all other possible actions. Love is like a fever, it is born and subsides without the individual will having played any part in the matter.' Which is what I myself was saying only a few minutes ago. Stendhal is repeating what fifty thousand poets, balladmongers, philosophers and story-tellers have said before him.

For thousands of years, indeed, it was believed that love takes possession of people by chance, sometimes even against their will, takes up its dwelling within them and remains for a year or two or ten, or even a lifetime. You are twenty years old (or thirty or sixty), and one evening, dining at the house of your friends the Champigneuls, you find yourself seated opposite a superb creature of forty-two with huge, adorable cow's eyes. Between courses you gaze at her open-mouthed and by the end of the meal you feel a kind of squashiness in the region of your ribs on the left side. The days that follow are delicious. You think incessantly of the beloved and whenever you do so it is like going up in the lift, your heart plunges to the depths of your body. Then one evening you declare yourself, because love will no longer be denied, and it turns out that she too has loved in silence from the moment of that first encounter. You go home and break the news to your family. 'Are you mad?' exclaim your parents, who are respectable grocers. 'A woman twenty-two years older than you whose father died in prison?' As if you cared about the father who died in prison. On the very day you come of age you marry,

41

you are happy and then unhappy and jealous. You work for twenty years without ever noticing that you aren't rich, but then one day your legitimate beloved, who is now sixty-two, takes it into her head to complain that she has never been to Bangkok or Valparaiso. It seems to you the most natural thing in the world that you should go off and rob the local pawn-shop, but as you bungle the job, incidentally killing the pawnbroker, you get ten years' imprisonment. When you come out you find your sweetie ten years more beautiful, and everything begins again and it's love for ever after.

This notion of love that is stronger than man, his master at all times, may appear correct at first glance. In any event, it has prevailed in the past and continues to prevail. The most common view is, moreover, that love is a fatality which it is vain to try to escape. One pictures a sort of parasite feeding on our flesh until it grows disgusted, the only way out that can restore our peace of mind. But truth is always slow to triumph over habits of thought. It is now some fifteen years since the great discovery was made which is destined to transform our whole theory of love. I refer to that innocent-seeming remark let fall by a scientist of world-wide repute to the effect that young ladies belonging to the privileged classes never fall in love with youths of lower social standing. I will ask the reader to ponder those authoritative words. He will not fail to perceive that they lead us on to new paths, far removed from our customary way of thought. We will suppose for example that I am a girl of eighteen named Eponine. Father is a permanent under-secretary in the Ministry of Noughts and Crosses, mother is the daughter of Isidor Kahn, the banker, and we live in a seven-room apartment, not counting the usual offices, on the Avenue Henri-Martin. Twice a day I go to the Lycée Molière, either by bus or on foot. I get to know a number of young men by sight and it amuses me to think of mother's occasional agitation at the thought of my walking unescorted through the streets, at the mercy of, perhaps even yielding to, the wiles of masculine villainy. I am amused because I know how well armed the girls of my world are against perils of this kind. In the first place, and this is something of which Mamma is unaware, there are almost no men in Paris. Naturally under the heading of men I do not include butchers' boys, messenger boys, clerks, commercial travellers, manservants and others. I do not deny that many of these may be my superior in intelligence or knowledge or looks, but still they are not persons with whom a girl of my background can fall in love. The fact is one that I do not seek to explain. In passing a certain provision-merchant's shop I often see a young assistant who reminds me of one of Poussin's Arcadian shepherds, and who smiles tenderly at me as I pass. But for my part, although the sight of that handsome and sensitive face gives me pleasure, I am otherwise unmoved, whereas when I meet Jean-Victor Chapolier, the son of the celebrated nose-and-throat specialist, and despite the fact that he bleats and looks like a moon-calf, I feel palpitations under my ribs and my flesh melts and, worst of all, I cannot restrain myself from giving him a swift glance below the belt, which causes me to turn crimson and babble; but thanks be to God he has never even noticed and if you want to know why, it is because he sleeps (Marie-Claude Popinard told me, and she lives in the same house) because he sleeps with the little housemaid (only think of it! a servant!) who works for Maréchal the privy-councillor and his wife, who also live in the same house.

I have sought to illustrate the distinguished professor's remarks in these homely terms in order to make clear the degree in which it does outrage to certain habits of thought which we are accustomed to take for granted. Is it the fact that he is male which causes Eponine's flesh to melt when she encounters young Chapolier? No doubt it is, yet we know that if he were a grocer's assistant, instead of the son of a nose-

43

and-throat specialist, Eponine would experience no sensation whatever. This alone is sufficient to prove that in the eyes of a woman a man's social standing is of greater importance than his male aspect, the efficacity of masculine charm being subordinated to a host of seemingly unrelated factors such as a sports-car, an address-book, a monocle, a necktie, an air of nonchalance, membership of a club, a hyphen, a family, business contacts, a gold wrist-watch, a coat of arms, a number of pairs of gloves, a cigar-case—all of which add up to a clear letter of recommendation. But I shall be told that I am arguing from the general to the particular and that the attitude to love and well-to-do young ladies must not prejudice our view of the behaviour of those in humbler walks of life. To which I reply from my own observation, living as I do in the Rue Saint-Martin, that it makes no difference. Once again my name is Eponine. I am a typist at the Laboratoires Bessières where my dad has been employed successively as cleaner, odd-job man, van-driver and finally night-watchman, age having rendered him useless for anything else. I have big eyes, small teeth, nice legs and a round bosom, rather sweet, really, if I do say so. Men are nice to me and I've been propositioned more than once. The men in the business can be divided into two categories—the lower grades, and the chemists and senior office staff. I'm not the least bit snobbish or up-stage and I couldn't care less about diplomas and the liberal professions. I'm quite at my ease with the laboratory assistants and the packers and van-drivers and so forth, most of whom are young; I'm on friendly and even familiar terms with them, but good-looking or not, there isn't one that attracts me physically. And on the other hand there's Lepandier, the chief chemist, whom I have a good deal to do with. Well, believe it or not, he's only got to look at me—he's about fifty and not a bit handsome, with a dirty yellow moustache, but it doesn't make the slightest difference—he's only got to look at me and it catches me right in the midriff. And Lepandier isn't the only one, there are others, all chemists or senior office staff. The man who makes my flesh melt is the man I could make a life with, and it isn't the money that matters most, but the social background and the job and the way of living.

In short the eternal feminine is not necessarily the yielding prey which the novelettes and women's magazines so often make her out to be, a predestined victim astray in the vapours of fatality, ready to surrender with sighs and sentiments to the first male appetite that comes along. She is very much the reverse. Make no mistake about it, for women love is primarily a social affair.

IV

I HAD just finished reading the first chapter in the blue exercise book when I heard the door of the apartment open and close. Michel looked up and shouted, 'For God's sake go away!' But a figure had already appeared in the doorway, that of a young man of about twenty-five, lightly clad for the time of year in a faded green shirt outside a pair of grey corduroy trousers with a black leather belt. His face was agreeable, blue-eyed, with a thick quiff of fair hair and a beard no less fair, carefully uncared-for and swept over to the left side of his face as though it had been blown by the wind.

'Sorry,' said Michel. 'I didn't know it was you.'

'I only came to bring you some money.'

'Thanks. Put it on the table.'

The young man put three thousand-franc notes on the table and went out, and we heard the front door close.

'An odd costume,' I said. 'He can't be very warm.'

'He never wears anything else, summer or winter.'

'What does he do?'

'He's studying an almost extinct east-African dialect.'

'Why did he choose to do that?'

'Because it interests him,' said Michel, 'and he's quite sure it will never be of the slightest use to him.'

This explanation, which seemed to call for footnotes, did not at the time arouse my curiosity to the extent it was to do later, when I thought about it. I was feeling rather at sea in my brother's life, and was trying ineptly to find my way in it without knowing how to make use of the opportunities that offered. I went on to talk about his first chapter, but with no thought of complimenting him, for he was without any kind of vanity—indeed, I might even say, without self-esteem.

'I don't see that your theory of love as a "social affair" for women is borne out in the case of Valérie when she got engaged to me.'

'Well, you weren't the Shah of Persia, certainly, but you were a chief accountant, which was a good match from her point of view. Anyway, what she saw in you was security, a safe fireside.'

'And what did she see in you?'

'Exactly the opposite. She realised that I was an incapable, born to be dependent on other people, and without even weighing the matter in her mind she set about saving me from disaster. A primarily social instinct, in every sense of the word. Incidentally, how are you proposing to fit in here? If you take her back there's no problem. But I shall have to ask you to share the bedroom with her in any case, because I always sleep in here on the divan. If you prefer you can have the big bed and she can sleep in the little one.'

The suggestion took me aback. During my time in prison I had never once envisaged the possibility of reconstituting my domestic hearth. After what had happened, and despite the affection I still felt for Michel, the thought of going back to live under the same roof with Valérie would have seemed to me absurd. But he treated it so much as a matter of course that I began to wonder whether I had really thought the problem over sanely.

'It isn't as simple as you seem to imagine. Valérie has to be considered. She's not likely to enjoy the idea of sharing her bedroom with me.'

'Why not? She told me what happened at the hotel. If you find her repulsive it's perfectly simple.'

'Apart from that there are the other people in the house. I managed to get in without anyone seeing me, but I don't know what they'd think if I came back to live here.'

47

On this point Michel was able to reassure me. The other occupants had not been unduly distressed by the death of Chazard, all having suffered from his bad temper. They even took the view that his persecution mania had begun to be dangerous, and although no one had come forward to say so in court they were all convinced that I had acted in self-defence. At the thought of his loneliness in death I had a twinge of pity for Chazard.

'Will you be moving in right away?' asked Michel.

I said no, not right away, as though it were merely a question of time. Before leaving I went and got some underlinen out of the wardrobe in the bedroom. It had been my parents' room and still contained the furniture which they had bought almost new in 1930, from a tenant who was leaving for Madagascar. The big bed was on the left of the attic window, the wardrobe beyond it, and facing them, against the right-hand wall, was a dressing-table with an oval mirror. The bedroom chairs and single armchair were upholstered in red velvet, worn and fading to pink. Finally, to the right of the door, which faced the window, there was a narrow brass bedstead bought by my parents in 1937 to lodge my cousin, Angèle, who had come from Bergerac to take a job as sales-girl at the Bon Marché, obtained through her father's political contacts, but had given it up after six months and married a captain of gendarmerie who was shortly afterwards posted to Tunisia.

I stood for a while trying to imagine what it would be like to share that room. Every evening at about nine, having had his supper, Michel would go out, leaving Valérie and me alone in the little two-room apartment. So great was my desire to live with my brother that Valérie's presence no longer seemed an insuperable obstacle. I told myself that although I had been her lover and her fiancé I had never really loved her, and this led me to wonder, as Michel had done in his first chapter,

48

what was meant by love. It seemed, after all, that I knew no more about it than he did.

As I was leaving the apartment I came face to face with another young man, this one comparatively well-dressed, with a round, pink face and thick-lensed glasses. Seeing me shut the door behind me he asked, 'Is Porteur in?' Porteur, as I luckily remembered, had been Michel's stage name. I replied that Porteur did not want to see anyone, and then, thinking of the previous caller, I asked him if he had brought any money. The young man flushed, looking greatly distressed, and it was some moments before he could answer.

'I'm terribly sorry but the fact is, I'm in a jam myself. I mean, I might manage a couple of hundred, but . . . I'm still at the Ecole Normale, you see. My parents are the worst type of working class, narrow-minded, socialist, patriotic—to hell with the working classes is what I say—and bloody tight-fisted. They were against my being a student at all. My school-teacher had to fight tooth and nail. And here I am, twenty-two and still not earning a living. It makes them sick. In consequence of which, not a bean.'

'You mustn't think that Porteur expects anything from his visitors.'

'You've no need to tell me that. I've never seen him, but I know all about him. I was the one who formed the Porteur group at the school. Well, to call it a group, that's going a bit far. There are only three of us.'

We walked together down the stairs, myself astonished at the fervour which Michel had inspired in this youth.

'You say you've never even seen Porteur. Then what makes you so enthusiastic about him?'

'At this stage it isn't easy to say. The fact is, I don't remember when I first heard of him. All I can tell you is that I know several people who have not only seen him but actually talked to him!'

Again the flush rose on his boyish cheeks and his eyes shone behind the thick lenses.

'Yes', I said, 'but what is there in what you've heard of him that excites you so much? Is it something special in his attitude to artistic or political problems.

He grinned. 'Well, since you ask, we might say that he has a doctrine. But don't try to go on with it. It's no use pulling Porteur to pieces. He's just *someone*, that's all. He's Porteur, and that's all there is to it.'

By now we had reached the foot of the stairs. The concierge, peering through her window, saw me pass her *loge* and I heard the door open. Since I was not alone she contained her curiosity, and all I could do was to look round and smile at her. At the trial she had spoken up warmly in my favour.

As we walked together along the street the young man grasped me suddenly by both wrists and cried:

'But look here, if you've just come out of his apartment you must know him! Tell me about him.'

'What do you want me to tell you? There's nothing to tell.'

'Nothing to tell! Well, that's just like Porteur. Nothing to tell! When I tell that to Forlon and Couture they'll go crazy. They never stop talking about him. Nothing to tell!'

He released me with those words and we parted, I in the direction of the Porte Saint-Martin. But for a moment he stood on the pavement staring after me, the man who positively knew Porteur. . . .

When at about seven I returned to the Rue Eugène-Carrière I found Tatiana at home, but not her mother, who had gone out and was not likely to be back until late. I had plenty of news for her and I began by telling her about my interview with Lormier. 'What did you think of him?' 'I don't much care for his looks.' 'There's a kind of force in him, you must admit.' 'You like him because he took a fancy to you.' We spent half an hour arguing about whether Lormier possessed any merit other than wealth, and any largeness except of body. I could see that Tatiana was tempted. Lormier had just sent her a basket of orchids. When she told me this I uttered a cry of alarm. 'Look at yourself!' I cried. 'Pull up your skirt. Your legs alone are worth all the kingdoms of the earth, and as for the rest, one daren't think of it. You aren't going to let yourself be had by that barrel of lard?' To which Tatiana replied coldly that it was precisely the thought of those eighteen stone weighing upon her body that excited her. We were sitting on the divan in the living-room, and her big, green eyes, fixed steadily upon mine, glittered with defiance. After all the years of struggle and poverty, the incessant problem of the new coat, she had suddenly reacted, seduced by the thought of ease and security. Still seeking to dissuade her I took her by the shoulders, but she wrenched herself away and slapped my face so hard that the heel of her hand, catching my nose, brought tears to my eyes. She tried to follow it up with the other hand. I made a hasty movement to parry this second blow and some-how caught her violently in the throat with my elbow, so that she turned pale and seemed on the verge of fainting. Then my heart went out to her, and I took her in my arms and talked softly to her. The colour came back to her cheeks and she knelt at my feet crying that she was a pig and a bitch to have treated me like that when I had only just come out of prison, and invoking all the calamities of Heaven upon her head. It was pure Dostoievsky, and suddenly this occurred to her and we both burst out laughing. So then I told her about Valérie and the hotel and the strip-tease act, which caused her to clap her hands and embrace me with enthusiasm. This made it easier for me to tell the rest, but I did not say anything about having waited an hour for Michel at the café. I simply said I had been to see him. Frowning a little Tatiana said, 'Well? And what do you think of him?'

'I found him rather puzzling, even more strange than he was

51

two years ago. In fact,' I added, smiling, 'he's very much Porteur.'

'Like Porteur? Michel? That flabby little scrounger, with no heart and no guts? Don't be absurd. Porteur's entirely different. I haven't met him yet, and I'm dying to. Someone has promised to introduce me. Porteur's a world in himself. If your brother talks to you about Porteur you should shut him up. It's pure affectation, coming from him.'

Evidently Tatiana had taken little interest in Michel's theatrical career and had forgotten his stage-name, if she had ever known it. I asked her what she knew about Porteur. Very little, from what I gathered, but he represented in her eyes, as though it were a presentiment or an aspiration, a certain moral attitude, largely aesthetic in origin. I felt that I ought not to disillusion her by divulging the hero's true identity. It seemed to me both useful and fortifying that one should admire a more or less imaginary figure fashioned out of the best in oneself.

But the worst was still to be told, Michel's proposal that we should resume our family life, and I did my best to make this sound as though it were the natural thing to do. I had expected Tatiana to be against the idea, but not that she would explode in furious indignation. Had I no pride? Did I intend to spend the rest of my life living in penury, in squalor, among the riff-raff? Hadn't I the sense to see that Michel, now he was tired of Valérie, simply wanted to throw her back at me? To say nothing of the fact that I should have to keep the two of them on the pittance paid me by Lormier.

'You're nothing but a great, sentimental oaf and I ought to hit you again, but I can't stand by and see you wreck your life by letting them exploit you. I won't have it. You're not to go near the place again. I forbid it!'

I put my side of the case. Rue Saint-Martin was still my home, and I had to have somewhere to live, even if it was only a servant's garret, which was not easy to come by. As for Valérie, I had settled that matter once and for all at the hotel. And again, I didn't like the idea of her keeping my brother on her earnings. Tatiana by now had jumped to her feet and was striding up and down the room showering insults and contradictions upon me. Valérie had betrayed me with Michel, and now let them get on with it. I might think I had done with her, but if I was fool enough to walk into the trap I'd soon find I was mistaken. Three days, Tatiana reckoned, was about as long as it would take for the worst to happen. And as for a home, there was one waiting for me here. Why should I go anywhere else?

'You've had two years of being buried alive. If you're to re-adapt yourself to the world we live in you need to be surrounded with trust and affection. Where could you be better off than with two women like Sonia and me?'

She was kneeling on the divan with her head pressed against my shoulder. It was a good way of persuading me. I caught the scent of her body and glimpsed the firm breasts under the thin stuff of her peignoir. I made her lie back on the divan and, in my turn, knelt beside her.

'Do you really think I could live with you without losing my head? Or are you ready to run the risk of finding me in your bed one night?'

Tatiana did not answer, but gazed at me with questioning, provocative eyes.

'If I lived here I shouldn't need to be handsome or seductive. I'd just be here. I'd be convenient.'

'Whatever happens, Martin, you'll always be more than that.'

'Do you know something? Michel is trying to write. He started a sort of essay on love and then gave it up.'

Regardless of her scornful laughter I told her of Michel's first chapter and repeated the last line. 'Make no mistake about it, for women love is primarily a social affair.' Madame Bouvillon entered just as I was speaking the words.

'That's quite true,' she said. 'A social affair. When I met Adrien, in 1919, I at once wanted him to marry me, for one thing because he was handsome but also because of his fine uniform. He's so good-looking, I thought to myself, and so smart, and all those medals—he must be rich. Oh, you mustn't think I was just being mercenary. I never tried to find out if he had any money, that would have been disgusting; but seeing him look so rich my head was enchanted and my heart too. And I'm bound to admit, because it's true, that I thought Adrien was very intelligent so long as I thought he was rich, but afterwards I didn't. I hope he'll forgive me for being so uncharitable, if he can hear what I'm saying.'

'Mamma, will you get us some dinner? I may mention that you went out without leaving the key under the mat. If I hadn't come home early Martin would have been waiting on the landing all this time.'

'So that's what it was!' cried Sonia. 'I've been feeling uncomfortable the whole evening. I meant to go to the cinema, but then I ran into Dunia Skuratov on the Champs-Elysées and she took me to tea. She talked to me for hours about her grandson, who has just passed into the Polytechnique, and about her grand-daughter, who's a film-star already. She's so proud of them, the silly old thing. I'm not in the least proud, but in the end I couldn't help telling her that you'd got your mathematics degree.'

'Mother, you're absurd. I often see Pierre Skuratov. He knows perfectly well that I failed.'

'You're quite right, darling, but Dunia didn't seem to know what a mathematics degree was and I'm sure she's forgotten about it already. It's like with your father. One day he was asking me about my aristocratic connections and just to get out of it I said that my family was related to Tolstoy. He'd never heard of Tolstoy and so of course he forgot. He was so sweet. Oh, I do wish I didn't tell lies, but they slip out for no reason at all.'

During supper Tatiana called upon her mother to agree that it would be the height of folly for me to return to the Rue Saint-Martin.

'But if he loves his brother,' said Sonia, 'it's natural that he should want to live with him.'

'A brother who betrayed and deserted him?'

'True affection doesn't remember things like that.'

V

AT nine o'clock the following morning I presented myself to Keller, the staff-manager at S.B.H., who received me coldly, evidently regarding me as a parasite, imposed upon him from above, for whom the business had no possible use. He handed me over to a secretary who made me fill in a number of forms. I gave my address as Rue Saint-Martin. Having concluded the formalities, the lady took me down a flight of stairs to an empty office, a small bare room furnished with an office-desk and chair. This was to be my abode, she explained, until the staff-manager had found a job for me. As to when that would happen, she could give me no idea at all, the fact being that the departments were fully staffed already, from which it appeared that where S.B.H. was concerned I was wholly redundant. My prison experience promised to be of great help to me in enduring days or weeks of solitude and inaction in that room, which was about the size of a prison-cell. At first sight there was nothing at all in it that could not be seen or discovered in the first two minutes, but one needs to have served a prison sentence to learn how to explore thoroughly an enclosed space. After looking through the window, which gave on to a yard, I sat down on the chair with my legs under the desk. It had three drawers on either side, all entirely empty except the last, the bottom drawer on my right, which I found to contain a ball-point pen, hidden right at the back and held in place by two drawing-pins. I did not need to reflect upon this for very long. Pulling the drawer out of the desk and turning it over I found what I had half expected, namely that the bottom of the drawer, normally invisible, was covered with very close handwriting, obviously done with the ball-point. I put the drawer back and pulled out the top one on the left, on the bottom of which I found the same thing. Without troubling to inspect the other drawers I settled down to read.

*   *   *

The first time I stole a car was when I was sixteen. Our chauffeur had taught me to drive father's Buick in the holidays. I saw a chap get out of his car in the Rue de l'Université and go into a tobacconist's and I was in and off before he could even look round. I headed west and drove back and forth all over the place and in the end I left the bus not far from our place in the Rue de Passy. It hadn't amused me much. For it to be really fun you want to have four or five others with you all a bit lit-up and singing and shouting like mad every time you graze something in overtaking. But apart from that it was a time when I was pretty browned-off anyway. I'd had one of those talks with my parents trying to persuade them that I was doing all right at school. 'You can't even spell let alone punctuate,' said father. 'That isn't giving me any complexes' I said. 'But what are you proposing to do in life?' 'The same as mother, have a nice time on your money living a comfortable, fashionable life.' End of conversation. But all the same I left the college and what bothered me was that I was just as bored as ever. Absolutely no point in staying at home, the place was like a graveyard, mother always out and father at the office being a top civil-servant as he said. Us civil-servants. The old square. He's been a top civil-servant ever since I was a kid and it was just the same then. I'd be left there alone with the maid and the governess who looked after my sister Flora (of all the corny names) and who was supposed to keep an eye on my home-work. She was a little dark-haired skinny bitch, all angles, who did nothing to spread sweetness and light. But one day when I was twelve, it was a Thursday, the school holiday, and Flora was having her after-dinner rest, she took me into the study to go over my essay and just to stir up a rumpus I put my hand under her skirt. Well I expected squeals and a box on the ears, but instead she spread her legs and sat there turning pale while she watched my hand moving up to her suspender clip and then grab hold of her pants. The end of it was I had her on the hearthrug and the same thing happened the next day and the day after that until in the end we were rumbled by the maid who couldn't stand her. So one afternoon when we were stripped one on top of the other the maid came in with Flora who was not quite five. They stood staring for the time you'd count three, long enough to have a good look, and then they cleared out. And me—I suddenly felt alone in the world as if everything was running away from me. 'Mademoiselle' I said 'get dressed you filthy slut' and as she was going out I punched her in the face. Since then I haven't had much use for women. I lay one now and then and feel I'd like to spit on her afterwards. After that business with Mademoiselle I got into the way of not hanging about at home. I went to the pictures every day. They taught me quite a lot, in particular that love is nothing but a lot of hooey for getting the broads on heat. I always cleared out before the final clinch and the horizon fading in. But I learnt a few other things that came in handy. All the same, as I said, after I left the college I was bored till the holidays came round. My father has a château in Burgundy but we scarcely ever go there. When it comes to the holidays mother always has some other idea. Two years running we went to Saint-Tropez; but she always left it till the last minute, and so we had one room here and another there, scruffy little rat-traps costing the earth. She'd be out every evening, dances, parties, friends coming to pick her up. There was nothing for me to do but drift round the streets. Saint-Tropez isn't what you'd call lively in the evening. I went to night places and cellars where they danced. I first met Germain on the circular staircase of one of the cellars. We were coming out with the music under our arses and he was a little ahead of me. Just as he was reaching the top he ran into a character in white flannels who was coming down. 'I thought I told you not to come here' Germain said and sat him down on the top step by butting him in the stomach. Then he looked round at me and said 'Help me get him outside.' We carted the type out into the open air. It was two in the morning, not a soul about. Germain beat this number up, he punched him and kicked him and to round it off he put his hand in his trouser pocket and ripped out the front of his flannel bags. We left him lying there and went for a stroll along the front without doing any talking. I could feel that Germain was happy. The next day at about five in the morning we went to the big car-park with a couple of bricks and smashed about fifty windscreens. Another character I met at Saint-Tropez towards the end of the holiday was Hermelin, the managing-director of S.B.H. It was the first week in August. Father had just arrived. He had to sleep on a li-lo in an attic, next to the chauffeur on a straw mattress, but he thought it was quaint. We were on our way to dinner, both parents and Flora and me, and we ran into this Hermelin. Father and he knew each other a little, not very well, but mother was wearing a pretty dress and you could tell from the way he looked at her that she'd got to him. I hated him right away. He was the typical good-looking type of fifty, the face, the voice, shoulders like a rugby footballer, but a sleazy side under all the classy manners, in fact, I'd say a swinish side. He had a villa, and he invited us to dinner next evening. The parents accepted, squirming with delight, but I said nuts and afterwards when father asked me why I said 'Because he makes me sick.' So the next night I had dinner by myself. I went on seeing Germain after we got back to Paris. He had other buddies and I got to know them but I was the one he liked best. We pinched cars just for the fun of leaving them somewhere else. Germain knew all kinds of ways of pinching cars.

Sometimes we jumped on solitary pedestrians at night and beat them up. One night round about midnight we drove a girl into the forest of Rambouillet, a big blonde with plenty of what it takes. Germain and me, we don't talk much, but she was the sort that never stops. Presently she started to get a bit nervous. 'Is it far to this Yugoslav cabaret?' she asked. Germain pulled up. The three of us got out on a narrow road in the middle of the forest. To start with Germain slapped her face. So then she pulled up her skirts and said 'Is this what you want?' So then we pushed her around a little, not very hard, and then we stripped the clothes off her, all except her shoes, and Germain knocked her into the ditch. By the time we'd started the car she was back on the road. We drove a couple of hundred yards and Germain stopped. 'This is going to be good' he said. The girl stark naked had started to run after us. There was a bright moon and you could see everything. We laughed so much it made our guts ache. She was running with her mouth open flapping her arms and her tits bouncing, we fair split with laughing. When she'd almost got to us Germain let in the clutch and drove on another two hundred yards. He did it three times until in the end she was kneeling on the road with her hands clasped wailing and sobbing. Quite a sight. But then we had an argument. Germain wanted to leave her there stark with an icy wind blowing but I wouldn't stand for that. It's all right being a shit but you've got to draw the line somewhere. I insisted on giving her back her clothes and he gave way. Hermelin, the managing-director of S.B.H., was sleeping with mother and he was always dropping in at our place for lunch or dinner. Father didn't see a thing, he hadn't a clue. Mother could have put on all her clothes inside out and he'd never have noticed even with spectacles on top of his monocle. One Sunday when we were lunching with Hermelin mother suddenly said that she'd decided to send Flora to a boarding-school in Neuilly. Just because Hermelin had his eleven-year-old daughter in the same dump. I'm not saying I'm all that keen on Flora, she may be only eleven but you can see the woman sticking out of her already, something dodgy about her and more character in her backside than her head, but all the same it got my goat hearing mother say that and I said to father 'Don't you count for anything around here, are you letting your wife's lover say where Flora's to go to school? I mean it, your wife's lover, you can stare at him like a bloody owl through your flipping monocle but that's the way it is. Well, I'm against it and I say Flora isn't going to any blasted boarding-school.' Well then of course they blew up and I was bawled out and even Flora the little bitch came in on their side. That evening I met Germain and I couldn't help it I spilt the beans. I'd never said a word about my family before or he about his. But he had his troubles same as I had mine. With him it was big money, half-a-dozen servants in Paris and as many more down in the south. His mother was forty, five foot ten tall and manners to match and gold-rimmed spectacles, she'd been left a widow a year after he was born. She didn't go for men. Her passion was good works, committees, meetings, conferences, breathing down the necks of the poor, always on the run from one committee to the next or going abroad to study pauperism in Japan or the Argentine. She was scarcely ever at home and if she did happen to have a meal there it was certain to be with a flock of other female do-gooders. Germain had spent his childhood getting pushed around by the servants who could do no wrong in his mother's eyes because one of the charities she sat on the board of was a society for protecting the dignity of the dependent classes. What with one thing and another Germain had had his belly-ful of charity and good works. When I told him this thing about Flora and the boarding-school he saw that my life wasn't working out either. 'You leave it to me' he said. The next evening he and some pals waited outside Hermelin's house and shook him down so hard that he didn't show his nose out of doors for a week. I stayed at home that evening with Flora and my ever-loving pa, saying that I didn't feel well. It was a cast-iron alibi but it didn't fool Hermelin. All the same he didn't squeal. And all the same when that Easter term ended Flora didn't go to boarding-school. Germain and I went on having fun. One night we loaded up the car with three girls we knew pretty well and drove to a villa some distance from Paris which Germain had spotted—a plushy dump on a side road with iron railings and the village nearly half a mile away hidden behind a curtain of trees. As we were pulling up at the gate we were caught in the headlights of another car coming up fast behind us and we waited for it to pass before getting out. Germain distributed the tools—big hammers for me and the girls and a big wrench for himself. We got the gate open easily enough, the door of the house took a bit longer but we managed that too. We went straight up to the bathroom on the first floor and smashed it to smithereens, bath, toilet, mirrors, bidet, the lot. In the bedrooms we smashed open cupboards and wardrobes, poured bottles of disinfectant over the underclothes, ripped up the bedclothes, gutted mattresses and pillows and all pissed together on one of the carpets. Down on the ground floor we drank whisky by the bottleful. It was hot thundery weather. The girls unzipped themselves and uncovered their breasts. One of them said she'd never felt so good in her life and it was true we felt bloody good. After we'd dealt with the pictures and hangings in the lounge we made a pile of everything we could find in the way of glass and china and pottery and then while we were busy smashing it up half-mad with excitement the gendarmes came bursting in with revolvers. We were taken off to the local lock-up. The coppers and the lock-up—not so funny. But as our families had influence and Germain's mother forked out in a big way for the damage nothing more happened except that the magistrate agreed to let us off on conditions. Germain had to go as a boarder to a school in England and I had to take a job with S.B.H. where Hermelin said he'd find something for me. I didn't like the sound of it but being in the lock-up had shaken me and I was afraid to say no. The day I went there a secretary showed me into an empty room the one I'm writing in now and told me I was to wait here until they'd decided what to do with me. I went out at lunch-time without seeing anyone and ten minutes after I got back Hermelin came in. He had a key and he locked the door behind him. He crossed over to stop me getting out of the window and he stood there grinning for a bit and then he told me how he'd had me followed by a private eye for nearly a month while he waited to catch me doing something sensational. I thought I'd play it tough and I told him his face made me sick so then he lammed me in the mouth with his fist and started to soften me up. Big and heavily built as he was I hadn't a chance against him. For a finish he sent me crashing to the floor beside this desk, with my head against one of the cross bars of the chair which had come down with me. It shook me pretty badly but I could have been worse. All the same I pretended to be half-stunned while I waited to see what he'd do next. And then the filthy swine started undoing his belt. He pulled down his pants and got out the works, staring at me. 'You little swine' he said 'you're going to get what your mother's had and so's your sister Flora.' Just saying it excited him and the machinery started to straighten up as he held it in his hand. Well, it would have annoyed me to get what mother'd had like he said so I started struggling to my feet acting as though I was still dopey and suddenly I straightened up and swung the chair at him .It took him by surprise and as he put his hands up to protect himself I let fly with my foot right into the equipment probably harder than I'd ever kicked anything in my life. It hurt him so much that he turned white as a sheet. He stood there bent double with his

63

teeth clenched and his hands on his thighs not daring to touch the part where it hurt. For just one second he closed his eyes and I let him have it again same foot same place and this time he fainted. I got the key out of his pocket and I went and unlocked the door leaving it half-open. When I saw he was coming to I went and opened the window ready to nip through it if he looked like starting anything else but he'd had it. He did up his belt and went slowly out walking with his legs apart. I locked the door behind him taking care to leave the key in the lock and spent the rest of the afternoon thinking over what had happened. I'd put paid to Hermelin for two or three days but I knew there'd be a comeback. The next day what with mulling it over and over and being so much alone I began to feel scared and that's what has made me write the whole thing down on the bottom of these drawers. At least if anything happens to me someone will end by discovering that it wasn't an accident. Of course I keep the door locked but there's always the risk that he'll get in here before me and hide till I come. Still that isn't what I'm really afraid of. I've been here four days now. I met him in the long corridor yesterday evening and today at lunch-time when I was leaving the building. He didn't look at me. If nothing happens to me, if I leave this room normally to go somewhere else, I'll make a cross on the underside of the desk between the two sets of drawers. If there's no cross I hope someone will pray for me.

Well after all I seem to have been exaggerating. When I got home at about seven yesterday evening I found my parents dolling themselves up for an official dinner. 'Hullo' I said 'isn't Flora here?' 'No' said my mother 'Monsieur Hermelin's chauffeur came for her, she's going to dine at his apartment with Janine.' Janine is Hermelin's daughter. I didn't say anything but I went to the other end of the apartment and called Janine's school. 'Monsieur Hermelin's secretary speaking. May I speak to Janine? I have a message for her from her father.' She

64

was on the line a minute later. No question of her going home or of a date with Flora. I hung up and tore back to the bathroom. Mother was doing her lips and father in his long evening coat was touching up his chin with an electric razor. I switched it off. 'Look' I said 'I've just called Janine's school, she's there and she isn't dining with Flora. The truth is your Hermelin's playing around with your daughter.' My father was like two cents worth of putty. Mother thought that maybe she ought to go after Flora but I said 'You wrap it up, you slut' and I turned back to father. 'Well what are you going to do about it?' 'Well really—well I mean to say—well I hardly know——' that's all I could get out of him, the author of my being. I pushed him out of the bathroom and dragged him along to the telephone to call Hermelin. Pop was trying to look tough but the moment his buddy comes on the line it was nothing but smiles and dear-friend-how-are-you. Janine's here, said Hermelin. The two girls are so happy together. And my bloody stuffed-shirt parent stood there simpering. It wasn't till I'd given him a bang in the ribs with my elbow that he pulled himself together. He started to clear his throat and hum and ha a bit but then mother came rushing in and snatched the receiver out of his hand. 'Dear Monsieur Hermelin we shall be late for dinner. . . . It's so very kind of you. . . .' And the two of them dashed off. I called them every name I could think of, shit, bitch, pimp, whore, I shouted after them all the way downstairs. A waste of breath of course. Where Hermelin's concerned my parents don't want to see or know anything. But I know and I shan't forget. This morning Saturday someone came and knocked on the door of this room at about half-past eleven. Although I knew it was locked I shouted 'Come in' but they didn't try to turn the handle and that was all that happened.

* * *

Here the writing ended, three-quarters of the way down the

sixth drawer. As soon as I had finished reading it I looked for the cross the writer had said he would make on the underside of the desk if, as he put it, he left the room normally to go else-where. I looked for it carefully, using the desk lamp. It shook me a little to find that there was no cross, nothing but an inscription in a different hand which read, 'Long live K! Long live Mao! Porteur for ever!' and which might have been written when the desk was being put together, since it was certainly not old. I spent the rest of the morning searching in vain for a clue, anything that would give me a hint as to what had happened next. Then I went out to join Tatiana at a snack-bar in the Champs-Elysées. We had arranged to meet at a quarter-past twelve, but she didn't turn up till half-past. There was a rush on, she said, and she had less than half an hour to spare.

'How was it?' she asked.

'They've put me in an empty room while they're finding a job for me.'

We hurriedly ate sandwiches and then went for coffee to a quieter place. When we had sat down Tatiana put her hand over mine as it lay on the banquette.

'Well, so this evening you're going back to your home. You needn't apologise, Martin. I'm not reproaching you, but I'm sorry. I should so have liked you to stay with us. Just to know you'd be there when I got back would have changed my whole life. Of course we'd have ended by sleeping together, but why not? I'm not in love with you, but I shouldn't have minded, I promise you. You're clean and you're solid. We'd have been a little bit married without meaning to be—in fact, without even noticing.'

I smiled at the day-dreams that floated through that pretty head.

'That's what you think, but I know that you're always on your guard. You'd realise one day that you were getting in a rut, and you'd go off and leave me there with your mother.'

'But I'd come back. Martin, I'm worried about your going home like this. I imagine that after two years in prison a person doesn't really know who they are.'

'That's just it. I was thinking about it this morning on the bus. To find yourself again you've got to come to grips with life and have contact with people.'

'Yes. Like going back to being a child that is shaped by its environment. And you'll be living with your brother, who's quite worthless, and anyway doesn't care and hasn't the slightest wish to give you anything. But the real truth is, you'll be living with Valérie, and she'll get her hooks well into you because she'll realise, if she's ever forgotten it, that you're someone she can rely on. I saw Valérie a few times when you were engaged. She's not a bad-hearted girl and she has some sense. But she's the kitchen-sink type, narrow, small-minded, full of touchiness and petty jealousies. She'll bring you down to her own level, and that's what I hate. You know it would be very different with me. I'm the sort that opens windows. Well, I've got to go. Will you walk along with me?'

We walked together to the Rue François-Premier and I asked her if we should be meeting again.

'Well, of course, but when? Our jobs take us in different directions. Our hours aren't the same and neither of us has a telephone. Anyway, do you think you'll still want to see me in two months' time?'

I said of course, of course I would, with great conviction, and then as we went on walking in silence I reflected that during the year before my imprisonment we had only met about three times. It was true that in those days she had been absorbed in her studies and her struggle to earn a living, but her present occupations, if more agreeable, seemed to be no less demanding.

We parted at the door of a studio where she was to pose for some publicity photographs. I wanted to thank her for all she had done for me, but emotion overcame me and I could say nothing.

From two to six I sat again in that empty room without seeing anyone, so I spent the time pondering over the mystery of the story written on the drawers and arranging the facts in my mind. The writer had been careful not to give his name or to say anything which might enable the reader to identify his family, except that he had a sister called Flora and that his father was a high-ranking civil-servant who wore a monocle. The name Flora might very well be an invention, and the same applied to the name Germain. Nor was there any way of dating the affair. It could have happened three months or as many years ago. There were points that could probably be cleared up by examining the office records, but for the present, at all events, I had no access to them. The first thing I wanted to know was whether there was any truth in the story at all, or if the whole thing was a fabrication, the work of a mytho-maniac or frustrated author, or even of a lunatic using these devious means to blacken the reputation of a man of good character. Which brought me to Hermelin. He at least existed. I had heard his name mentioned that morning while I was filling in forms, although I had not known what his position was. This seemed to be the one positive fact that the narrative contained. I sat brooding over the mystery, wishing that I had had time to discuss it with Tatiana. I was fascinated but uneasy, and very anxious to discover more.

VI

THAT evening, while I was travelling home by métro to the Saint-Denis station, a couple got on the train to whom at first I paid no attention. The woman was a red-faced, bosomy blonde, going on for forty. I had no recollection of having seen her before, but she stared fixedly at me and when our eyes met a look of intense aversion appeared on her face. Keeping her eyes upon me she leaned towards her companion and whispered in his ear, nodding towards me as she did so. I could feel myself turning pale. They evidently knew who I was and were talking about my crime. While they both stared at me I forced my way backwards through the crowd of passengers, jostling several people because I could not turn my head away. I got out when the train stopped and let two others go by before continuing my journey.

Back at the Rue Saint-Martin I went straight into the concierge's *loge*. Madame Letord, a small, thin, grey-haired woman with a resonant masculine voice that had startled the judge at my trial, proceeded, after greeting me warmly, to tell me what she thought of the jury that had convicted me.

'I never saw such a collection of dunderheads, Monsieur Martin. They didn't know the first thing about life. They had never reflected on the human passions.'

When I asked how the other tenants would view my return she said emphatically that I had nothing to worry about. My treatment of Chazard had made me the hero of the entire building. Despite these consoling words I felt decidedly low-spirited as I went upstairs. I was thinking of Tatiana, her solicitude and tender forthrightness, and wondering whether it was not the sense of my own failure that had caused me to reject all she offered me. I hurried up the stairs nevertheless, still afraid of meeting the neighbours, and by doing so overtook Fondriant, who lived on the fourth floor, an elderly man who had known me since I was a child. He looked round at the sound of my approach, recognised me and turned to greet me with a smile that made me blush with pleasure.

'I'm delighted to see you again,' he said, shaking me warmly by the hand. 'I have often thought of you and your bad luck in having such an unimaginative jury.'

He, too, had come forward as a witness to character, but for all his good intentions he had said nothing strong enough to impress the jurors. Everything I knew about him led me to suspect that if he had been one of them, and someone else had been in the dock, he would have seen nothing wrong with the two-year sentence. Standing outside his door I thanked him for having spoken up on my behalf, and he said as he put his key in the lock, 'Well, don't let's have any more foolishness, and mind you keep a guard on that quick temper of yours.' I promised to do so with a meekness that did not bother me even after we had parted, so relieved was I by the way he had greeted me.

Michel, sprawled on the divan in the living-room, was reading a book entitled *Lolita*. He looked up as I entered and remarked that it was unlike anything he had ever read, a most astonishing novel. I made no comment. I am not interested in novels—or, for that matter, in literature in general. Remembering this, Michel gazed at me for a moment in silence. 'It's the story of a man of forty who's the lover of a girl of twelve,' he said. At which I could not help making a movement of impatience. You sweat your guts out at school and college, you toil through hundreds and thousands of lines designed to shape and edify your tastes and sentiments, and then you're expected to plunge into a kind of literature that contradicts everything you've ever been taught. I said this, and went on to say that if it was little girls today no doubt it would be octogenarians tomorrow. 'A literature of piss-houses and drains and looney-bins, that seems to be what you enjoy,' I said. 'When are we going to have a world best-seller which is entirely about life in a cess-pit?' My sudden exasperation made Michel laugh and I ended by smiling myself, with an effort. I have a puritanical streak, like so many sons of poor parents who acquire a certain amount of education and try to discover, in teachings that take them out of their own world, the austerities of that other order of teaching which is summed up in the word poverty. But Michel, who had never had any part in the financial worries of my father and myself, and in any case was more or less indifferent to material matters, had done his reading as an amateur. Returning to the subject of *Lolita*, and finding me still angry, he said that in literature, as in other domains, one must always press on further in every direction, and that in one direction or another there must exist a sort of sound-barrier beyond which the spirit would acquire an unimaginable agility—a view which seemed to me scarcely in keeping with his general nonchalance.

Valérie came in, wearing a kitchen-apron over her dress, and seemed in no way put out at finding me there. I apologised for moving in sooner than I had expected, but she replied amicably that everything was ready for me and there was plenty of supper for three.

'Afterwards I'll make up the big bed. It makes no difference to me because I always sleep in the little one anyway. We can arrange about washing.'

Here, as in Tatiana's apartment, one had to wash at the kitchen-sink. Valérie cleared Michel's books and papers off one end of the table and proceeded to lay three places. When she went back into the kitchen I got up and offered to help, but she smiled and said not to bother. I had gone with her as far as the door, and when I turned back I found Michel again immersed in *Lolita*. I went and stood at the window, which looked on to an interior courtyard already plunged in dusk. Of the seven attic windows opposed to ours, two were lighted, with shadowy figures to be seen moving behind their curtains of tulle. They must be those of people I had known a very long time, if the inmates of the house had not changed during my absence. One of the attics had been occupied by an old woman who never showed herself at the window except in summer, another by a man with a bald head and a black moustache who knelt on the window-seat every morning and prayed with clasped hands, finally crossing himself. This ostentatious display of piety had intensely irritated Chazard, whose apartment, just below ours, also looked out on to the courtyard. It had also incurred my father's displeasure when he learned that the man was merely a waiter. 'I ask you,' he said. 'A waiter in a café!'

As we began our meal I asked Michel if he had become a Communist while I was away. He shook his head, and I told him of the inscription I had found underneath the middle part of the desk—'Long live K! Long live Mao! Porteur for ever!' He was amused at first but then he looked thoughtful. The mention of Porteur had caused Valérie's expression to harden. I seemed to discern that for her the pseudonym represented a side of Michel's life which was outside her control and to which she had no access.

'Why?' Michel asked. 'Have *you* joined the Communists?'

'Oh lord no. In prison you're completely cut off from everything. You don't feel that politics concern you in any way at all. In any case, I'd never been able to get interested in them, even before I went to prison. I felt that all that business was nothing but a fly-blown stage-setting, and that what really mattered was scientific know-how—electronics, nuclear physics and the rest of it.'

'Just the same,' said Valérie, 'if we didn't have men like Pinay at the helm we should be in a fine old mess.'

'For God's sake!' said Michel. 'You're crazy. Our father's political notions used to make me sick, the typical lower middle-class view of the Right as the safeguard of wisdom, security, sound currency and a peaceful old age.'

'They were better ideas than any of your friends have,' snapped Valérie. 'All your dope-fiends and dirty Yids!'

The outburst did not surprise either Michel or me. Ever since I had known her, and probably long before that, Valérie had been an anti-Semite. I remember that once, some years ago, I found among Michel's school books a volume by Sartre containing some brilliant pages on the subject of anti-Semitism among the wealthy bourgeoisie. But I am afraid Sartre was not very well-informed. The immense majority of our wealthy bourgeois families get along very comfortably with the Jewish bourgeoisie. The real anti-Semites in Paris are the shop-assistants, office-employees and people of that sort, not because they have any particular racial theories, or because they are concerned with defending the Christian faith, but simply because for them the Jew is the boss. The same applies to a great many small independent tradespeople who were once on somebody's pay-roll, and to their children, who, although they may have risen into the ranks of the liberal professions, continue to think, or rather to talk, as their parents did. But it is the clerks and shop-assistants who remain the solid core of anti-Semitism. Valérie's case was rather special. She had once been passed over for a secretarial post, to which she had some reason to consider herself entitled, in favour of a relation of one of the partners in the firm, two Jewish brothers. Not only Valérie, but her mother, a domestic servant in Belleville, and both her brothers, one a lorry-driver and the other a mechanic, had become furiously anti-Semitic when this happened.

I asked Michel if he had heard any news of Dépardon, a former schoolfellow of mine who had become an official in the Préfecture de la Seine. He said he had seen his mother, who lived near us, not long ago. Dépardon, taking the view that France was growing increasingly effete, had left for Caracas last September. After supper was over, at about nine, Michel put on an old duffel-coat and left us without a word.

'He's going to join his Yids,' said Valérie. 'He's Porteur now. Oh, I'm fed up with it. Porteur!'

'Why are you so fed-up?'

'Well, of course, you don't know. I'm even astonished that when you found the name Porteur written under that desk you should have connected it with Michel. But you'll be even more surprised when I tell you that there are people for whom Porteur really means something. It's a thing I'm always coming up against—for instance, only last week. One of the girls who works in our office, Emilienne, has a brother who was on leave from Algeria, and on his way back from Saint-Hilaire-du-Harcouet—that's where the family lives, at Saint-Hilaire-du-Harcouet—he spent a couple of days in Paris. Emilienne wanted to show him round a bit and she asked me to help, so one night we all went to Saint-Germain-des-Prés. I may say I'd never been there before. Heavens, it was boring! Anyway after we'd been to the historic cafés, the Deux Magots and all that, we went to a little place in a side-street where two or three couples were dancing to a juke-box. The boys were students and so were the girls, I suppose. Me, I can't stand students, the sort of show-off look they have and still not really sure of themselves or fitted into life, which they can't possibly be at their age. We just had one drink and then we left. It was only a little after eleven. We strolled along the boulevard and then on the other side we saw a place with a terrace above the level of the pavement. La Rhumerie, I think it was called—would that be it?'

'I don't know. But it's a name I seem to have heard.'

'Well anyway, we went there. There were six at the next table, five boys and a girl who wasn't badly dressed. They were all arguing together, and suddenly, although I wasn't paying any attention, I heard the name of Porteur.'

'It's a common enough name,' I said. 'There must be thousands of Porteurs.'

'I know. But one of them said, "Try to see things the way Porteur does." So then they all started shouting each other down about the way Porteur saw things, and people from other tables came and joined them and said what *they* thought about Porteur and his point of view, and suddenly this well-dressed girl asked if any of them actually knew Porteur. Dead silence. "Well, I do," the girl said. "That's to say, I know someone who knows him. Porteur lives in the Rue Saint-Martin." At this they all looked respectful and there was another silence, except for someone who said, "Good lord—fancy!" '

'But didn't you ask Michel why his name, and presumably his person as well, should be held in such reverence?'

'Of course I did. He just didn't seem to understand. But you know what he's like when he doesn't want to say anything.'

I followed Valérie into the kitchen and we went on talking while she washed up. I asked her if she often went out in the evenings and she said she couldn't afford to. Once a week she went to see her mother. I told her that from now on I would pay the rent of the apartment and the cost of keeping my brother. She made no objection to this but I felt that it did not greatly please her.

We talked until ten, and then, when she saw me yawning, Valérie said that it was time for bed.

'As we're sharing the bedroom,' she said, 'we'd better decide how we've to arrange matters. There are only two ways. Either we don't undress at the same time, and take care never to see each other stark, or else we just don't bother one way or the other, which would be much more convenient, considering how small the apartment is. Seeing that you find me repulsive I don't imagine it will worry you.'

75

'I didn't say I found you repulsive.'

'Never mind. Which way do you prefer?'

'Better choose the one that's most convenient.'

'All right.'

Valérie went into the kitchen to take off her make-up, while I started to undress. I had my shirt and vest off and was unlacing my shoes when she came into the bedroom. By the time I had taken off my trousers, folded them and hung them over a chair, she was in nothing but her pants and stockings. She was standing directly in front of me, but when she spoke I was afraid to look at her.

'Don't worry about me if you want to read,' she said. 'The light won't keep me awake.'

'Thanks. I don't want to read tonight.'

She got into bed naked, explaining that pyjamas and night-dresses cost too much. I found at the same moment that my own pyjamas were missing. Michel had worn them out all the faster because they were too small for him. So I too slid naked between the sheets, beneath the gaze of Valérie, who, sitting up in bed, reached out an arm to switch off the light. I had been afraid that her presence would cause me a restless night, but in fact I fell asleep almost at once. When I got up next morning she was washing at the sink, stripped to the waist. She dressed while I washed and then got breakfast for the two of us, since Michel, who had come home late as usual, rarely awoke before midday. We breakfasted in the kitchen, and I was the first to leave, having further to go than she. It was clear that we were going to have to live together on terms differing only in one respect from those of man and wife.

VII

My second day at S.B.H. was passed in solitude as complete as the first. I had brought with me a book of Michel's entitled *In the Cause of Uselessness*; a philosophical essay, printed in large type and bearing a flowery inscription in the author's hand, devoted to the proposition that the performance of 'useful work,' in the ordinary sense of the words, served merely to debase humanity, to disfigure it and speed its progress to an ignoble end. The first chapter began as follows: 'I use the word "parasite" to denote the man of superior qualities who leaves it to others to provide for his material necessities on the severely restricted scale which is all he requires.' I read the whole of it during the day, but not all in one gulp. After getting down two or three chapters I allowed myself a long pause during which my thoughts were divided between Valérie and the mysterious writer of the story in the desk. Where Valérie was concerned I marvelled at my sobriety and self-control. No more than two or three times the night before, and once that morning, had I needed to resist a passing impulse to fling myself upon her. But I was very much struck by the change that seemed to have come over her during my absence, the courage and sturdiness which had enabled her to keep her singular ménage going for two years, the clear-sighted detachment with which she viewed herself and her situation, and her rather crude frankness of a woman who has nothing to hide. All this was very different from the old days, when she had constantly exasperated me with her anxiety to make much of herself by striking attitudes and enacting elaborate falsehoods that as a rule were quite pointless except for her desire to impress. Being accustomed to take people seriously I had often quarrelled with her about this.

But it seemed that living with Michel had taught her the vanity of lies and pretentiousness. One of the ways in which he was my superior, and that of a good many other people, was in his capacity for seeing through affectations at a glance, and ruthlessly demolishing them, often with no more than a grin.

As for my unknown story-teller, I was no wiser than I had been the day before. But the presence of that riddle, in the room where I was sitting, began finally to prey upon my mind. Once again I meticulously examined the desk to make sure that I had overlooked nothing, and then the room itself, which was so small and bare that it seemed to offer no hope of a clue. There was no cupboard in it, not even a shelf. On the other hand, there was a coat-stand with three arms, and this, too, I examined minutely, searching for a mark, a name scratched on the wood. It was on the face of it an unhopeful quest, since if the writer had wanted to be identified he could have written his name on one of the drawers, or on all of them, together with any details he cared to add. Finally, having found nothing, I turned in irritated frustration to the fourth chapter of my book. My eye ran over the following sentences, without my mind really taking them in: 'Let us now seek to distinguish beyond all possibility of confusion between the useless and the useful thing. The components of appreciation, for those content to accept superficial evidence, would seem to be innumerable. . . .' This fourth chapter, in short, promised to be at least as boring and pompously written as the others, and before grappling with it I allowed myself another breathing space. As I sat staring rather blankly at the unpolished panes of the window the last words of the first sentence I had just read, and the opening words of the second, occurred to my mind—'The useful thing the components.' It sounded a little more like sense. I repeated the words, and this time added something to them, for no reason at all except that my eyes happened to be absently dwelling on it at the time—'The useful thing the components of the radiator.' There was a radiator in the room, fixed to the wall but standing an inch or two away from it: and suddenly I experienced that slight, subtle thrill that I had known in my student days when I found that I was in sight of the solution of a problem of mathematics. I went and stood over the radiator, knowing in a flash what the 'useful thing' was, and where I was going to find it. I reached down behind the radiator, and my hand came up with a nickel key fitted with a hook made of stout wire. The method of keeping it in place was ingenious. It had been hanging by its hook from a thick elastic band attached by similar hooks to two of the inner flanges of the radiator. The key fitted the door of the room, as I at once ascertained.

Greatly heartened by this discovery I sat down to think it over. The key was a piece of concrete evidence enabling me to believe that the story in the desk must at least be partly true. Allowance had still to be made for exaggeration, and even for pure invention designed to further some purpose of revenge; but there must be some compelling reason why this youth should have found it necessary to lock himself in the room. It was really only on principle that I went on raising objections in my own mind. The story itself, with its uncouth vocabulary and slapdash style and punctuation, was enough to convince me that it contained an element of truth. I had known semi-literates of this sort at school and in the army, scarcely capable of composing a grammatical sentence. They hated having to put anything on paper, and only a very powerful motive would have driven any of them to write so long a tale.

It was not hard to understand why the youth had hidden the key before leaving the room. He must have been afraid, if he kept it in his pocket, that he might meet Hermelin outside and have it taken away from him. And one day, at the lunch-hour or in the evening, he had put the key in its hiding-place and left the building, never to return. Perhaps he had simply gone off on a Saturday meaning to return on Monday, but after thinking it over during the week-end had told his parents that he would rather go to prison. Perhaps he was now in prison, or had joined the paratroops or the Foreign Legion; or perhaps he was dead.

Before going out for lunch I too fixed the key behind the radiator. A young woman emerged from a door across the corridor at the same moment as I, clutching her overcoat about her. 'This place is like an ice-chest,' she said to a plump, middle-aged man who had also just appeared. It was true that the building was far from warm. He rubbed her back, taking the chance to sniff her neck in the furtive manner not uncommon in men at his time of life, tormented with the itch. 'Mademoiselle Chardon,' he said, 'I bring glad tidings. They're lighting the furnace now.' The people I passed in the corridor ignored me, and I was as offended as though it were a deliberate slight. In the enclosed world of prison every new face had been an object of intense interest, as a rule favourably disposed. Here nobody cared. As I drew near the stairs I saw the young woman who had dealt with my papers in the staff-office and I tried to catch her eye, but she went by without giving me a glance. In this case it must have been intentional, and it did not seem to me to augur well for my future in S.B.H.

Out in the street I found Tatiana waiting for me in a taxi. I got in with her and we drove towards the Rue Saint-Honoré, where her place of business was.

'I had twenty minutes to spare so I thought I'd pick you up,' she said. 'I wanted to ask you to come to supper this evening. You will? Good. And how did you get on yesterday evening at home?'

'Very respectably. Michel went out after supper as usual and didn't get back till two or three in the morning.'

'How charming of him! The very night you arrive. How lordly and distinguished!'

'Tatiana, you're wrong about Michel. He has his faults, but he's really quite incapable of vanity or affectation. That's what makes him so easy to live with. So Valérie and I were left alone. We talked for a time about money and practical arrangements and then we went to bed, she in the little bed and I in the big one.'

'And weren't you tempted?'

'Very much less than I had expected, although we agreed that we weren't going to fuss about undressing in the same room.'

'Don't flatter yourself, Martin. You'll be caught out one of these days. I'm a little consoled by the thought that Balzac in his *Physiologie du Mariage* comes out strongly against separate beds, which he says are the worst possible thing for marital harmony and good-will. But then, writers often talk nonsense. I do hope you aren't going to be silly.'

I promised with a light heart and, dropping Tatiana outside Orsini's, took the taxi on to the Bourse, whence I went on foot to the Rue Saint-Martin. Valérie was back from work already and laying the table in the living-room. Michel, still in bed, opened one eye and then turned over and buried his face in the pillows. I waited for Valérie to go out and promptly stripped the bedclothes off him, leaving him naked.

'Up you get! Surely you don't expect Valérie to serve you in bed with me here?'

He pushed me away, retrieved the blankets and lay down again.

'Why should I get up? She likes bringing me meals in bed, and all the more because it's an excuse for giving me a piece of her mind—waster, loafer, idle clod, and I'll be the death of her only she'll clear out one of these days and leave me to rot in my own squalor, and so on ad lib. She knows insults don't worry me and she can say whatever she likes. I daresay your being here will make her pipe down a little, but of course that'll soon wear off.'

Valérie returned and planted a dish of steak and fried potatoes on the table. She then threw a couple of pullovers at
Michel and he pulled them on, one on top of the other. She
gave him the largest portion of the meat, but when he asked
for potatoes she said shrewishly:

'You eat your meat first and you'll get your potatoes afterwards.'

'Just two or three. Just to taste. Please.'

'I said no. If you want to eat like other people you must get
up like other people.'

To change the subject I raised the question of heating the
apartment. It was no problem in Valérie's eyes. They had had
no heating of any kind during the two years they had been
together, not even in the depth of winter, and they were none
the worse for it. Michel finished his steak and held out
his plate for potatoes, and this reminded me to mention that
I should not be in for supper that evening. Valérie received
the news with manifest displeasure. She did not love me,
perhaps she even detested me, but I had become a member
of the household and she intended to order my life so far as
she was able. However, Michel was the immediate victim of
her wrath.

'Here you are, take the potatoes, take the lot, since it seems
I'm not even expected to eat anything. I think I ought to
have my head examined, getting up at seven and doing the
housework, and then the office, run off my feet from morning
to night, while you do nothing but eat and sleep and out all
night with a crowd of Yids and sluts. I'd like to know what I'm
supposed to be, nothing but an unpaid maid-of-all-work with
two great useless louts on my hands, and if I want a man to
go to bed with I can darned well go next door!'

Michel retorted that if this was meant for me I was under no
obligation to keep her company in the evenings, still less to
pander to her lascivious furies.

82

'It's a pity he finds you so unattractive,' he said, 'but it can't be helped.'

Valérie made no reply; but the remark had done nothing to improve the atmosphere, as I pointed out to him when she had gone to make the coffee.

'If you turn her against me,' I said, 'life will become impossible.'

'Don't you worry. The only thing you have to fear is that she'll assault you in your bed. You'll see.'

I left the Rue Saint-Martin at a little after one and returned on foot to the S.B.H. building. Paris at that hour is still at table, and it was pleasant to walk through the relatively quiet streets. Contemplating those long, open vistas I had a slight pang, a momentary return of my absurd nostalgia for prison, where for two years I had rejoiced in an incomparable freedom of spirit, life in that place being so tranquil and restricted that it called for no exercise of judgement or decision. I had never been one of those prisoners who live with clenched teeth, their heads filled with memories and evocations of the outside world.

When I got back to my room I was struck at once by its unaccustomed warmth and a smell of scorched rubber. The central heating, as I now recalled, had been started that morning, and the radiator was already very hot. I managed to retrieve the key, burning my fingers in the process, and I also removed the rubber band from which it had been hanging. This turned out to be a strip cut from the inner-tube of a bicycle-tyre. I found, as I examined it, that it was scarcely affected by the heat. It was not at all perished, as must have happened had it been left in contact with the heated radiator for any length of time. The smell, in any case, would have been likely to give away the hiding-place of the key. It seemed certain, then, that it had been put there when the radiator was not in use, which meant that my unknown author must have occupied the room since the ending of the winter. I tried to remember if there was anything in the story indicating a particular time of year, but being unable to do so I locked the door and copied the whole thing out. I had taken up shorthand while I was in the army, with a vague idea that it might some-day come in useful, so the job did not take me very long. While I was doing it I noted a phrase referring to the night when the party of young vandals had wrecked the villa—'It was hot, thundery weather.' Such weather is uncommon in the Paris region before the end of June, and this, taking into account the likelihood that Flora and her mother had later gone away on holiday, made it seem probable that the incident had occurred early in July—that is to say, about three months ago.

I finished my copy at about three, and being then in a state of some excitement I soothed myself with the remaining chapters of *In the Cause of Uselessness*. When I had finished this, too, I suddenly remembered that the door of the room was still locked. I unlocked it and put the key in my pocket, together with my sheets of shorthand and the strip of rubber. And about ten minutes later the door opened and a man walked into the room, tall, powerfully built, with stiff grey hair, regular features and a heavily-boned face—in short, the 'typical good-looking type of fifty' described in the narrative. Even the hint of swinishness was not lacking. Leaving the door open he walked past my desk, then turned abruptly and said in a harsh, deliberately loud voice:

'You're just out of prison, aren't you? You murdered a man called Chazard.'

'Quite correct. And who are you?'

'I'm the Managing Director of S.B.H.'

I picked up my book, took my raincoat down from the peg and walked out of the room without looking at him. In a towering rage I ran upstairs to the second floor, darted across the lobby, where a porter in a blue uniform shouted at me, 'Where are you going? What do you want?' and burst into the Chairman's office. Lormier, seated at his huge desk, looked up with a frown. I stopped a few feet away from him and said:

'I don't know what you're playing at. You seem to have got me here simply for people to call me a murderer to my face. I'm clearing out—and you can keep my two days' money.'

'Who called you a murderer?' asked Lormier, coolly surveying me.

'The Managing Director—with your approval, I suppose.'

At the mention of the Managing Director a light shone in his eye and the sudden tightening of his jaw caused his flabby jowls to tremble. He touched a bell and a messenger entered.

'Lambert, tell Monsieur Hermelin I would like to see him at once.' Then he turned back to me. 'Which department have they put you in?'

'None at all. I've spent these two days sitting in an empty room waiting for a job to be found for me, if there is one.'

'Do you mean to say the staff-manager hasn't given you anything to do?'

'Nothing whatever.'

The messenger must have met Hermelin in the corridor, for at this moment he entered. He was carrying himself very erect, with an expression on his face of mingled disdain and defiance. Lormier did not look at him but went on addressing me as though he had not noticed his arrival.

'You have high professional qualifications,' he said in a formal tone, 'and, as I have already noted, remarkable maturity of judgement for so young a man. We are regrettably lacking in men of your type in S.B.H., where, I am sorry to say, authority does not always go with merit. In a large concern like this, principles have sometimes to be sacrificed to expediency, greatly though I deplore it.'

He then affected to become aware of Hermelin's presence, and turning to him said sharply:

'I understand, Monsieur Hermelin, that you called Monsieur Martin a murderer.'

'Was I mistaken?' asked Hermelin with an unabashed grin.

'Let me remind you that you were guilty of an offence punishable by law. We will inquire later into your reasons. For the present, Monsieur Martin, since I am finally responsible for what goes on in this place, I will ask you to accept my apologies for any discourtesy that may have been shown you, and in particular for the insufferable conduct of my Managing Director.'

'One minute,' said Hermelin, flushing crimson. 'As Managing Director I am responsible——'

'That will do, Hermelin. You can go.'

'I have the right——'

'I said, you can go!'

After a moment of hesitation, during which the two men glared at one another, Hermelin turned and walked towards the door, still with his head held high. Lormier watched his departure with a smile of triumphant malice, but without, as it seemed to me, being wholly satisfied. He spoke into the house-telephone.

'Odette, will you please ask Monsieur Keller to come here immediately?'

We waited in silence. The Chairman was fidgeting with his small, puffy hands, pressing the tips of the fingers together. A door at the far end of the room opened, and Lambert showed in Keller, the staff-superintendent, who had received me upon my arrival the day before. He was a man in his thirties, fair-haired, with a thin, shrewd face. He glanced at me, but did not acknowledge my greeting.

'You wanted to see me, Monsieur le Président?'

'Yes, Keller. It appears to me that you are neglecting your

duties. For the past two days you have kept Monsieur Martin sitting in an empty room without giving him any work to do. You're wasting the company's money.'

'I can assure you, sir, I have only done what I normally do in the case of a person joining the company on a personal recommendation. We wait until a suitable place can be found for them.'

'Another thing, Keller. When I mentioned Monsieur Martin to you the day before yesterday I told you that you need not include any mention of his police record in his dossier.'

'Quite so, sir. I gave orders that this formality was to be dispensed with.'

'But you took care to see that Monsieur Hermelin was informed.'

'It was not a matter that I felt able to conceal from the Managing Director, in case he later held me responsible.'

'And your own slight trouble with the police a few years ago, in which I had to get my brother to intervene—something to do with a young man in a public lavatory, was it not?—did you feel unable to conceal that, too, from the Managing Director?'

Flushing scarlet, his shoulders sagging, Keller had for a moment the tormented and furtive look that I had seen on the faces of well-dressed men in my own quarter as they lurked near the public urinals.

'Did you in fact inquire into Monsieur Martin's past, Keller?'

'No, sir, I did not,' replied Keller eagerly, happy to be able to defend himself on one count, and with his strained face already relaxing.

'Then it can only have been Monsieur Hermelin. I would like you to note that Monsieur Martin will in future be working directly under me in the capacity of—well, let us say, as my personal assistant. I will ask you, as staff-superintendent, to ensure that he has free access to all departments, including your own. He will be acting in my name and he will be entitled to know about everything that goes on.'

After Keller had departed Lormier warned me that he had saddled me with two vigilant enemies whom I must never for an instant overlook. In fact, they were his own enemies; for Hermelin, as I realised, aspired to the office of chairman, and Keller, whom Lormier had thought he had under his thumb, was now revealed as one of his supporters.

'You must watch those rats very closely. Hermelin is a dull-minded brute, but cunning and tenacious. He has made trouble for me before now and he'll do so again.'

Lormier then took me into the adjoining room and introduced me to his private secretary, Odette, a woman in her thirties, sturdily built and flat-chested, with the calves of a long-distance runner and a candid, intelligent face. She showed no great pleasure at the news that I was to work with her in close attendance on the Chairman. My build, my look of a transplanted peasant and my unprepossessing countenance, did little to predispose women in my favour, a fact to which I had grown accustomed. Two other women shared Odette's room, an assistant-secretary, Jocelyne, thin and unbeautiful, aged about twenty-five, and a youthful typist name Angelina, a graceful, pretty child. They looked at me with mistrust, if not hostility, and when Odette introduced us, after Lormier had left the room, they were civil but no more.

VIII

TATIANA—I was conscious of it the moment I entered—had the slightly shamefaced, evasive look of a child conscious of ill-doing—of clipping the cat's hair, for instance, or locking her old uncle in a cupboard. I also noted that the table in the living-room was laid only for two. Watchfully observing my expression, Tatiana blushed, and her lips quivered slightly as she spoke.

'Mother isn't here. She's having dinner with Dunia Skuratov.'

Whereupon she flung herself upon me, a good three inches taller than I, and with her lips pressed to mine bent me backwards as though she were the male half of the act. For a moment I felt humiliated and ridiculous, but then my vexation melted and I went with her into her bedroom. We were there for more than an hour, side by side in her narrow bed, and finally she leaned on one elbow, gazed into my eyes, and said:

'You aren't going back to the Rue Saint-Martin. I'll fetch your things. You're staying here.'

I said no, calmly and firmly. Seeing that I really meant it she cried in despair—'Then it's been no use!' I buried my face in her hair to hide the smile prompted by this revealing outburst. Tatiana wept on my shoulder and I talked softly to her, saying that I loved her.

'I'd be ready enough to be your sheet-anchor, but it wouldn't work. My being here wouldn't stop you doing the thing you're afraid of—the reverse, if anything. Nothing can prevent you except yourself.'

'Rubbish. The truth is, you'd sooner live in the Rue Saint-Martin. Oh, why won't you marry me?'

89

I got dressed and Tatiana, after covering herself with a peignoir, suddenly changed her mind and decided to honour me by putting on a very pretty dress and subduing the fiery tangle of her hair. Before putting on the dress she paraded herself almost naked, in nothing but shoes and stockings and a white, embroidered suspender-belt. No doubt she had been told many times that she looked enchanting like this. I said it again, and it did indeed seem to me that she made the American pin-ups look dreary by comparison.

The living-room was filled with flowers in vases and pots. There were flowers everywhere, even in the kitchen, expensive flowers, and I did not doubt that they came from Lormier. Tatiana was giving me a cold meal. While she bustled to and fro laying the table I told her about Hermelin and that he had asked me if I was Chazard's murderer. She was furiously and volubly indignant, which pleased me, but when I went on to tell her of the sort of defensive pact between Lormier and myself she became thoughtful. Nor did she react as I had expected to the news that I was to be Lormier's personal assistant, but only congratulated me in an abstracted, non-committal way. This so surprised and disappointed me that I very nearly didn't tell her the rest of my news; but as we took our seats side by side at the table she got up abruptly and pressed my head to her bosom, saying with every appearance of meaning it:

'Oh, I can't tell you how delighted I am!'

We started on the oysters which she had opened before my arrival, as badly as possible. Nearly all had bits of shell in them, some had been drained of their liquid and others had been mashed into a pulp.

'Tatiana, there's something else I want to tell you about. Since I got to S.B.H. I've been sitting in an empty office in front of an empty desk with six drawers, three on either side. Well . . .'

I told her of my discovery, and then got out my shorthand

copy and read her the story. She was as passionately interested and full of questions as I had hoped.

'Did you find the cross on the underside of the desk?'

'No. There was nothing but an inscription—"Long live K. Long live Mao. Porteur for ever." But it was in a different handwriting.'

'Porteur a Communist? Well, that's a joke! Weren't there any other clues?'

I produced the key and the strip of rubber, and explained why I had concluded that the story must have been written about three months ago. She was now very excited.

'But we've got to find out who this boy is. We've got to do something. That story's a cry for help. You don't seem to realise!'

'Believe me, I've thought a lot about what one's duty is after making a discovery of this sort. I'm not trying to get out of it, but as a convicted killer I'm not so keen on going to the police to report a crime that may never have been committed. Suppose the boy has simply returned to the bosom of his family or joined the paratroops, I'd look silly, to say the least. Before I start anything I want to be able to say definitely, "So-and-so has disappeared, and his family have had no news of him. I think I can shed some light on what happened." Even then I shall be lucky if I don't come under suspicion myself.'

'Why don't you tell Lormier?'

'I've thought of that too, but I don't trust Lormier any more than I do Hermelin. There seems to me to be very little to choose between them. S.B.H. reeks of intrigue and blackmail, from what I've seen of it. Suppose Hermelin has had a hand in a murder and Lormier finds out—do you think justice would be done? I'm not so sure. Lormier might find it more convenient to use it as a means of keeping his Managing Director under control. That is to say, the whole thing would be discreetly buried, and my own position—well, there's really no knowing.'

91

191558

'Prison has put a lot of ideas into your head,' said Tatiana in an awed voice. 'But still you can't just leave it at that. What are you going to do?'

'I thought I had an idea when Lormier told me what my job was to be. I'm to have access to all departmental records, including personnel, which means that I should be able to find out all about anyone who joined the company during June and July. But thinking it over I doubt if that's worth very much. Of course I'll see what there is, but with Hermelin and Keller working together the chances are that this youth's record will have vanished from the files.'

'But you've still got his story.'

'Yes, and that is where you can help me. You meet a lot of people in your job. I want you to try and identify a family living in Passy, the husband a senior civil-servant with a monocle (but the monocle may be just a trimming), the wife very flighty, a daughter named Flora and a Buick, with chauffeur.'

At this moment—we were now eating cold chicken—Sonia Bouvillon burst into the room. She came towards me smiling, but as I rose to greet her Tatiana sprang up and seized her by the shoulders.

'What has happened? You're supposed to be dining with Dunia?'

'Heavens!' exclaimed Sonia. 'May the Lord take pity on his miserable servant! Dunia Skuratov—I'd forgotten all about her. Oh, why did Adrien have to die before me? It would never have happened if he'd been here.'

'This is the second time you've stood her up. Well, come on. You needn't think you're going to eat the rest of our chicken. Hurry!'

A minute later we were all running down the stairs with Sonia pursuing her monologue.

'I wouldn't have dared forget while Adrien was alive, and yet he wasn't as hard on me as my daughter. But he was the soul of neatness and order. "Your slip's showing," he'd say, or, "Your seams aren't straight." Well, of course, he was so used to women.'

While she and Tatiana went into a café to telephone I ran for a taxi. I had to go as far as the Place Clichy before I found one. We drove Sonia to the Skuratovs' dwelling in a small street near the Place des Ternes. She continued to argue and protest at length, saying that it would be better if she didn't go, that Dunia wouldn't really mind and that anyway everything blew over in the end.

'Mother, you're going!' Tatiana finally cried in a tone of such exasperation that it silenced us all for the rest of the journey. I was watching her and trying to guess what was in her mind. She had a hard expression, almost fierce, and I fancied that she was now angrily reproaching herself for the folly and fruitlessness of our proceedings before supper. I, too, was sorry I had given way, the more so since I was now sure that I loved Tatiana and was likely to lose everything, even her friendship. When we arrived she said that she would wait in the taxi while I took Sonia up to the Skuratovs' apartment and saw to it that she didn't come down again without ringing the bell.

'You know,' said Sonia, as we climbed the stairs, 'I didn't exactly *think* of forgetting, but I daresay I should have done it if I had. My poor mother, who must surely be seated at God's right hand, often used to say to us, "If you forget a thing it's because you really want to."'

I watched her press the bell and waited just long enough to see the door open and a woman rather older than herself appear. They fell into each other's arms crying, 'Darling! Darling!'

Tatiana, when I rejoined her, told me that we were now going to call upon her friend Christine de Rézé and her husband in the Rue Spontini. She had rung up after telephoning to Dunia, while I was looking for the taxi.

'Rézé works in the Foreign Office, at the Quai d'Orsay,' she said. 'He's rich. He only does it to amuse himself, and perhaps also because it looks well. Anyway he may be able to tell us about your high official in Passy.'

It was Christine de Rézé who opened the door to us, a pretty woman about as tall as Tatiana, but slimmer, less solid, less richly curved. Her face was soft and secret. Tatiana introduced us in terms which made it clear that she had spoken of me already, and she offered me her hand after a very slight pause, not, as it seemed, because she was reluctant to do so, but because she had needed a moment to consider, the gesture not coming quite naturally. Tatiana took off the grey coat with its rabbit-skin collar which still troubled her. Looking each other over in the lobby, the two women told each other their respective weights, patting each other's hips, waist and bosom as they did so. Then the Count de Rézé came out into the lobby. He was a man of about forty with slender hands, refined features and intelligent eyes in which there was a slight cast, most elegantly dressed with, I thought, a preference for being behind the times. He clasped my hand warmly and his words of greeting were no less cordial. Evidently he was proud and delighted to be receiving a convicted criminal in his home, and I think he rather admired himself for it. We moved into a small drawing-room, comfortable and luxurious. What most impressed me was that there was nothing on the walls except a single line-drawing, signed Etienne Dupont, casually affixed with four drawing-pins. I realised, thinking it over later, that if the name had been that of a well-known artist the whole effect would have been spoiled. It would then have been an affectation amounting almost to bad taste. And in a conventional, middle-class drawing-room, of course, the off-hand gesture would have been meaningless. One needed riches and a degree of civilisation to be master of these subtleties.

94

'I know you think I'm as crazy as a coot,' Tatiana said, 'and what I've come to talk about isn't going to make it any better. Martin and I have reasons for believing that a youth whose name we don't even know has disappeared in suspicious circumstances. Our only clues to his identity are as follows. He's a rather bad boy of about seventeen. His father is a high official who wears a monocle—but we can't be sure about the monocle, it may be real or just a figure of speech. His mother's a cocktail-party snob who has had a great many lovers. There's also a twelve-year-old daughter named Flora. The father has a castle in Burgundy, which doesn't prevent the family from going to Saint-Tropez for their holidays and paying enormous prices for attic bedrooms. Oh, and they have a Buick and a chauffeur.'

There was a pause while de Rézé thought this over. Christine was the first to speak.

'A Buick—would it be Bijoux?'

'No, definitely not,' said de Rézé. 'Bijoux isn't the monocle type and he hasn't got a castle in Burgundy. Besides, he has two sons and no daughter. This isn't a riddle you can answer in a flash. Paris is bulging with high officials. It's a case for systematic inquiry. You're in a hurry, I take it?'

'A great hurry,' said Tatiana.

'Well, tomorrow I'll get my secretary on to it. She can start by finding out which high officials own Buicks. There can't be very many.'

'There's another problem, connected with the first. This boy had a friend about his own age whose mother is an extremely wealthy widow with a house full of servants in Paris and another on the Riviera. She's a tall woman with a passion for good works.'

'Well, I can guess who that is. She's a Madame Cousin, the widow of Léopold Cousin, who owned *Pâtes Alimentaires Coucou*—spaghetti and so forth.'

'Her son's name is Germain.'

'H'm ... Cousin Germain. That has a phoney ring to me. It sounds more like a joke.'

'It very likely is a joke,' I said. 'His friends may have nick-named him Germain because of his surname.'

'Well anyway, your charitable lady can only be Héloïse Cousin. At present she's touring South America, where, to judge by the reports that come in, she's making life a hell for our diplomatic representatives by trying to drag them into the slums of every capital she visits. She's known to a good many Ministries here in Paris as the most formidable of all our charity-loving ladies.'

It was unfortunate that this Madame Cousin should be abroad, but nevertheless Tatiana and I both felt that we had made some progress. The name of Cousin alone had estab-lished a link between us and our unknown author.

Having exhausted the subject the de Rézés went on to talk of other matters.

'You know,' said Christine to Tatiana, 'you made a great impression on Anglaz the other evening.'

'It's true,' said her husband. 'He really means it. With a little encouragement he'll propose marriage.'

'Let's have some figures,' said Tatiana promptly.

'Seventy-five acres of vineyard. Shares in the engineering firm for which he works. And prospects.'

'Is that all you think I'm worth? Prospects! As though I were the daughter of a bank-clerk with a moustache. Tell your *vicomte* that the daughter of the steppes is daily expecting the arrival of a caravan of merchants who will cut their throats for the glory of offering her their loads of silk and gold! But now we must leave you. It's nearly a quarter to, and Martin has to change on the métro. Come along, darling, we ought to be going.'

The de Rézés showed no surprise at hearing Tatiana address me as darling, but I turned crimson. I was embarrassed on her account, in case they should get it into their heads that we were lovers. Christine gave us each an apple, and we made for the Victor-Hugo métro-station. Tatiana asked me what I thought of the de Rézés and I said that they were completely beyond me, the lady hidden behind her long black eyelashes and he behind his money, his education and his air of imperturbability. To me they were like beings from another planet. Tatiana bit into her apple and I bit into mine.

'It's queer. I scarcely know Rézé and yet he seems to me as transparent as a pane of glass. I think men are always pretty transparent to women. Social distinctions make no difference. Christine's parents are working people in Ménilmontant, but it didn't take her long to get the measure of her Rézé. And yet I'm sure she's as puzzling to him as she is to you.'

Occasional cars swept past us down the Avenue Victor-Hugo, travelling very fast, but the pavements were deserted. Tatiana suddenly asked me to kiss her. I felt as I held her in my arms how she flexed her body so as not to oblige me to raise my head.

'Why did you call me darling just now in front of the Rézés? Do you remember?'

'No, but it must have slipped out quite naturally. Don't you want me to call you darling?'

'To be frank, I don't think it suits me.'

We had reached the station, and as we walked down the stairs Tatiana kept her eyes fixed on my face. Suddenly she burst out:

'Oh, you make me cross! Even if you don't talk about it you're always thinking about that silly crime of yours. You let it get in the way of everything. But what does it matter now, Chazard and your two years in prison? All I wish is that you'd killed half-a-dozen people, instead of only one.'

An elderly lady, slowly climbing the stairs, overheard these last words and gazed at me with the utmost horror.

'You're quite wrong,' I said. 'I wasn't thinking of that at all. When I do think of it, it's because of the difficulties it makes for me, which I have to take into account. I know it hasn't harmed me in your eyes, but I still don't think darling is the right word for me.'

'I can't help what you think. I've got to express my feelings in my own way.'

'You don't have to go dressing them up. Darling is just parrot-language. What do you suppose Porteur would say?'

'Porteur? Well, there you are—he'd be in favour of darling if it was really meant. Oh, darling, don't you see how much more convenient it would be if we were living together? For instance, if we're to solve this mystery of yours we shall have to be seeing each other all the time. Oh, won't you come and live with me? . . .'

It was after midnight when I got back to the Rue Saint-Martin. I undressed in the dark so as not to disturb Valérie. Someone was still up in an apartment across the courtyard, and there was just enough light from their uncurtained window for me to be able to see what I was doing. My mind was filled with thoughts of Tatiana and our evening together. When I got between the sheets Valérie, who had been stretched at the extreme edge of the bed, came and pressed herself against me, disconcerting me with her warmth, the return of old memories, the very shape of her body, which was better adapted to mine than that of a taller woman. It was without shame that I yielded to a temptation against which I had thought myself well-armed. After a time, however, I sent her back to her own narrow bed.

IX

ODETTE spent part of the next morning telling me about the activities of S.B.H. Founded in 1898 by the father of the present Hermelin and a gentleman named Bertin, who sold out three years later, the corporation (its full title was the Société Bertin-Hermelin) had originally specialised in the manufacture of wheel-hubs. Bertin's shares, representing 60 per cent of the total capital, had been bought by the father of Lormier, a manufacturer of horse-drawn vehicles with a sturdy disbelief in the future of the automobile. During the 1914 war the company, working on government contracts, had extended the range of its products first to shell-cases and then to spares and fitments for army-trucks. It was this expansion, directly due to the enterprise of the original Hermelin, which had laid the basis of its subsequent growth and prosperity; but it had also given rise to the intense antagonism existing between the Hermelin and Lormier families. The Hermelins, in a nutshell, found it unjust that Lormier, who was still obstinately manufacturing horse-drawn vehicles, should be getting more money out of S.B.H. than the real creator of the business. In 1920 Hermelin started to build his own factory for the manufacture of motor-lorries, but before it could go into production he had suffered a cerebral thrombosis which put an end to his active career. The Hermelin family, brought to the verge of ruin, were rescued by Lormier, who took over the factory and incorporated it in S.B.H., which was reconstituted on terms reducing the Hermelin holding to 25 per cent. At the same time, old Lormier gave up the manufacture of horse-drawn vehicles. S.B.H. thereafter expanded with great speed, manufacturing motor-coaches and omnibuses as well as lorries, and starting local transport companies in France and Algeria. It acquired real-estate, land, mines and office-buildings, and in the course of time gained control of a number of smaller concerns whose financial difficulties, more often than not, had been brought about by itself. I learned from Odette that, apart from its own widespread activities, S.B.H. now held the controlling interest in twenty-three other companies, several of them of considerable size. The original Lormier, a widower, had not troubled to make a will, and his share-holdings, after a great deal of family bickering and horse-trading, had been divided between his two sons. The position now was that the present Lormier held only 45 per cent of the ordinary shares in S.B.H. while the present Hermelin held 25 per cent, the remaining 30 per cent being divided between a Dutch syndicate, an American bank, an industrial concern in the north of France and an Algerian wine-grower.

It was Lormier himself who eventually told me most of this back-history and divulged his position in relation to Hermelin. Odette merely explained the organisation and functioning of S.B.H. As I have said, she had shown no sign of welcoming me as the Chairman's assistant, but she was a person incapable of ill-will and after we had talked to-gether for a while she seemed to forget her prejudice against me.

'You must call me Odette,' she said. 'Then I can call you Martin.'

I was impressed by her quickness of mind and grasp of detail. In particular, she helped me to understand the Chair-man's problem, which was to decide matters of policy and then ensure that the Managing Director did not sabotage his decisions. Lormier was in touch with everything that went on, and it was the business of his personal staff to see that he was kept fully informed. Where S.B.H. was concerned, Odette and Jocelyne were walking encyclopaedias.

'Did the Chairman tell you that I've just come out of prison, and why I was sent there?'

'He told Jocelyne and me. In fact, it was Jocelyne who went through the newspaper files to give him the details. But Angelina, the typist, doesn't know anything about it.'

'I think you should tell her. I'd rather it came from you than from some friend of the Managing Director.'

'Well then, I will. She's very young, but she's a sensible child. You needn't be afraid that she'll pretend to be scared of you or be too inquisitive.'

Odette then passed me over to Jocelyne who, for my information, was to take me to visit certain departments. She was sadly unprepossessing at first sight, tall, thin, round-shouldered and pale-eyed, with big hands and feet and skinny legs.

'I'll take you to the staff-office,' she said. 'We thought we could count on Keller, but after what happened yesterday we know that he's one of Hermelin's stooges. It's rather serious from our point of view. We don't know how long he has been staffing the departments with people who take their orders from Hermelin, or who the people are. It's not going to be easy for us to find out.'

Keller greeted me with the utmost affability, assuring me that he would be only too happy to tell me anything I wanted to know. He went on to give me a rather vague account of the work of his department, and from this he was proceeding to describe the system of insurance benefits when Jocelyne interrupted.

'Forgive me, Monsieur Keller. The Chairman is anxious for Monsieur Martin to have an exact knowledge of how everything works. Perhaps it would be better to begin at the beginning. Suppose we take the case of someone who joined the corporation at the beginning of this year. How did they come to join and what were their references and qualifications? What dealings have they had with your office since then, and where are the details to be found?'

Keller accordingly selected the case of a typist who had entered the business in February. He showed us her file, containing various forms and other documents, and the general staff-list, where her name appeared under that of the department to which she had been appointed. I asked if a register was kept recording not only the entry but also the transfer or re-allocation of staff within the office. It seemed to me, as it did to Jocelyne, that Keller was somewhat disconcerted by this, and it was only after hesitation that he produced what I asked for. The register was in six volumes covering the past ten years. While Jocelyne looked through one of the earlier volumes I examined the one for the current year. It seemed that very few people had joined the corporation during the period from May to August, and these were all over twenty-five except one girl of eighteen. I had evidently been right in assuming that there would be no record of my unknown author in the files. Jocelyne then asked for the dossiers of a number of senior members of the staff, and while we were studying these, and making notes, Hermelin entered the room, having presumably been tipped off by one of Keller's subordinates. He took strong exception to my intrusion in a domain where, so he said, my ignorance could only lead to confusion. To which Jocelyne replied firmly:

'Monsieur Martin is here under my supervision at the personal request of the Chairman.'

'If the Chairman has given you instructions of this sort he should, if he did not consult me first, at least have informed me in writing. Please go and ask him for a signed office chit. In the meantime, Monsieur Keller, perhaps you will be good enough to let me see this gentleman's dossier.'

'Wait for me here,' said Jocelyne to me. 'I won't be a minute.' ·
She left the room, and Keller asked a clerk to fetch my file.

He was looking extremely uncomfortable. I stood facing Hermelin, gazing at the door through which Jocelyne had departed.

'Have you been following the Lieboeuf trial?' Hermelin remarked to Keller while we waited. 'The verdict's due today. That man ought to be condemned to death, don't you agree?'

'I'm afraid I don't know very much about it,' said Keller in evident embarrassment.

'The judges are much too soft with murderers in these days. It's simply encouraging crime.'

Jocelyne returned just as the clerk put my file on the table.

'Monsieur Hermelin, the Chairman has asked me to tell you that an official note will be sent to your office immediately. He also asks me to give you his kind regards.'

The final words caused Hermelin to stare blankly, while his ears turned first red and then purple. I saw that his hands were quivering with rage as he picked up my file. Even in relation to his tall stature the hands were truly gigantic, in thickness no less than in their length and breadth. The file contained the two forms I had filled in, together with a handwritten note by Keller.

'But this isn't complete,' exclaimed Hermelin. 'It contains no mention of your police record.'

'That is unavoidable at present, Monsieur Hermelin,' said Jocelyne. 'A summary has to be procured from the court where the case was tried, and this normally takes at least a week. Monsieur Martin is not to blame for the omission.'

'Perhaps not, but clearly it is a matter about which the corporation needs to be fully informed, especially if it's a question of his doing work of the kind you seem to be engaged on. The files contain confidential reports on persons of good standing whose reputations we are bound to protect against indiscretion or malice.'

'I quite agree. Well then, I will take these files to the

Chairman himself. Monsieur Martin, will you be so kind as to help me?'

Since the Chairman had been invoked Hermelin could raise no further objection. Jocelyne and I left with our arms loaded with files which we carried straight to Lormier's room. He listened with intent interest to her account of what had taken place and was particularly anxious to hear about the colour of Hermelin's ears at the moment when she had delivered her message of good-will.

'They turned purple, Monsieur le Président,' said Jocelyne. 'And then when we went off with the files they turned red again.'

Lormier gave a sharp laugh, his eyes gleaming with spite, and I saw Odette and Jocelyne smile fondly at his gratification, gross creature that he was. I wondered if a time would come when I should find myself talking, as they did, of 'our interests', when I simply meant those of the Chairman and not necessarily of the corporation as a whole. Despite my first dislike of Lormier, Hermelin had already done much to bring us together. Daily work and association might well end by achieving this everyday miracle, that of the employee who devotedly serves the interests of an employer he does not even like. As I turned to leave the room with the two women Lormier called me back.

'We still haven't settled the matter of your salary. You have thought about it, no doubt?'

'Yes', I said, 'but after being out of touch for two years I don't know much about salary rates. I think, as you are putting me in a position of trust, that I should be paid at least sixty thousand francs a month.'

'Yes. That is about what I should like to see you getting. But the fact that you have just come out of prison makes a difference. I can only justify my confidence in you by treating you as a person of exceptional attainments and paying you accordingly. The rest of the staff won't be impressed by your merits unless they know that you're getting a large salary. So I shall pay you a hundred and twenty-five thousand, and I may say that it greatly annoys me to have to do so. I get no pleasure out of pampering my employees.'

Lormier was silent for a moment while he regarded me without kindness, if not with actual distaste.

'You're the type that was born to be poor but honest. It's really rather shocking to think of you getting as much as a hundred and twenty-five thousand. On second thoughts, I'll make it a hundred and twenty thousand. That relieves my feelings a little. It shows that I haven't quite lost the ruggedness so essential to the owning class.'

But then he sighed and went on, playing with his small, puffy hands:

'No, I'm fooling myself. The truth is that I'm as feeble as all the other owners. I've fought against it, but the socialist disease is everywhere, in the air we breathe, in the changeable, hazy meaning of every word we speak. I find myself openly admitting that all men have a right to live and a right to work. Even worse, I sometimes treat an employee with positive benevolence. That is why we owners as a class are destined to disappear. The danger is not that the Russians will clear us out. The mortal danger is this contagion of weakness which causes us to doubt our divine right and treat the workers as though they were human. Well, there it is. Are you in favour of an independent Algeria?'

'Yes, Monsieur le Président, I am.'

'Then we'll make it a hundred and fifteen thousand, just to remind you that S.B.H. has very considerable interests in that country. That's another case of our being too benevolent. We——'

However, the Chairman decided not to give me his views on Algeria at that moment and with a wave of his hand dismissed me. The time was ten past twelve. I went into the next room, where Odette and Angelina were powdering their noses and patting their hair. Jocelyne, who was immersed in one of the files, looked up to say that she could find nothing in it which enabled her to determine whether the subject was one of Hermelin's henchmen or a supporter of the Chairman. I suggested that we should study the photograph it contained. It was that of a man of thirty-seven, good-looking with carefully brushed black hair and large dark eyes—a disarming countenance, but with a peculiarly suave and glossy smile which I was inclined to regard with suspicion. 'But I know him quite well,' said Jocelyne. 'I can even recall the sound of his voice.' It seemed to me that this could be misleading. A man in the flesh can put on a performance which will cause you to forget the look of his face. In a photograph he is immobilised. He cannot prevent his face from being exposed, naked and fixed, to the cold scrutiny of the beholder. I suggested that at least we should include this person in our list of suspects, but Jocelyne was not much impressed by the argument, saying that the question of whether anyone was on the side of Lormier or of Hermelin depended on something more than their looks.

'Only a person of exceptional intuition could decide a thing like that on the basis of a photograph,' she said. 'Someone like Porteur, perhaps.'

'I shouldn't think Porteur had ever had anything to do with that kind of people,' said Angelina.

'Porteur knows everything and understands everything,' said Odette decidedly.

Porteur was sound asleep when I got home. He had opened one eye and told Valérie that he didn't want anything to eat. There was a *pneumatique* from Tatiana asking me to call her at an Etoile number between one-fifteen and a quarter to two.

Valérie laid our luncheon on the small table in the bedroom. We were finished in a quarter of an hour, and then, as I got up, she came and put her arms round me. I kissed her lightly, meaning to rebuke her, but the glow in her eyes and the urgency of her body were too much for me, and it was I who undid her dress. Afterwards I was at first thoroughly angry with myself; but then I gave myself the benefit of extenuating circumstances, the fact that I had been taken by surprise and was in any case not made of wood. It seemed strange, none the less, loving Tatiana tenderly as I did, that I should have given way twice in the twelve hours since I had been with her.

I went down to a nearby café to telephone.

'Tatiana? Are you there, Tatiana? Is that you?'

'Yes. Why are you shouting at the top of your voice? I can't hear a thing. It sounds as though you were furious with me.'

'No, it's not that, but listen. When I got home last night I undressed in the dark and then I found Valérie in my bed, and—well—there it was.'

'I quite see. Is that all?'

'No, it isn't. Just now Porteur was asleep and——'

'Who was asleep?'

'I mean, my brother, Michel. He was asleep and so Valérie and I had lunch in the bedroom, and then—mark you, I never meant to, I wasn't even thinking of it, but . . .'

'It couldn't matter less, particularly with Valérie. All I care about is that I love you. I'm at Christine's. Rézé has started making inquiries but we shan't know anything until this evening. Perhaps I'll come and see you. Good-bye, darling.'

She rang off before I could say any more. Through the glass pane in the door of the telephone-box I could see into the little café. Seated on the banquette nearest to me was an aged pair of lovers, she about sixty-five and he seventy or more. The woman was thick and shapeless with a worn face, pouches under her eyes and a plain felt hat from beneath which wisps of hair escaped over her forehead, leaving traces of black dye. The old man was skinny and frail, with a nodding head. They were holding hands and gazing into each other's eyes. I had a better view of them as I went out. Neither was smiling, but their faces were illumined as though from within, and the light in their eyes seemed to me something not of this world. Such was the impression they made on me that I mentioned them at supper that evening to Michel and Valérie.

'But I can't describe them,' I said. 'It was something you have to see for yourself.'

Valérie said that she envied the old dears and her heart went out to them, in demonstration of which she pressed my knee between her own under the table. I rather irritably moved my leg aside, but without letting anything show in my face.

'I can picture them,' said Michel. 'I've seen the same thing at least twice. Last summer I saw a couple sitting with three other people outside a café near Saint-Germain-des-Prés. The *terrasse* was crowded, but they sat there gazing into each other's eyes quite oblivious of everything that was going on around them. People were turning and craning their necks to stare at them, and telling each other their names. The man was a well-known racing-motorist, a foreigner, and the woman was a French ballerina, also very well known. What struck me particularly was their absolute unconsciousness of everything except themselves and a sort of mystical radiance in their faces.'

'Eat up your spaghetti or it'll get cold,' said Valérie.

Michel with a remote expression did as he was told and then came back to his lovers.

'I thought to myself, if love really exists, that must be it. I wanted to know, and I took a lot of trouble to find out. I managed to make the acquaintance of another dancer who was a close friend of the ballerina. To make her feel at home I made love to her here on the divan, and then I got the story out of her. It seems that they had run into one another quite by chance one evening in Bourges, just outside the cathedral. They knew each other slightly, having sat next to one another at a public dinner the year before. Neither of them wanted to stay in Bourges—he had only gone there for a funeral and she had been visiting a relative in a mental home. So he drove her back to Paris and they stopped for dinner at a small country inn and shared a room for the night. The encounter of a single night, they thought, no more than that. He was due to fly to South America, where he was racing, in a couple of days, and he was not very happy about it. Before they left the inn in the morning he stole her handkerchief, telling himself that if she didn't miss it by the time they got to Paris it would be a good omen.'

'I call that ridiculous,' said Valérie. 'I remember a friend of mine, Chantal Guerillot——'

'Please let me finish. Well, so the racing-driver had the handkerchief. As they said good-bye to one another in Paris he made her a little speech—"When I get to South America I shall look at the Southern Cross and think of you and your ballet. I know you're going to have a great success." A quarter of an hour later they were both thinking of other things, but the next day, on board the air-liner, he felt in his pocket to make sure he still had her handkerchief. The plane put down at Dakar and he bought a magazine in which there were two pages of photographs of her. And some days later, when he was practising on the track where he was to race, he had a sudden vivid recollection of the morning when they had woken up together in that little country inn. There had been a steep hill-side beyond their open window, and a meadow sparkling with dew in the early sunshine. She had danced barefoot, a dance ending in a passionate climax. So she had become for him a sort of divinity, at once fortifying and inspiring. But meanwhile in Paris things were not going so well. The new ballet was giving a lot of trouble in rehearsal, the sets were haywire, the orchestra was ragged, and worst of all our ballerina was simply dancing in a competent, orthodox way that quite missed the spirit of the piece. In her distress at the reproaches and meaningful silences, she thought now and then of the Southern Cross and was comforted. One evening, when something particularly unkind had been said, she flew into a passion and declared that she was sick of the whole business and would never dance the part again, or anything else, and that she hated everyone. She then burst into tears, turning her back on the orchestra, and as she did so she saw in the wings the figure of her racing-driver holding a glittering Southern Cross with his arm outstretched. As a matter of fact (I asked particularly) it was simply the electrician checking a lighted contraption which was part of the set. But after seeing that vision she recovered her inspiration or self-confidence or whatever it was and had a splendid success. So you see how a quite unimportant little roll in the hay, brought about by boredom and mere chance, may in the end be transformed into something quite different; and how a deviation of the religious impulse, concentrated upon a human object, may give birth to a great love.'

'Well!' exclaimed Valérie. 'I didn't know the religious impulse even existed for you.'

'Yes, but also as a deviation. I can admire a great novelist in the same way that I admire your talent as a cook. But when it's a musician or a poet I'm taken out of myself, I rise above myself, I lose myself utterly in the exaltation I feel.'

A new note had suddenly entered Michel's voice and was manifest in his expression, a note of warmth and genuine emotion, strikingly different from his ordinary tone when talking to me. The thought occurred to me that perhaps I had long been mistaken in him, and that his usual utterances, cool and precise as they always were, might conceal something deeper than indifference.

'I got some brie,' said Valérie. 'I thought it looked rather good.'

At this moment we were invaded. Tatiana and Christine de Rézé appeared in the doorway of the living-room. Tatiana, wearing an ice-blue mink coat which she had borrowed from Christine for the occasion, was dazzling in her elegance. It was evident to me that, whatever the pretext, she had really come to overwhelm Valérie and rejoice in her confounding. Christine was more simply clad in a suit and a racoon stole. The three of us had risen to our feet, but Valérie's expression was instantly aggressive. I was feeling uncomfortable myself. It was Michel who went forward to welcome the visitors.

'I rang but nobody answered,' said Tatiana, 'and as the key was in the door I thought we might venture to walk straight in.'

'Quite right,' said Michel. 'The bell doesn't work. Come and sit down.'

Introductions were performed and the ladies begged us to go on with our meal. Valérie helped herself to cheese. She then stared fixedly and sourly at Tatiana's coat and said with a titter:

'How nicely dressed you are!' (Here the titter) 'I didn't know models were so well paid.'

'We aren't at all well paid,' said Tatiana, 'but of course we do have the chance of meeting rich gentlemen. Even a simple girl like me—well, there was the Shah of Persia and the Aga Khan and Colonel Nasser. It's an amusing life.'

Christine giggled, Michel burst out laughing and so did I, despite myself. Tatiana went on with the greatest amiability:

'I don't think I've seen you, have I, since you were engaged to Martin? Two years ago, but you're as fascinating as ever.'

'You needn't think I imagine it's me you've come to see.'

'But I'm delighted to be doing so, and the Countess, I know, is most happy to make your acquaintance.'

Tatiana then opened the mink coat and pushed it back, disclosing a white silk dress with bare arms and a deep décolleté. Angry though I was with her for this assault upon Valérie, the sight of her beauty did not leave me unmoved. She turned slowly towards me, letting her eyes stray from one bare shoulder to the other across the white expanse of bosom which she offered me; and she addressed me in a voice of such melting tenderness that I was utterly bowled over, at least for the moment.

'Darling, I just couldn't wait to let you know the result of Count de Rézé's inquiries. That is why we have come dashing over here. Christine, tell him.'

'It doesn't amount to much. There are only two high officials who own a Buick or have owned one in the last three years. One of them is a widower with no children. The other is a colleague of my husband's at the Quai d'Orsay who lives in the Rue Vaneau. He's always called Bijoux, but his real name is Alfred de Birul de Carjoux. His wife is very pious, very fashionable and rather eccentric. There are two sons, one aged eighteen and the other a year or two younger. He has a castle, but in Périgord not in Burgundy. That's as far as we've got so far.'

'But it's something, isn't it?' said Tatiana. 'We're getting on. Come to supper tomorrow night and we'll talk it over.'

The ladies then rose and effected a rapid withdrawal. I went with them on to the landing, and a last look from Tatiana bowled me over again. Michel was preparing to go out when I returned to the living-room. He had evidently made some favourable reference to Tatiana, because Valérie was saying acidly:

'I'm blessed if I know what you see in her, that great mare, just the type of tart you see around the Madeleine. But you men are all the same. Those Yiddish sluts always knock you endways, and if they've got a bit of mink draped over their bottoms you go raving mad.'

'What are you talking about? Tatiana isn't a Jewess.'

'It doesn't make the slightest difference, a lot of foreign lay-abouts from God knows where, all battening on us French. I'd turn the whole lot out of the country.'

Michel went off shrugging his shoulders, and I reminded Valérie of what she knew already, that Tatiana had been born in this house and was at least as much a part of it as she was herself. To this Valérie chose to make no reply, nor would she even look at me. She went out to do the washing-up, leaving me to reflect upon the problems which Tatiana had created. Then I noticed the blue exercise book on the table and settled down to read Michel's second chapter.

X

THE BLUE EXERCISE BOOK—CHAPTER TWO

WE have seen that in women the social instinct is sufficiently strong to influence the reproductive instinct, bearing in mind that the word 'instinct' is here used as a figure of speech having no very precise meaning. In any event, in referring thus to the social instinct I have no thought of calumniating the female sex, or of attributing to it over-narrowly practical or self-centred views in matters of love and marriage. On the contrary I am disposed to believe that women in their love-life are unconsciously influenced by an exaggerated sense of social necessity, at least at the outset (I say at the outset because it appears to me that there are disappointments, discoveries and orders of experience which often eventually distort this natural sense of vocation). In the case of men, on the other hand, the social sense is entirely lacking. My name is Alfred Lambulant and I am eighteen years old. Father is a large-scale exporter of alarm-clocks and frying-pans. He must be doing pretty well, considering the way he goes on about the taxes. We live in Passy, in the same house as the Comtesse de Villemeuse, who can't stand mother at any price. Six months ago—that is to say, at the beginning of October—the Countess had a little maidservant called Janette. I got to know her in one of the local cafés, playing one of those electric bagatelle games with lights and bells and scores running into millions. She was a dark-haired, pretty little number from Finistère and I liked her a lot. Come to that, I'm not so bad myself. So one night I sneaked up to her room on the top floor, and the next day I was so worked up about it that I dashed right off to the Champs-Elysées where father has his alarm-clock-and-frying-pan business. He didn't seem too pleased when I told him I wanted to get married. He was talking on the telephone at the time, and when he had hung up he said—who? When I told him he said, For crying out loud can't you see I'm busy, clear out before you get the toe of my boot. When he came home to lunch he and mother both pitched into me. Mother was hopping mad because she'd rung up the Comtesse de Villemeuse to ask her to get rid of her maid and had got the reply that she (the Countess) didn't interfere in her servants' love-affairs and anyway she thought that for Janette to marry the Lambulant boy would be a very suitable match. So my loving parents called me a half-wit and a disgrace to the family and a no-good oaf and said it was bad enough to go round sleeping with servants without all this talk about marrying them. Well, me being a minor all I could do was shut my trap. That afternoon I went into Passy cemetery to think the situation over and while I was walking among the tombstones I made up a story to myself about how father had gone broke and we were all out on our ears begging in the streets and Janette was set up in a nice little provision merchant's shop and she offered father a bit of sausage out of charity and then she noticed I was there and smiled at me and father said, 'Why Alfred, I believe she's taken a fancy to you!' And I said, 'A girl that used to be a servant? Are you crazy? I'd rather starve!' And we would have starved, what's more, but in the end I married her to save the family. Well, I was making up tales like this when I came upon a young widow who was bending over one of the tombs trying to shift a big bronze urn with poppies in it. So I lent her a hand and she told me about her husband, Alexis, who'd passed away in a car smash. 'Oh, Monsieur,' she said sobbing, 'he was so handsome and his kisses tasted of honey and he was wonderful at backgammon.' I took her hand in mine and stroked and patted it, and there we were kneeling on poor old Alexis's grave and her skirt was rucked up so I could see her knees and part of her thigh and a nice bit of cleavage down her front. And I blushed and said I was pretty nifty at backgammon too, and then there was a long, long kiss right on top of the inscription, 'Alexis Dupont. 1931-1957. May he rest in peace'. And at supper that night father said, 'Well, are you still determined to marry that serving-wench of yours?' and I said, no, I was going to marry a young widow instead. Well, of course, father's one of those old squares, born before the first war, who have spent their lives jeering at everything and just don't understand that young people nowadays are serious. 'You young devil, you think you can pull my leg,' he said, laughing while he said it, 'but anyway you'd do better to marry a respectable young widow than to go round with a lot of anarchist bees in your bonnet.' I just let him talk, him and mother. I didn't care what they said. I was head over heels with my widow and there was nothing I wouldn't have given her, the whole of father's fortune and even his life, come to that. It was her birthday two days later and I went to buy her some flowers. Anemones, I rather thought. There was a girl at the florist's with dark eyes with a golden gleam in them. She was bare-legged and wearing an old pair of slippers and a crumpled skirt and a jersey that absolutely moulded her. She was smashing! So I said moo, sort of, and she said moo back and then we both knew and I pushed her into the back room and—well, I just knew that this was love at last, the real thing, I mean, that ends in marriage. All of a sudden she cried, 'Heavens, I've forgotten the post!' and she shot out. And a minute later her sister came in, fair hair, blue eyes, and a very nice shape. So I couldn't help saying moo again, and she said moo, and I pushed her into the back room and this time I knew that there was no doubt about it, this was the one I'd been looking for all my life. Well, she went out too, and a third sister came in, with a figure like a sack of coke and a face like the back of a bus. Just the same, moo-moo and I pushed her into the back room, and—etc., etc. . . .

You will no doubt object that this Alfred Lambulant was not a truly serious-minded young man. To which I reply that he was just as serious-minded as any other young man, but fortunate in love. Setting luck aside, they are all like him, all ready with the slightest encouragement to discern a twin soul in every new bosom or behind. Not a shred of social sense or regard for the future. They see no further than the thing they covet, and filled with good intentions are ready to throw everything overboard if they may plunge into the first petticoat that offers. If the male animal were not subjected to a stern educational process curbing his desires he would go from crime to crime, merely for the brief appeasement of an itch which, most happily, is still not publicly to be avowed. And in the middle class, although he is conditioned to hypocrisy, the male takes no account of social distinctions, whether it is a matter of union for life or for an hour. The unmarried woman whose name appears in the social register will not marry her social inferior, but the Duc de la Marsière marries the daughter of his concierge, the Baron Dolbach marries a girl off the streets, the Abbé Rondeau throws his cassock to the winds and goes off with a trapeze-artist and Colonel Lefranc resigns his commission to marry a waitress.

In these days women, whether they have achieved independence by earning their living, or whether they merely devour women's magazines which arouse in them irresistible instincts of cruelty and domination, are free to choose their own mates. In theory the men are no less free, but since, for the reasons given above, they are incapable of choosing, it is the woman who gets the best of it.

Things customarily work out as follows (the example applies to all ages). A youth of no marked physical attractions but with the prospect of a successful career (a high rating in chemistry, the promise of a job and a little money behind him) is acquainted with a dozen girls. Being a hard worker he has little time to spare for pleasure, but he is nevertheless ready to discern in any one of them the woman destined to him for all eternity. One day he melts in the arms of Ernestine and they experience a moment of blazing passion. I stress the word moment. He has, I repeat, little time to spare. Ernestine, although she holds him in high esteem, is also interested in Eugène and Victor, two equally promising young men, one of whom in addition plays the guitar while the other is a hurdles champion. And while she is weighing the respective merits of all three, our young gentleman, with his flair for rapid decision, discovers that Léonie Jalavoine is his true soul-mate and the girl who makes the blood thunder in his veins. Léonie is at least a girl who knows what she wants. Having decided that he will do she proceeds to take him firmly in hand. She disposes of Ernestine with the remark that she is one of those girls who take up with boys for the sheer pleasure of making them fail their examinations, a thought that fills our young man with alarm. Léonie, on the other hand, helps him to pass his chemistry exam. Also, prior to the moments of blazing passion, she conveys to him that other girls' bosoms and behinds are lamentably defective whereas her own are precisely what the Creator intended. He, being modest (in matters of love most men are extremely modest), believes and admires so fervently as to cause him to wonder whether he is truly deserving of such riches. He even starts believing in God, since there seems to be no other way of accounting for the miracle that has befallen him, and in this he is warmly encouraged by Léonie. She weaves about him a network of daily habits shrewdly mingled with the strands of her own hair, and so contrives matters that whenever he opens his eyes to look about him her bosom (or behind) is well within the dear boy's field of vision. But Léonie Jalavoine's master-stroke is to have sublimated in the mind of Eleuthère (did I mention that his name was Eleuthère?) the bond that really unites them, and transmuted it into a matter of conscience. She has done this without effort because she is perfectly sincere in saying such things as, 'No one will ever love you like I do. . . . I almost wish something terrible could happen to you because it would make me love you more than ever. . . . Our love isn't just physical. . . . Even if we both died tomorrow I know our love would last for ever. . . : Everything that happens, I think of it in terms of our love. . . .' To all of which Eleuthère replies amiably 'Me too' until in the end he really believes it and falls in love in the manner of women, seriously and solidly. And now let us suppose that one night he happens to be walking alone along the Rue Pigalle and encounters Nana la Myope who murmurs, 'Tu viens, chéri?' just at a moment when his conscience is a bit off the boil. Nana la Myope is a cute little piece with everything it takes, the curves, the legs, the lot, and a gleam in her eye that makes Eleuthère's breath come faster and causes beetles to run up and down his spine. But then, at the crucial moment, Conscience sounds the alarm. The figure of Léonie, the bosom or the behind, arises before his eyes, and uneasily considering what Nana has to offer he takes the high-minded line and says to himself, 'How squalid are these mercenary loves!' not pausing to reflect upon the spurious association of the adjective 'mercenary' with the word 'love' as he elects to use it at that moment. Thus he triumphs over temptation and strides hurriedly on, pleased with himself and more than ever beholden to Léonie who in the moment of peril has inspired him with such exalted sentiments. Twenty years pass. They have two children, an apartment in the Avenue Mozart, a refrigerator, a foreign car, a uniform edition of the works of Victor Hugo and a respectable visiting list; and this is the account of their youthful romance which Léonie dishes out to the children: 'Well you see we met when we were both at college. Eleuthère wasn't a bit interested in girls, because of working so hard. He was such a handsome boy, with a dear little moustache. And then one day when we were having lunch in the refectory I saw him looking at me and I blushed to the roots of my hair. We hadn't even spoken to one another, but I knew at once that I was the one he had chosen. . . .' But let it be repeated, the male is not the one who chooses. He devours every female he can lay hands on until the day when one of them—it may be one he has never even thought of— decides to become his wife or permanent mistress, or anyway does the choosing. There are of course exceptions to the rule, among whom the reader will not fail to perceive himself. Rare though they are, there are men who elect to choose their wife or mistress (I say nothing of the marriage of convenience, which is a different matter entirely). Either because they are too conceited or too timid to let nature take its course they actively pursue women possessing some remarkable endowment, whether of beauty, birth or fortune. The least of the risks they run is that of failure.

My name is Pierre Meublé. I am twenty-seven and very rich. Nobody can fool me. When I want a woman I just grab her and pinch her bottom, so she knows exactly what to expect and no room for any misunderstanding. All the same I play it cool and walk out after a fortnight. But I'm an only son and I don't want the line of Meublé to become extinct, so I've decided to get married. I go around looking the girls over and finally I choose Hélène. She's pretty, she seems to have plenty of commonsense, and her father's an army officer with no private means and five daughters to dispose of. So I ask for her hand in marriage. The parents are in raptures and we have a white wedding, choir, bridesmaids and everything, at Saint-Honoré-d'Eylau. And then it turns out that Hélène, in spite of her religious upbringing, has a temperament like a volcano, practically a nymphomaniac. She's at me every minute we're alone together and I lose fourteen pounds in six weeks. It scares me and I say I've got to get some rest. So then she takes a lover, and where does that leave me?—in love, jealous and mortified. I go and see her father and he says, 'For God's sake can't you handle your own wife?' I go back and plead with her, I say how much I love her and how I'm suffering, and I make pretty speeches about her eyes and her hands and her breasts, and she opens up her pyjamas and says, 'Well, here they are if you want them.' That's all love means to her. And tonight she's out again with her lover, and I'm left alone in our princely mansion, which, as you might expect, our friends call the *Hôtel Meublé*. So now I'm writing a letter to the coroner. 'Dear Sir, I've had all I can take.' And now I've blown my brains out. Signed, Meublé.

Were I called upon to instruct a class of very innocent children in the nature of love I should take pains to avoid drawing upon the philosophers, novelists and poets—the latter, perhaps, most of all, for it is not sufficiently realised how revolting these poets are in their sensuality. I would teach my innocents love-songs, but not the realistic kind with their flavour of mattresses and couplings; the songs of those idyllic times when lovers, apparently sexless, seemed to be creatures of light and air, and love achieved its consummation with the merest touching of the lips or, better still, the finger-tips. 'That is all very well,' you may say to me, 'but you do not seem to be closely in touch with current thinking on the subject, and those songs of yours, however charming, are a trifle on the corny side and wholly lacking in educational value.' With this I disagree. I maintain, on the contrary, that by disregarding sexual love, by dwelling upon the state of the soul rather than the vital statistics, my songs express an essential truth, which is that love and physical desire are separate matters and not to be confused, whatever the subject may think. (This is so profoundly true that there are women, possessing two lovers, who will explain to you that one is for love and the other for pleasure; and this fact may be related to another, no less significant, namely that women are often jealous of a husband or lover whom they do not love. I mention it because jealousy is very generally held to be a natural extension of love.)

Having stirred the imaginations of my innocents with my songs, and after they have made their first fleeting contacts with the tangible reality, I shall come to the root of the matter. Striding to the blackboard I shall write and underline with coloured chalk the Axiom propounded by the illustrious savant to whom I referred in my previous chapter—'Young ladies of good social position never fall in love with young men of inferior status.' Having done so I shall make a dramatic pause, commanding absolute silence, and then turning to my flock I shall address them as follows:

'My dear children, you are now aged between eleven and fifteen, and before achieving your earliest aspirations, which will be, according to your sex, to tumble any girl you can lay hands on, or to go up in smoke with some ravishing hero of fantasy, you will devote much thought to the subject of love. Let me urge you never to lose sight of the Axiom here inscribed, of which no one will ever remind you, for the doctors, novelists, psychiatrists, philosophers, poets and economists are in no way disposed to scrutinise a revelation which would oblige them to revise venerable opinions and certainties related to a thousand problems, and furthermore to burn a positive mountain of books on which they repose their material comfort and their reputations. On the other hand, you must guard against drawing excessive conclusions from the Axiom. You must not deduce from it, for example, that women love whom they choose, or that they are diabolically clever in matters of love. If you feel the need for a formula of more immediately practical value, then you should confine

122

yourselves to saying that women are so contrived that only men in a certain social category, or who represent it in their eyes, can inspire them with feelings of love. And in this context you must strive to see men as they really are, like large and noisy bluebottles that have got into the room and continue to hurl themselves against the window-panes, the walls and the furniture, bouncing from one thing to another until the mistress of the house disposes of them with a duster. In the same fashion you may see men bounce from blonde to brunette careless of everything that does not speak directly and crudely to their male instincts—in short, careless and blind, or very nearly so. Let me suggest an experiment. Question your friend Gontran on his return from some fashionable beanfeast and ask him how he found Madame Ortanbois and the Baroness Empédocle, these being the two ladies who principally engaged his attention. He will tell you of the one that she was a blonde with superb hips and bosom, and of the other that she had the finest legs you ever saw. And that is as far as you will get. In the case of Madame Ortanbois, who is in reality a synthetic blonde, he will not have noticed the shape of her face, the colour of her eyes, or the colour of her dress, or even the famous emeralds which she got from her first husband, the heavyweight boxing champion. As for the Baroness Empédocle, who is noted for her beauty of countenance, her dresses and her jewels, he will have seen nothing of her but her legs. Until some woman has pinned him down, choosing him for her husband or her lover, the entire feminine world will be nothing to him but a sea of bosoms, buttocks, waists, hips and thighs. (You women who so suffer to be beautiful, who dream of dazzling *toilettes*, of furs, of the jewels of a-thousand-and-one nights, opals of fatality, diadems bleeding with rubies, when will you learn that men have no eyes for these marvels and that all they look for is the smooth white flesh beneath?) Dear children, I hope I have now made the matter sufficiently

123

clear for you to understand how this great Axiom enables us to draw the dividing line between the sexes.

'To those of you who are girls I would say that your part in the duet of love is precisely laid down and in not unhopeful terms. One of these days you will be attracted to a young man whose situation seems to promise well for the future, and he, finding you neither more nor less seductive than any other young woman, will at once try to get you into bed, without any thought of long-term policy. This is when you need to know how to put the matter on a serious footing and persuade him that something of profound significance is taking place. When you have succeeded in teaching him the use of a high-flown and poetic vocabulary in all matters affecting your romance, you will have transformed him into a sincere and devoted lover, thus achieving what is known as the union of souls. But you must never relax this discipline of language, whereby even the most trivial of your shared interests is discussed in terms that are at the least elegant, when they are not positively exalted. The male sex being credulous and readily susceptible to lofty sentiments, this will not be difficult to do; but you must be careful to keep him up to the mark by ensuring that his innocent delight at the uniqueness and harmony of your union is constantly nourished with well-chosen words.

'And now I must address myself to the boys. It is a somewhat ticklish undertaking, in view of what I have just said to the girls. For it is true, dear lads, that your part in the business is to hover like the butterfly, to sip, to revel until such time as a pretty girl—or an ugly one, for that matter—chooses you and turns you into a beatific lover, a true knight, a sayer of the ineffable and an exponent of all high principles. Not a brilliant role, and we may as well admit it. You must face the fact that, despite appearances, for you the marriage of inclination does not exist and that you have got to put up with what you get.

It is with an eye on your sex that the wisdom of the ages has declared marriage to be a lottery. You may at least account yourself fortunate that your wife does not eat you at the conclusion of the nuptials, as happens here and there in the animal kingdom. Undoubtedly it is humiliating to reflect that in this matter of the union of souls one of them, namely yours, has exercised no freedom of choice but has been merely impounded by the other. But be consoled: in the world you live in everything conspires to make it appear that it was you who did the choosing. It will be said that you asked for your wife's hand in marriage, which implies initiative on your part, and later that you married her. However much the position of women may have changed in recent years, we seem to be no nearer the day when the woman will ask for the man's hand in marriage—and why should she, when she takes it anyway? But your greatest consolation will be your privileged position in the home. You will be the head of the family, the seat of authority, the chooser of wines, the proclaimer of political opinions, the pundit, the master. Your wife and children will hang upon your lightest word. Gone will be the heedless nincompoop you once were, pursuing and clutching at every petticoat in sight and never dreaming that one of them would eventually make of you the object of veneration you have now become. Surely a trifling humiliation is a small price to pay for so enviable a destiny.'

XI

OUR study of the staff-files left Jocelyne and me little the wiser. It merely confirmed what we already knew, that Keller had a free hand in engaging new staff and to a large extent in authorising transfers and promotions at the higher levels, although in theory everything he did was subject to Lormier's approval. It occurred to me to wonder whether Lormier would be much worse off even if—to put the thing at its worst—the senior members of the staff were all Hermelin's people. The struggle for power between the two men did not depend on the quality of the work done at any level but solely on the shareholders, and was finally a question of money.

'But it's not so simple,' said Jocelyne. 'The Chairman has to prevent the other shareholders ganging up against him, which is what Hermelin wants. So Hermelin goes out of his way to oblige them, and the variety of S.B.H. undertakings offers him a good many possibilities. For instance, we manufacture speedometers and so does the Dutch group which is one of our largest shareholders. They would like to cut us out in the Belgian market, and Hermelin might be able to help them by reducing our Belgian sales if he could get the sales-manager for that territory to co-operate. The trouble is that the control we exercise in this office is based largely on results. It doesn't operate until after the damage is done.'

Odette, who was engaged at that moment in studying the returns from one of our subsidiaries, looked up and said:

'You might add that it is very difficult to prove sabotage if it has been cleverly carried out, however much you may suspect it. So you see, Martin, how important it is for us to have reliable people in the key positions.'

I opened one of the dossiers we had taken from Keller's office the day before. It was that of a man named Maxime Andrillot. The first document it contained was a form similar to the one I myself had filled in, on which were inscribed, as required by the corporation, the full names of his father and mother.

'It seems,' I said to Jocelyne, 'that the maiden name of this Monsieur Andrillot's mother was Eléonore Dubois.'

'Well?'

'You'll think I'm being foolish. But yesterday when we were looking through the files in Keller's office I had a glance at Hermelin's file. His mother's name was Louise Dubois. I don't know why I remember it—perhaps simply because the name is so common.'

Angelina, the typist, laughed, and Jocelyne remarked that there were Dubois to be found in every street. But Odette was looking intently at me.

'There can't be anything in it,' she said slowly. 'Andrillot has been with the company over ten years. All the same, one or two strange things have happened in his department. There was something at the beginning of this year, Jocelyne—some important orders cancelled in the South-West. You must remember—that business of the dynamos.'

Jocelyne remembered; but before she could say more a gentleman entered the room without knocking, elegant, slender, aged about forty-five, with a lively, agreeable countenance. He extended his arms crying:

'Well, my loves, how are you?'

'Why, Monsieur le Ministre!' exclaimed the three women, and they ran to embrace him. 'Monsieur le Ministre! But what are you doing here? Why aren't you at the Delbrousse wedding?'

'I cried off. It's going to be such a bore. I pleaded my duties as a senator.' The gentleman then smiled amiably in my direction.

'This is Monsieur Martin, who joined us yesterday,' said Odette. 'He's very nice.'

'I felt sure he was. I, Monsieur, am Lucien Lormier, the younger brother of the great Lormier. Of course you don't know my face. The Fourth Republic is now forgotten. Yet for nearly fifteen years I figured in nearly all the ministerial combinations—in unimportant offices, I do not deny. I was Commerce, at one time, and Health and Public Works. I was known to be quite negligible but the deputies loved me. And now it is over. Even the Resistance, in which I played so noteworthy a part, has cast me aside. Ministers in these days are required to be something more than performers. They're expected to have ideas. Well, we shall see. Believe me, I speak without bitterness. I went into politics solely because I had to earn a living. Before the war I was a poet. Among other things I published under my own name a little volume of erotic poems entitled *Prologues* which caused my family great dismay. Decency forbids me to quote from it in the presence of these ladies, but there was one poem in particular, relating to the clergy and to choir-boys, which I fear hastened my poor old father's end. And yet you know, such is the contradictory nature of things, during my political career that poem ensured me the unswerving support of the Radical Party. My dear Monsieur Martin, what a wonderful thing radicalism was! It understood nothing of economic problems—indeed, it ignored them. Its power was spiritual. The Radicals were responsible for a moment unique in the history of the world. Do you realise, young man, that it is to the Government of Justin Louis Émile Combes that we owe surrealism, cubism and the free flowering of paderasty in lay circles?'

Lucien Lormier here paused for breath; but seeing that he was about to resume Odette broke in.

'Monsieur le Ministre, were you acquainted with the family of Monsieur Hermelin?'

'I knew them. To tell you the truth, my father, who came of middle-class stock, taught us rather to look down on them. The old man, who as you know was the founder of S.B.H., was originally a factory-foreman. However, there was some contact between the two families, and my brother and I went there to lunch occasionally.'

'Do you happen to remember if the present Hermelin had any female cousins?'

'He certainly had! There were three of them. Lucienne, Armande, and the eldest, who was over twenty at the time I'm talking about, 1922 or '23—her name was Eléonore.'

'Eléonore?'

'Yes. She had splendid thighs, I remember, which the fashion of the time enabled me, despite my tender years, to admire extensively.'

'Do you happen to remember her surname?'

'Of course. It was Dubois, Hermelin's mother's maiden name. But why do you ask?'

Jocelyne told him of our speculations concerning Maxime Andrillot and showed him his file, which contained an identity-photograph taken when Andrillot joined the corporation, at the age of twenty-five. Lucien Lormier studied this with particular interest.

'That's Eléonore's nose,' he said. 'I'd know it in a thousand.'

It was true that the shape of Andrillot's nose was a little unusual, but I had seen others like it. Odette, however, was sure that the eyes in the photograph resembled those of Hermelin, and Angelina professed to see a family likeness in the ears. Jocelyne then wondered whether we should send an urgent message to the Chairman at the church of Saint-Pierre de Neuilly, where he was attending the Delbrousse wedding.

'But why?' said his brother. 'He'll only spend a frustrated week-end nursing his fury with Hermelin.'

Odette looked at her watch.

'Yes, it's nearly half-past eleven. Hermelin will have left the office before the message could reach him.'

'Particularly as it's a fine day. He'll probably leave early to take his son into the country.'

'His son?' I exclaimed. 'You mean, his daughter?'

'No, no, his son. Hermelin hasn't got a daughter.'

My astonishment was so apparent that Odette asked me what was the matter. I was thinking of the anonymous story, in which the writer had so definitely stated that the chauffeur had been sent to fetch his sister, Flora, to spend the evening with Janine—Janine, the daughter of Hermelin. While the three women gossiped and laughed with Lucien Lormier I sat trying to work it out, wondering why a daughter should have been substituted for a son. It could not be simply a mistake. The writer had described how he had rung up the school and talked, first to the headmistress and then to Janine herself. Even if this particular episode were fictitious, he must surely have known the sex of Hermelin's child. It was a deliberate substitution, the reason for which was beyond me.

I was still thinking of it when I left the office, but in so much bewilderment that it was not until I was on board the métro, hedged in among the midday crowd, that I began to grasp what it implied. If there was no Janine there was presumably no Flora either. Instead of a sister the writer must have had a twelve-year-old brother. I recalled the words Hermelin was supposed to have used, 'You little swine, you're going to get what your mother has had, and your sister too.' For 'sister', it seemed, we must substitute 'brother'. Perhaps we should also substitute 'father' for 'mother'. This took a lot of swallowing, but it opened up so unexpected a train of thought that I got out at the next station, which was Havre-Caumartin. I wanted to see Tatiana.

Orsini's establishment, in the Rue Saint-Honoré, was only five minutes' walk. I had not foreseen that when I got there I should be brought to a stop in the courtyard, suddenly afraid to enter. The gilt metal grill framing the doorway was a warning in itself, and as I watched a young South-American couple come out, the woman luxuriant and laughing, the man handsome and extremely well-dressed, I realised how very inappropriate to this setting was my own shabby appearance. Confronting the golden gates in my cheap, readymade suit I felt more squat and uncouth than ever, a thousand leagues removed from the rich and lavish world represented by this temple of the *haute couture*. The distressing thought occurred to me that Tatiana might be embarrassed to see me there. I was about to turn back when a party of women came out of a side entrance. I went up to the youngest of them, a little wisp of a thing who looked no more than fourteen but was in fact a married woman, as her wedding-ring proclaimed, and asked her if she knew Tatiana.

'The model? Do you want to see her? I think she's still working. I can't speak to her myself because we aren't allowed upstairs, but I'll ask one of the sales-women. What's your name?'

'Martin. I'm sorry to——'

'Oh, it's all right, but don't stand there in the middle of the courtyard. Stand close to the wall beside the door.'

I nearly called her back to tell her not to bother, feeling more than ever an intruder after this piece of advice. But Tatiana came very quickly. She was wearing her everyday coat with its rabbit-skin collar, and her face had the taut expression it wore on bad days.

'You wanted to see me? You know I'm not free to do as I like here.'

'I'm sorry. Some other time.'

'No, you'd better tell me now that you've brought me downstairs.'

'Well, it's about that business. I've discovered that Hermelin has a son, not a daughter.'

'A son? Is that all you had to say?'

There was a note of exasperation and faint mockery in her voice. I couldn't bear it. Distress and anger caused a lump to rise in my throat.

'No, it isn't. What I came to say was, I shan't be coming to supper this evening. Goodbye!'

'What!' cried Tatiana. 'You're most certainly coming to supper. Now don't argue—you're coming. The cheek of it! An ugly, dingy, scruffy little man, not a penny in his pocket and a two-bit crime on his two-bit conscience, and he can have the prettiest girl in Paris, and then he says——'

'All right, all right. I know I'm lucky. Just don't shout so loud.'

'I'll shout as loud as I like. So you're going off in a huff just because I didn't fall on your neck. It doesn't matter that I've got a job to do and a living to earn and that——'

'For heaven's sake! People are listening at the windows.'

'Well, let them. The lordly male! I'm supposed to fling myself into his arms whenever he chooses to show up. They can all listen and I'll tell them what I think of men, this one in particular. I think——'

However Tatiana broke off abruptly as the great Raphaëlo Orsini himself appeared in the doorway, a plump little man enshrined in the golden gates and escorted by a gaggle of women, one of whom was carrying a white silk shawl with a fringe which she was trying to put over his shoulders.

'Monsieur Raphaëlo! Oh, he mustn't! He'll catch cold!' And the rest cried in chorus: 'Oh, Monsieur Raphaëlo! Monsieur Raphaëlo!'

'Stop fussing, all of you,' said the little man, 'and leave me to talk to Tatiana. Tatiana, how dare you create a disturbance in the courtyard of the greatest couturier in Paris, enough to lose us our entire American trade?'

He had now come up to us, and while he addressed Tatiana

his eyes were fixed upon me in something like stupefaction, as though he were contemplating a phenomenon outside nature for which he found it impossible to account. Tatiana was very much aware of this, and I thought for a moment that we were in for another explosion. But suddenly her face cleared.

'Monsieur Raphaëlo, may I introduce my friend Professor Martin, one of the greatest mathematicians of our time.'

This quite changed the situation. My disreputable aspect was now accounted for and Raphaëlo, bowing with respect and even with a hint of awe, offered me his hand. The duenna with the shawl, who had kept at his heels, seized the chance to wrap it round him, and Tatiana clinched the matter by explaining that we had been having an argument about binomial differentials or some such matter.

'I'm afraid I always tend to shout when I'm in the wrong,' she said.

Feeling, evidently, that the recondite nature of the dispute did credit to his establishment, Raphaëlo raised his arms as it were in a gesture of benediction, the effect being much enhanced by the dangling ends of the shawl. The harpies of the escort clasped their hands in ecstasy, and I took leave of him and Tatiana came with me to the doorway of the courtyard. We had both recovered.

'You can think yourself lucky,' said Tatiana. 'If Raphaëlo had given me the sack I should have married you to keep myself off the streets.'

'You looked wonderful when you were scolding me—like a cavalry colonel. May I see the dress you're wearing?'

Tatiana undid her coat saying, 'It's an old model called "Lady in Waiting".'

She was in fact not wearing a dress at all, nothing but a gauzy petticoat and a brassière. She laughed and did up her coat again.

133

'Did you say that Hermelin hasn't got a daughter?'

'Yes. Which must mean that the sister Flora in the story is a boy as well, and could even mean that the youth was really writing about his father when he said his mother. I hope you follow me. Well, according to de Rézé, there are only two high officials who own a Buick, one being a bachelor and the other one of his colleagues at the Quai d'Orsay, Birul de Carjoux, known as Bijoux. We ruled him out because he has two sons but no daughter and his wife doesn't go in for lovers. But now we've got to start thinking of Bijoux again. You ought to telephone the Rézés as soon as possible.'

'They flew to Nice this morning. They won't be back till Wednesday or Thursday.'

'How tiresome. Well, see if you can find out if this Bijoux is a queer, and if he's lost track of his elder son. That's the line to work on. Please will you undo your coat again!'

'Not on your life. You'd be making a dive for Valérie the moment you got home. See you at seven.'

I arrived at the Rue Saint-Martin half an hour late. Valérie was also late as it happened, and I heard her singing to herself as she got the meal. This unaccustomed light-heartedness caused me to wonder whether she was dreaming of a new love or at least had a date. Porteur, propped against the pillows, was reading the morning paper. He was only really interested in the miscellaneous news items and except for these merely glanced at the headlines.

'Listen to this,' he said. ' "Two murders have been committed on the same day in Ambarès-le-Rotrou. A cobbler named Deblouse, aged forty-two, who had been living separated from his wife for eighteen months, waited for her late yesterday afternoon outside the municipal wash-house and cut her throat with his paring-knife. He then went and gave himself up to the police saying, 'I loved her too much, you see; I loved her too much.' And scarcely two hundred yards away, at almost the same time, another murder was committed. A farmer named Auguste Chalendieu sold his horse a month ago to another farmer, Ernest Aubriot, because he was hard up; and after that he constantly hung about outside Aubriot's farm. Yesterday evening he hid behind a hedge, and when Aubriot came out of the house on his way to the stable, he shot him. 'I couldn't bear the thought of my horse belonging to him,' he said." '

'Two crimes of passion, it would seem.'

'In other words, love and jealousy are inseparable. There is nothing to be said about the cobbler's crime that does not apply equally to that of Chalendieu. Both men had been deprived of a daily contact, a presence, and could not endure the thought of the beloved object being possessed by another man.'

'You're pushing it rather far,' I said. 'The word "possessed", has a different meaning according to whether you apply it to a woman or a horse.'

'That's only hair-splitting. A man sleeps with the woman he possesses, whether he satisfies her or not. But there's nothing to prevent a man sleeping with his horse if he feels like it.'

'Still, that's where the difference lies. Male desire is more readily appeased by women than by horses.'

'Yes, and that's all that distinguishes the cobbler's love from the love of Chalendieu.'

'You can't rule out a certain mystical or religious element in the love of a man for a woman, as there was for instance in the story you told me about the racing-driver and the dancer.'

'There could have been something of the kind in Chalendieu's love for his horse. Incidentally, when I was talking about the mystical element in love I said I had seen two cases. The one I told you about was the second.'

'What was the first?'

'The first happened much earlier, and it happened to you.

Yes, it did. You were eleven, and you were in love with a girl of your own age called Assunta, the daughter of the Italian grocer down the street. I was only seven, but I could see that you were in love. You were transformed. There was a glow in your face, a radiance—well, a mystical light is all I can call it. In the end it enchanted me too. Don't you remember?'

Suddenly I did remember. I recalled that poignant love, so long forgotten, and was astonished that I should never have thought of it in all the time I was in prison. Assunta was a little girl with brown hair and dark blue eyes whom I had known all my life. One afternoon, urged on by Tatiana who adored violence and heroism, we had played a cops-and-robbers game, girls as well as boys. I was an officer of the mounted police, and Assunta one of the passengers in a coach. We were captured together by bandits as I sought to rescue her, and confined in a make-believe prison which in fact was a small, dark alleyway off the Rue du Grenier-Saint-Lazare. Assunta, ill-at-ease, perhaps coquettish, gazed anxiously at me and I seemed to see her for the first time. For a minute or two the battle raged furiously outside our prison, and then it passed on down the street and we were forgotten. She took my hand and we walked out on to the pavement. I remember her showing me a mark on her shoulder and saying, 'Tatiana's awfully rough sometimes,' in a voice so musical that it was like a voice in a dream. I knew when I went home that evening that I loved her, and I felt as though I belonged to another world. There was a lightness in and around me, a kind of unreality like that of dancers or horses in a slow-motion film (I often dream of a film made entirely in slow-motion, with a setting and scenario devised to suit it). All through that year I fell more deeply in love, but I never spoke of it to Assunta. In my eyes she was so lovely, so exquisite a being that I thought of her as though she were a goddess. And I remember that in my class at school there was a boy of fourteen called Maroche, a wonderful blockhead, but since he was a head taller than the rest of us and moreover professed to be well versed in matters of love we were in the habit of confiding our secrets to him. Once when I happened to be alone with him I suddenly overcame my shyness and told him rhapsodically of my love-affair. Maroche, nothing if not a realist, cut short my lyricism by saying, 'Brunette with blue eyes. No need for any fancy stuff. Just whip the pants off her.' I ran from him in horror and when I got home knelt on the stone floor of the kitchen in penance for the insult done to Assunta.

Michel asked:

'Do you love Tatiana in the way you loved Assunta?'

'No.'

'In other words, you just sleep with her.'

The matter-of-fact conclusion did not please me. Something was lacking. Upon reflection I knew what it was. My feeling for Tatiana was one of the warmest affection, tenderness and gratitude, but it was clear and readily defined, with nothing mystical about it, nothing of the marvellous. I was quite sure that where she was concerned I had never, not for an instant, known that wonder and soaring of the spirit that had captivated me when I was eleven. Having reached this conclusion I said, not altogether convinced:

'The love I had for Assunta, and the love of your racing-driver and ballet-dancer, are extreme cases.'

'Probably,' said Michel, without much conviction either.

After our meal, which she enlivened with bursts of gaiety, jokes, puns and stories about Jews, Valérie went out clad in her Sunday dress and her Sunday coat. Michel, who had had luncheon in bed as usual, went and washed rapidly in the kitchen and then got dressed. For him the day was just beginning. I had intended to spend that Saturday afternoon with him, and I had hoped by discreet means to clear up something of the

137

mystery that surrounded him, but when he came back and sat down at his writing-table curiosity drove me to a direct question.

'It's less than a week since I came out of prison,' I said, 'but I've constantly heard people talk about Porteur, and in terms of great admiration. Why is that?'

'Frankly,' said Michel, 'I've no idea. I realise that for a large number of people, young ones especially, I have come to stand for something—hope or truth or the meaning of life, or whatever it may be. But I can't tell you the reason. You know what I'm like—I haven't changed in the last two years. I don't talk much, even when I'm feeling sure of myself. I'm not the kind that broods over world problems. I don't take myself too seriously and I don't make pronouncements. When I'm with the people I usually go around with I don't even encourage serious conversation.'

'Do you read them the things you write?'

'God forbid! That's the last thing I'd do.'

'Well then, how has it happened? There must be a reason.'

'I wish I knew. I think it may be that people are so saturated with publicity, so sick to death of all the names and faces, all the public performers, whether they're politicians or boxers or comedians, who crop up in every newspaper and magazine, on the telly, on the radio, on gramophone records, on the screen and on the hoardings, that they need to be able to admire someone obscure and repeat a name that is still veiled in mystery. I don't mind telling you, in my own case, that the very sight of the names of Sartre, Montherlant, Vadim, Mauriac and Sagan makes me feel so tired that I wish I were illiterate—to say nothing of Princess Margaret and Marilyn Monroe.'

'I don't know if you realise how well your own name is known in Paris.'

'It may be a kind of snobbishness, in which case sooner or

138

later I shall have the camera-boys after me. And that will be a pity. The day it happens I shall kill Porteur.'

There were other questions I should have liked to ask, but Michel, seeming already put out by my interest in the subject, had picked up a book, and so I did not venture to pursue it.

XII

'You must not mind, dear child, if I call you Volodia. It's because you're so like a boy who used to live in Kharkov, in a shabby old house almost opposite our own. He was a simple soul and his eyes were exactly like yours. Volodia used to come to us every day for vegetable parings to feed the two or three rabbits his mother tried to fatten in their poor lodging. The father had gone to the war and been taken prisoner by the Austrians. And listen, there was a schoolmaster living in another house in the street, a shy man fifty years old and when he looked at a woman there was such longing in his eyes that he made himself blush. It's so nice when men have eyes like that. Women don't know they're growing old, all they know is that men grow stupid and change more and more. For twenty years Dunia Skuratov has been saying that nowadays men are all dummies, and when she first said it I didn't understand because I was only thirty-eight at the time and she was fifty, but gradually I came to have the same feeling, that men are all dummies, and now I know what she means. And the other evening when I was having supper with Dunia I was naughty and said what is true, that when the men stop looking at us that is when death starts to make eyes at us. Sometimes I think of my funeral, and I'm glad there'll be a few people there. There'll be a few French people I hope, and I know my Russian friends won't fail me. It's a consolation for an exile to know that other exiles will follow her coffin and grieve for her death. And listen, I had a friend called Natasha Cherchev, and she got the sort of cancer that kills you in three months, and she knew and she said to her husband, "I want you to sprinkle a handful of our Russian earth on my coffin." So off he went to the Soviet Embassy and a clerk took him to another clerk and the second one took him to a third and the third one asked, "Where were you on the 8th of September, 1918?" And Captain Alexei Cherchev replied, "I was serving in Kolchak's army." And the Bolshevik said, "I was fighting with the Red Army against Wrangel, in the same regiment as my brother, and on the 8th of September the White cavalry raided our outposts and cleaned up the one he was commanding. Two days later I found my brother's body hanging naked from a tree. It was hanging by the feet and the head was charred by a wood fire lit by Wrangel's bandits, the ashes were still warm. So go and tell your slut of a Natasha that there isn't a grain of Red Russian soil for White Russian pigs and that her stinking body can rot in six feet of bourgeois earth." And Alexei went home and said to Natasha, "It's all arranged. They were very kind. The earth will be sent round on Wednesday." And then I wasn't able to go to poor Natasha's funeral after all because I sprained my ankle the day before and if you want to know how that happened. . . .'

'We seem to have rather lost track of Volodia and the schoolmaster.'

Sonia Bouvillon smiled. She was seated at the table in the living-room, with a plate at her right hand on which were the remains of a dish of pigs' trotters and on her left an open book. So as not to dirty the pages of the book with her greasy fingers she had taken the easy course of putting on her gloves. I fancy she had come in at about six and had been unable to resist cooking the pigs' trotters. It was now half-past seven, and I trembled for her at the thought that Tatiana might appear at any moment and find, not merely that she had committed this crime but that she had been too lazy to go and wash her hands afterwards. I felt that at least we ought to clear the table and wash up.

'The schoolmaster had come to Kharkov in 1915. His landlady found him a housekeeper who left him after a little while for a better job and he asked my mother if she knew of anyone. My mother recommended Mariushka, Volodia's mother, who came to do cleaning for us. She was a big, strong woman with rather uncouth manners. She and the schoolmaster met at our shop to arrange matters between them. I was there. When he saw her the schoolmaster's eyes nearly popped out of his head and he turned a deep crimson and so Mariushka went to clean and cook for him, and then, one day. . . . Ah, here's Tatiana!'

The bell had rung. I went and opened the door, but it was not Tatiana. I found myself confronted by a man in his sixties who evidently had not expected to see me, for he looked startled, as though wondering if he had come to the right floor. He was poorly clad, and his thin face, with strongly-marked features, was irradiated with a gentle warmth, a sort of anxious benevolence.

'This is Madame Bouvillon's apartment? Then that's all right. I'm a relation.'

I stood aside for him to enter the living-room. He had a parcel under his arm.

'Good evening, Sonia. I happened to be passing and I thought I'd look in to ask how you are. I'm not disturbing you?'

'Of course not, Jules. I'm always glad to see you and you come so seldom.'

The name Jules enlightened me. Tatiana had talked to me in the old days about Jules Bouvillon, her father's cousin. Unlike that steady-going shop-walker, he had picked up his living in haphazard ways, largely by repairing clocks and electrical appliances. When his cousin died he had come to the help of the widow and daughter with such money as he had, and had encouraged Tatiana in her resolve to go on with her studies. Himself self-taught, he had a passion for learning and above all a passion for goodness, which was the subject of all his meditations. He lived simply, and the greater part of his earnings went in the purchase of books and reviews. I like the self-taught for their earnestness, even though this is sometimes oppressive, and for their interest in ideas and their intolerance. The knowledge which they acquire with labour and with love is more deeply rooted in their minds and hearts than that of university graduates, and since they have never had to submit to any discipline of prescribed forms they look for nothing but truth in the books they read, and run less risk of being led astray by the smoothness of words.

Sonia introduced me.

'We used to live in the same house in the Rue Saint-Martin,' she said. 'The poor boy has had a very bad time.'

Cousin Jules' extraordinary gaze dwelt fixedly upon me, as though he were peering into the depths of my eyes to discover the extent of my burden so that he might share it; and I felt that I should be displaying an unworthy lack of trust in him if I sought to hide the truth.

'Two years ago I killed a man called Chazard in that house in the Rue Saint-Martin. I only came out of prison on Monday.

Still with his eyes upon me Jules Bouvillon gave an approving nod of his head, and said, placing his hands on my shoulders:

'My boy, it is a good thing that you have committed a crime. It is a good thing that you have been in prison.'

He uttered a laugh which lit up his strained face and then turned to Sonia.

'These hopeful signs are to be seen everywhere. In Algeria, for instance—all the misery, the people suffering and afraid, and the soldiers being killed on both sides. That's a good thing too—yes, a good thing! The world is turning and twisting, and in doing so it is finding its soul. To my mind, Sonia, there are another fifty years to be got through, hard years—I would

143

even say, very hard—but humanity will emerge triumphant at the end. Of course, not wholly triumphant. That would never do.'

Tatiana now entered. A single glance, as she stood in the doorway, was all that was needed for her to take in the story of the book, the pigs' trotters and the gloves, but the presence of Jules prevented her from saying anything. She greeted him gaily and affectionately.

'And are you still teaching mathematics?' he asked after she had kissed him.

'That just shows how often you visit us! No, I've given up mathematics and gone into the dressmaking business.'

'Well, that's something I hadn't expected. And what do you do in the dressmaking business?'

'I'm a sales-girl,' said Tatiana without hesitation and with nothing in her candid gaze to betray the untruth. I could understand her reasons for not wanting the old man to know that she was a model. It is a calling which the ill-informed are inclined to consider no calling at all, and I thought it very likely that this was Jules' view. I could sympathise with Tatiana's wish not to incur his disapproval; yet, knowing her character and the particular kind of moral forthrightness which was natural to her, I was astonished that she should have told a deliberate lie when there was no real need. I think Sonia was equally startled. The smile vanished suddenly from her face and she looked sharply and distressfully at her daughter. Seeing us both dismayed Tatiana became extremely talkative. She launched into a long and voluble account of the *haute couture*, the 'rag trade', describing it as a racket and, to please her cousin, becoming excessively indignant at the way the sewing girls were treated. This moved Jules Bouvillon to a profession of faith.

'We must not pity the oppressed,' he said. 'Their souls flower in the light of suffering. Those whom we have to pity

144

are the oppressors, the tyrants, the capitalists. Even if they are conscious of the harm they do to others, they have certainly no inkling of the fact that they do a thousand times worse to themselves. That is why they must be rescued from opulence and banged on the head if necessary. But do not misunderstand me. Anyone who studies, reflects and penetrates to the heart of things is bound to discover that Marxism is impossible. A beefsteak for everyone! They make me laugh, those imbeciles whose only thought is to fatten the poor, to stuff them with food and distractions so that they no longer have anything to fight against, no need to struggle or wring their hands while they moan, "Dear God, why was I born?" Because that is the question. That is what really matters. *Why was I born?* But a lot they care, those self-pleased party-members, for the hopes and tribulations of the human spirit!'

His voice trembled with emotion, but his thinking, as I was to discover in the course of the conversation, was not very consistent. In a general way he believed in the flowering of humanity under the stress of hunger and oppression, but at the same time he reproached Tatiana for giving up her mathematical studies, which he felt would have ensured her a more safe and honourable career than she was likely to achieve in the dressmaking business. And then he went on to praise Sonia for her serene temperament and aptitude for happiness. However at this point my attention was distracted by a sound of ticking coming from the parcel he had brought with him, which now lay on the table; and suddenly—the time was eight—we all heard the striking of a clock, somewhat muffled by the wrappings. Jules Bouvillon made a gesture of vexation. The clock had only struck six. He undid the parcel and got out a cardboard box containing a somewhat old-fashioned time-piece dating from about 1925. It was of imitation marble with a hexagonal face, tinted pale blue, on which the hours were inscribed in Arab numerals inside a circle of chromium.

Jules turned the hands to nine o'clock, whereupon it struck seven.

'There's certainly an error of adjustment,' he said. 'Nothing serious, but it's a nuisance. The last time I went to see my old friend Moncornet I took this clock away with me and said, "I'll bring it back in a month, and at the same time I'll bring you a surprise." '

He laughed and produced another package out of the parcel, wrapped in paper but not tied.

'This is the surprise. I have been writing down my meditations. To tell you the truth, they are more than meditations, they are my whole philosophy. The argument is developed after the fashion of Spinoza, but it is better. Well, when I say better I do not claim that it is as well arranged. I mean that it goes deeper, very much deeper. I have called the work *God*. I should like you to read it some day, Tatiana. I think you need it.'

'I will read it whenever you like, Jules. I long to read it.'

'You others should do so as well. I am sure that this young man would profit by it.'

He asked me whether I believed in God and I was obliged to confess that I was an atheist or at the best open-minded. Contrary to what I had feared he was pleased to hear this, explaining that it was precisely for people like me that his work had been written. I think he would have liked me to read it on the spot so that he could watch and rejoice in the good he was doing me, the glorious transformation which must infallibly result. Unfortunately he had to take it away with him to give to his friend Moncornet. However, he insisted on showing us the manuscript, which he unwrapped with great care. The single word 'God' was inscribed in large letters on the stout grey cover, this title being enclosed in a circle of daisies painted in water-colour, with beneath it his own name in a circle of roses. He stood gazing with soft, glowing eyes at this

146

decorative scheme while a smile of beatitude spread over his face, and then with a regretful sigh he wrapped the manuscript up again.

'I don't know what Moncornet will think of it. I'm afraid it may be too strong for him. Moncornet, you see, is nothing but a poor old anarchist who has always clung to the material aspects of this world. He'll be furious, I'm afraid, when he sees the positive proof of God's existence set down in black and white.'

Sonia tried to persuade Jules to stay to supper, but Moncornet, who was expecting him, had promised to cook a special *ragout* of mutton, so he had to go. He said to me as he left:

'I hope you will come and see me. I'm in the Impasse de la Baleine, in the Folie-Méricourt quarter. Anyone will tell you where to find me.'

I promised in all sincerity that I would do so. He went off, enveloping the three of us in a gaze filled with warmth and kindness. Directly he was gone Tatiana took her mother by the wrist, dragged her to the middle of the room under the light, and pulled off one of her gloves. Sonia's hand was shining with grease, and the interior of the glove, still retaining the shape and warmth of the hand, exuded a smell of fried pork.

'Disgusting,' said Tatiana in an icy voice, throwing the glove on the floor.

I picked it up and rather sharply told her to be quiet.

'Never mind, Volodia,' Sonia said. 'She's quite right. I'm a wretched creature, a bad mother, idle, useless, good for nothing——'

'Go and wash your hands,' interrupted Tatiana.

Sonia went off with a bowed head to the kitchen, and in my indignation I sought for something unpleasant to say.

'It seems that it would have been better after all if I hadn't come this evening,' I remarked, and added with a sarcastic laugh: 'I gather you've given up modelling to become a sales-girl.'

A flush rose on Tatiana's cheeks, and I think she came near to slapping my face.

'Come into my room. We can talk better there.'

She led the way. I knew what was going to happen in her room and I was not much in the mood for it. I told myself that I was about to undergo the operation known as brain-washing by love. I determined to be on my guard whatever happened, but when she turned and smiled at me as she opened the door I felt all my wrath and indignation melt away. She took my hand, standing in the doorway, and pressed it to her cheek. Her bedroom was very small. Looking over her shoulder I saw on the chest of drawers, only a few feet from me, an open, silk-lined case, bearing inside its lid the name of a celebrated jeweller in the Rue de la Paix. I withdrew my hand, and as I did so Tatiana saw what I was looking at.

'It belonged to my sister Katia,' she said in a perfectly natural voice. 'It's a bracelet that her fiancé gave her before he went to the war.'

I had not heard that her sister had been engaged, but it could have happened. Katia, who was ten years older than Tatiana, would have been seventeen in 1939. However, that was not the point. Whether she had been engaged or not, the case had certainly not belonged to her. I could see at a glance that it was nothing like twenty years old. The leather was bright and unfaded, the silk lining immaculate, the gold lettering of the jeweller's name untarnished.

'You're lying,' I said without anger. 'That case didn't belong to Katia. It's new.'

Although she was so accomplished a performer, Tatiana did not like lying. She sat down on the bed without saying any-thing.

'I'm not making a jealous scene,' I said. 'I'm not going

148

to preach morals either. I know that when you gave up serious work to become a model it was with an idea at the back of your head. I can understand that a very pretty girl should want to escape from poverty and dazzle the other girls by driving round in a luxury car, wearing the sort of clothes that so far you've been merely showing off to the public. It's a bit cheap, to my way of thinking, but I can quite see that it's a great temptation to the sillier kind of female, the child-women and peacock-women. If that's your heart's ambition, to be rich and have a cook and a lady's maid for your closest friends; and if the sort of flummery that you see all round you at Raphaëlo's makes your eyes pop out of your head, well, for God's sake, why not? But in your own interest as a strumpet I do beg you not to sell yourself to Lormier. I agree that the fact that he's a monstrosity and physically repulsive is beside the point if you're in that line of business. All that matters is that he should be very rich, which he undoubtedly is. But I'm warning you against Lormier because I'm beginning to know something about him. He's a very nasty man, at least as unpleasant as Hermelin, if not worse. He'll keep his side of the bargain, no doubt, and pay the agreed price, although it almost certainly won't be as much as you're hoping for; but you'll find that he'll want much more than you reckon in exchange. You aren't the sort to kow-tow to a man who is fundamentally crude and brutish. You'll fight him and in a very short time the thing will break up. And he's vindictive. When that happens he'll certainly get his own back.'

I had set out intentionally to wound her pride, which was great, choosing the harshest words I could find to express a contempt which, in fact, I did not at all feel. (I try to despise no one, and generally succeed: to me the attitude of contempt is a deliberate blindfolding of the consciousness, to spare oneself the effort of understanding.) I knew from her pallor and the widening of her eyes as she looked at me that my words

149

had had all the effect I intended, but I had made the mistake of going on too long. By the time I had reached the end of my speech Tatiana had recovered and was ready with her reply.

'Well,' she said, 'at least I now know your opinion of me. I must say I had no idea it was as low as that. I thought, I don't know why, that you had a certain regard for me. Well, it can't be helped and I must try to make the best of it, but you're an idiot, Martin, all the same. That case doesn't come from where you think. It belongs to Christine de Rézé, who lent it to me yesterday, as well as the bracelet I'm wearing at this moment.'

She pulled up the sleeve of her coat to display a heavy gold bracelet ornamented with a large ruby and some small diamonds.

'If it belongs to Christine,' I said, 'why did you say that it belonged to Katia?'

'I guessed what you were thinking when I saw you looking at the case, and I let you catch me out in a lie just to make you say it.'

I was not quite convinced. Tatiana stood up and said in an intense voice:

'You still don't believe it belongs to Christine? Martin, I swear it's true.'

To me a solemn oath of this kind, although it has no religious connotation, is one of the few human conventions entitling the individual to a generous measure of credit; one based, moreover, on a sense of honour which is not merely due to the arrogance of caste. I marvel that there should still be so many people capable, in the midst of a dispute, of becoming suddenly grave and saying in an entirely changed voice, 'I swear it' or 'I give you my word'. Whether they are sincere or not I find it wonderful that in order to convince someone, or merely to gain the advantage in an argument, they should take it for granted that there exists in their conscience a sort of Sunday-pigeonhole, the contents of which everyone is prepared to take on trust. Tatiana's oath convinced me utterly, and so I had to admit that I had been abominable. I begged her to forgive me for the things I had said and the words I had used.

'You have hurt me very much, Martin. What wounds me particularly is that you should have been so quick to jump to the wrong conclusion, as though you were waiting for the chance.'

'You can't really believe that. The truth is that I'm frightened for you, in case you're too tempted by money. You must try to understand me. I'm nothing but a shabby little office-clerk—no, I mean it, that's what I am—narrow-minded, opinionated, stuffed with small logic. I try to follow you into a world which is quite strange to me, and I ask myself all kinds of questions about you to which I can't find answers. For instance, what made you take up modelling, of all things, when it's a kind of work that can only last a few years? What do you hope to get out of it? And this world you live in, the world of Raphaëlo and the de Rézés, and snobs and queers and window-dressing and money—have you really accepted it? Are you a part of it?'

'Darling, you're fussing for no reason. If you'd think for a minute you'd remember that I answered all the questions before you even asked them. But talking of Raphaëlo, I had the chance of a few words with him today, which doesn't often happen, because he generally treats us models as though we were part of the furniture. The name of Bijoux cropped up. He said something about Christine, who isn't one of his customers although he'd very much like her to be, and I said that they'd gone to Nice with Bijoux and his wife. So then he told me how absolutely devoted he is to dear Bijoux and it was quite obvious from the way he talked that Bijoux is another high-ranking queer, like he is himself. That's all it amounted to, I think—oh, and he told me the names of the two boys.

The older one is Jean-Pierre and the younger one is Yorick.'

This fitted in with what I had already surmised. It seemed, then, that my unknown writer must be Jean-Pierre de Birul de Carjoux. He had wanted to expose Hermelin and be revenged on him, perhaps posthumously, but had been restrained by shame or a sense of loyalty from giving an account of his family which would enable them to be identified. So he had turned his invert father into a faithless wife, his pious mother into a gentleman with a monocle, his brother Yorick into a sister Flora (two equally affected names), and the château in Périgord into a château in Burgundy. The one authentic detail was the Buick.

'Why don't you ring him up now,' said Tatiana, 'this Jean-Pierre de Carjoux? Go down to the café.'

'What good would it do? He's certain not to be there. Anyway I don't know the number.'

'The name may be in the book. Don't forget that they live in the Rue Vaneau.'

The small café was empty when I went in, but I heard the proprietor in the kitchen shout in a husky voice, 'Rita, you'll have to fix me a hot-water bottle. It wouldn't surprise me if I died in the night.' The distant voice of Rita answered, 'All right.' I consulted the directory in the telephone-box and found 'Carjoux (Baron Gratien de)' in the Rue Vaneau. The lines seemed to be crossed. Directly I had dialled the number a voice yapped, 'This is the Comtesse Piédange. Is that you, Noémie?' I hung up, dialled again and again heard, 'This is the Comtesse Piédange.' Forgetting that I had the receiver in my hand I said 'Hell!' to which the Countess replied, 'Offensive brute! Get off the line!' I left the box rather depressed. The *patron* was back behind his counter, and forgetting that he was in danger of dying in the night I asked for a beer without worrying about his look of suffering. I was irritated by the delay and replied abstractedly to his remark about the penetrating dampness of the night air. When I dialled the number the third time I heard the ringing tone and the voice of the Countess asked who I was. 'Monsieur Cousin speaking. I want to speak to Jean-Pierre de Carjoux.' She replied, 'Will you please hold on,' and I heard her call, 'Jean-Pierre! It's some cousin of yours.' I waited a few moments and then a youthful voice asked again who I was.

'Your friend Germain Cousin. We met in Saint-Tropez, remember?—on the stairs leading to that cellar.'

'I'm afraid I don't get it. I don't remember your name or the cellar either.'

'Come off it. You can't have forgotten our last party, the time we smashed up the villa with those two girls. My mother sent me to school in England but I lammed out of it. What about you? I heard you had to go to work for S.B.H.'

'Sorry, old boy, you've got it all wrong. I've been at the Collège Saint-Evremond since the beginning of this term. I admit it's the fourth college I've been to in two years, but I've never smashed up a villa. You must have the wrong number.'

'But you are Jean-Pierre de Carjoux, son of the Baron of that name, who drives a Buick?'

This he agreed was the case. But it was all. There was nothing else, and my whole theory collapsed. I went back to Tatiana and during supper we talked of nothing else. She felt that I should not abandon the youthful Bijoux without finding out more about the family. What had so put me out, as she said, was the discovery that Jean-Pierre was not dead or disappeared. I had to admit that this was the case. I had made up my mind that someone had been done away with. Indeed, I had set my heart on it, and I imagine professional judges must sometimes meet with a similar temptation. I no longer believed that the Bijoux family was involved, but we agreed that in any case Flora must be a boy, and after going through the whole story again we felt that we could still believe that the flighty mother was really a disguise for a homosexual father. But now the Buick became a matter for misgiving. Might it not really have been a Chrysler or a Cadillac or a Mercedes or perhaps just a Renault Dauphine? Here sex was of no assistance to us. Could we even be sure that the homosexual father was a high official, or an official of any kind? It was impossible to tell how far the camouflage went. We talked and talked while Sonia sat and suffered in enforced silence. Knowing her perfect inability to keep her mouth shut we had thought it dangerous to tell her what it was all about. I felt for her in her suffering, passionately interested though I was in the matter. When the meal was over Tatiana said firmly:

'Martin and I will do the washing-up. You're not looking well tonight, mother. You're very tired. You must go to bed.'

'But, darling,' said Sonia, 'I'm feeling perfectly well. I'm not in the least tired.'

'You're not to argue. I want you to go to bed.'

I nearly gave way to cowardice, but it seemed to me that I owed Sonia something in the way of reparation.

'I think you're mistaken,' I said to Tatiana. 'Your mother's looking perfectly well.'

'Of course I am, Volodia, I never felt better. I'm as strong as a horse and sometimes I feel ashamed when Tatiana comes home worn out in the evenings.'

Tatiana jumped up, her face scarlet. She crumpled her table-napkin and threw it on the floor.

'All right, so I'm the one that's tired. So I'd better go to bed. Well, I'm going!'

She went into her bedroom slamming the door behind her. I started to get up but Sonia held me back.

'Let her get over it. If you go in she might say horrid things, the sort that can't be taken back. She's so tempted, you see, because of wanting a new coat and because of everything. And I'm so tiresome. She's still angry about the pigs' trotters

154

and especially the gloves. It was such a disgusting thing to do, and I'm always doing them. I'm naturally dirty, Volodia. I hate washing, and I know that if I were by myself I'd always be dirty and I wouldn't mind in the least. So it's one long battle with Tatiana because she's always clean all over, even the places you don't see. She looks at me and she asks me and I tell lies and say I've washed my feet when really I haven't at all, but she nearly always guesses. If I was a good mother I'd wash all over every day so as not to make her unhappy about me, but I'm not a good mother. I'm bad. I'm a monster.'

The tears ran down Sonia's cheeks and fell on the banana-skin lying on her plate. I said in a loud voice:

'You mustn't cry. I'm sure Tatiana isn't cross with you.'

'Dear boy, you're talking loud for her to hear, but she doesn't get over her rages so quickly, particularly when it's with me. I've been a trouble to her for so long, much worse than a child and no hope of improvement. But come and see us again soon. Don't wait for her to ask. She's very proud.'

Before leaving I tapped softly on Tatiana's door and murmured her name but without getting a reply. I could hear her pacing up and down her room and moving things about. When Sonia had gone into the kitchen I tried again and this time she answered.

'Good night, Martin. Forgive me, but I need some sleep. You were right. I really am tired.'

There was no more to be said, but the fact that she had spoken to me was a little reassuring. I arrived home at about half-past eleven. Going into the bedroom I switched on the light to make sure that Valérie was not in my bed. Then I looked at hers and started. Valérie was there, naked as usual, and at the extreme edge of her narrow bed, against the wall, was a man with a crop of dark hair, sound asleep. I was as outraged as a householder who catches someone in the act of stealing the spoons. Seizing Valérie by the shoulders I dragged her out of bed and thrust her into the next room, after which I locked the bedroom door. Her cries caused the man to turn over sluggishly in bed. He opened and shut his mouth, clicked his tongue and blinked his eyes. He was a youth of about twenty, rather plump, with an agreeable baby face and the general look of a heavy eater who has already had trouble with his liver. Valérie was banging on the door and calling me a rotten bastard, which was natural enough. The young man, after puffing and grunting, managed to get his eyes fully open. My presence at the bedside seemed to alarm him.

'Get up,' I said. 'Get up, get dressed and get out.'

He stiffened in consternation and I slapped his face, not viciously but simply to wake him up. He scrambled out of the bed naked, and never taking his eyes off me moved sideways towards the chair where his clothes were piled. Valerie, from the other side of the door, was shouting to him to bash my face in because I was a dirty Jew and a communist riff-raff. 'Go on, Gilbert, beat him up! He isn't as strong as you.' Gilbert shrugged his shoulders to indicate his disapproval of these sentiments. In the course of dressing he found his tongue.

'Well, naturally, if I'd realised. . . . But you know how it is. You see a girl and she takes a fancy to you and you know it isn't going to cost anything. Well, I ask you, what would you have done?'

I remained coldly silent, and Gilbert, again apprehensive, sought to appeal to my better nature.

'I shall be getting my call-up papers any time now. Twenty-eight months in bloody Algeria chasing the bloody Arabs. A nice lark that is, and maybe you come back alive and maybe you don't. Well, of course, you've got to take the rough with the smooth in this world, but all the same it's a bit hard. I've got a poor old mother. . . .'

'Hurry it up,' I said. 'I'm losing patience. You can put your tie on outside, and your shoes as well.'

156

When I opened the door, thrusting him out ahead of me, Valérie flung herself upon him with such vigour that he staggered back three paces. She clung to him crying:

'Gilbert, stay with me! You mustn't leave me alone with him. He's a gangster and a murderer, and the proof is that he's only just come out of prison.'

'Quite right,' I said. 'I came out on Monday, and I may add that prison turned me pretty sour.'

The terrified Gilbert got rid of Valérie by shoving her violently on to the bed, and he was off and out without a backward glance. Valérie decided to get back into bed and there was no further conversation between us. The next morning, Sunday, we had breakfast together in the kitchen and she asked me if I would rather she left the apartment.

'I wouldn't do anything to stop you going,' I said. 'But I should be sorry if you did.'

XIII

DURING the next month, helped by Jocelyne, I made great efforts to acquaint myself with the organisation and ramifications of S.B.H., but in doing so I constantly encountered veiled hostility and obstruction on the part of senior members of the staff, probably inspired by Hermelin. To some extent these more or less open manifestations of ill-will were of value to us in the Chairman's office as a means of detecting Hermelin's supporters. The corporation as a whole, with its numerous inter-related departments and their outside connections, formed an elaborate complex which occupied my mind even when I was away from the office, and left me little time for thinking about the mystery of the unknown writer and his story. Apart from this Lormier often kept me back after office hours to talk about schemes he had in mind, or developments which he feared, or simply to discourse at large on the state of the world. He did not like me and was shrewd enough to know that I did not like him, but he preferred my company to that of Odette or Jocelyne, no doubt because I was a man, but also perhaps because my argumentative disposition afforded him something more positive to bite on than the rather syco-phantic acquiescence of the two ladies. His favourite topic was the cowardice of the possessing class, their criminal and suicidal sentimentality. Communism, he maintained, was not merely at our gates but in ourselves (meaning the owners). From this he would go on to discuss the children of the well-to-do, educated on too-liberal lines, soaked in socialist doc-trines, the betrayers of their parents. I was cautious in what I said when he asked me my opinion, but he forced me to form one. Those conversations, which I found extremely wearisome, had the effect of causing me to look for precise answers to questions which I had never troubled to formulate clearly. In his relaxed moments, when he let himself go to me with a coarse frankness in which there was an element of personal hostility, Lormier was like a mirror reflecting on a considerably enlarged scale the attitudes of his own kind. As I listened to him I realised, once and for all, that the rich, even the best of them, the most benevolent, the most truly Christian, are persuaded in their hearts that they belong to a species so different from my own that, to their way of thinking, there can exist no common ground between us. It was as though the mere possession of money was enough to prove to them that a different blood ran in their veins. And perhaps it was at the instant of grasping this that I also realised why I was not a Communist. That profound conviction of the superiority of wealth was essentially the same as the feeling of the militant Communist for the unitiated, whom he tends to treat with the condescending disdain of the wide boy who knows all the answers. Like the bourgeois enriched with money and privilege, the man enriched with Marxist certainties holds himself aloof from the common run of men.

I got on well with the women in the office who, by the time we had worked together for a fortnight, seemed to have accepted me entirely. We were a team wholly devoted to the interests of the Chairman, although our personal feelings for him differed a great deal. Odette had been with Lormier for more than twelve years, and although she was too clear-sighted not to see him as he was, she had come to accept him. Long association must have dulled her reactions where he was concerned, and her gaiety, vitality and practical good sense inclined her in any case to tolerance. Angelina, the youngest, had only been there eighteen months, and was still treated by Odette as a sort of apprentice. She did her best to adopt Odette's attitude to Lormier, but I detected in her, or thought

I did, a young girl's distaste for the Chairman's physical presence. As for Jocelyne, although all her intelligence and vigour were dedicated to the service of Lormier, it was clear to me that she had made up her mind and would never accept him without reservation. Everything about him affronted her natural delicacy and humanity, and I think she secretly hated him; unless she took the line of regarding him with detachment as a social phenomenon. In any event, by tacit consent we never exchanged a word on the subject of the Chairman's moral outlook, and so this matter caused neither dispute nor embarrassment between us.

However, apart from office matters there was one subject on which I found the three of them arrayed against me. It was that of Porteur. There were occasions when, exasperated at hearing the name crop up so constantly in their conversation, vested with an inexplicable authority ('Just the line Porteur would take. . . . The sort of thing Porteur might have said. . . . A typical Porteurism. . . .') I was moved to protest at this apparently groundless affirmation of faith, and I tried to pin them down by asking them to define what they called the 'Porteur spirit'. To this they replied that for people capable of understanding it the Porteur spirit defined itself, and that it would be rash to say more. It was not difficult, by repeating remarks and opinions which they had attributed to him, for me to confront them with their own contradictions; but they merely laughed indulgently, telling me that I was a philistine, a backwoodsman, a low-brow, a country cousin, a square, a provincial, a typical average Frenchman and a telly-viewer.

Among the hundred-and-thirty or so employees of all ranks who constituted the headquarters staff of S.B.H. there was one whom they held in boundless esteem. His name was Faramon and he was in charge of office equipment; but his unique distinction in their eyes lay in the fact that he had positively seen Porteur. I might well have spared myself a visit to his department, which was of little importance, but apart from my desire to see everything that went on I wanted to hear what he had to say about the phenomenon. So one afternoon I went down to the basement and into a large square cellar with whitewashed walls, where a solitary assistant was moving about amid rows of office chairs, tables, typewriters, desk-lamps, filing-cabinets, electric bulbs, brooms, brushes, soap, toilet-paper, ash-trays and packages of stationery. The office of the head of the department was a glass-walled enclosure by the door. Faramon, who was evidently not in the habit of being visited, looked up sharply as I entered and drew a newspaper over something he had been writing, which led me to suspect that he was attending to his private correspondence in office hours. He was a man of about my own age, twenty-eight, tall and thin, wearing ill-fitting clothes, but with an intelligent face in which there twinkled a pair of alert and wary dark eyes. I introduced myself and asked him to tell me about the work of his section, which he did with perfect good humour; and then I broached the matter which was the real reason for my visit.

'They tell me that you are one of those rare people who have actually seen Porteur.'

'Yes, I've seen him,' said Faramon, 'although I can't pretend to have met him. I've never spoken to him, and I only saw him for about a minute. But I did hear him speak. It was—let me see—yes, it was in the Rue Mabillon, a little after midnight, when I was coming away from the Boulevard Saint-Germain, seeing a friend home. I don't know if you know the Rue Mabillon. For a distance of about twenty yards the roadway is separated from the houses on that side by a wide deep trench with footbridges over it. The effect is rather charming. There was a party of about half-a-dozen people crossing one of these bridges, all talking and laughing, and as we came up with them a young man broke away from the group and said to my friend, "Don't you remember me? I'm Luc Blanchon." They hadn't met since they were at school together. They exchanged a few words and then Blanchon said in a low voice, "I'm with Porteur, the tall one in the leather jacket who's holding the girl by the hand." Naturally I looked at Porteur. He's good-looking, with a nice face, and, I'm bound to say, with a hint of mystery about him. I heard him say, "As for pastries, the only kind I like is apple-tart." Then they moved on across the bridge and into the house. That's all that happened.'

I could not doubt the truth of the story. The mention of apple-tart was enough to identify my brother. I asked him what he thought of Porteur.

'Oh, well,' he said, 'I've no need of Porteur. Mine isn't the sort of job that strains the brain. People ring down from upstairs and say, "Madame Chambrier's chair's broken and Monsieur Letort's bulb has burnt out, Room 67," so I come out of my hutch and I get a chair and look it over and I test a bulb and I say to Ernest, "Take these up to Room 67. The chair's for Chambrier and the bulb's for Letort," and Ernest says, "Sure the chair's all right? You know the size of Ma Chambrier's bottom." We have our jokes. He comes back with the broken chair and the burnt-out bulb. We take it in turn to explode the bulbs. Now and then the carpenter calls to see to anything that wants mending. He likes it so much down here that he can hardly tear himself away. We're a bit like that ourselves, never in a hurry to leave in the evening. It's a retreat, this place, a hermitage. So you see, Porteur. . . . Although, of course, that doesn't stop me sympathising with the people upstairs as they sit there brooding, far from it.'

This conversation at least shed a faint light on the pheno-menon of Porteur. What most surprised me was the picture of Michel with a group of people at midnight on a footbridge in the Rue Mabillon. Curious to know how he spent his evenings, which ended between two and four in the morning, I had several times asked him about them, but he did not seem to know very much himself. 'Nothing special . . .' was all he had to say; or 'Well, it depends, but I can't say exactly. . . .' I don't think he was trying to evade my questions, which meant no more to him than if I had asked him what he did in the afternoons. We had passed the afternoon together the first Saturday after I came out of prison, and really there was nothing much to be said about it. People had come and gone without saying hullo or good-bye, perhaps to foster an illusion of never parting company. The conversation had not followed any prescribed course and nothing out-of-the-way or really significant had been said. Moreover there had been long silent periods during which Michel worked at the play he was writing. The youth in the green shirt who had left three thousand francs on the table had arrived at about four. He had sat down on the floor with his back against the wall facing Michel, and had settled down to the study of his African dialect, referring to a sheaf of notes which he pulled out of his pocket. Then there had been a girl whom Michel had kissed, ruffling her hair a little, but nothing more. It seemed to me now that this had been the most notable event of the afternoon. For me the only mystery had lain in the subtle, easy understanding between Michel and his visitors, who had treated him with no particular veneration, nor done anything to suggest that they looked up to him.

After taking leave of Faramon I went back to my ladies and repeated what he had said about Porteur. He had already told them of the encounter, but, perhaps for fear of disillusioning them, he had not repeated the remark about the apple-tart. I was less considerate. I wanted them to hear a positive statement by Porteur of which the authenticity was not in doubt. Faramon's tact turned out to have been quite unnecessary. Contrary to my expectation, they were charmed and delighted by the utterance, particularly Jocelyne, who positively wrote it down to make sure of getting it right. Once again I strove to understand.

163

'For heaven's sake, can you explain to me what sort of thrill or inspiration you get out of the words, "As for pastries, the only kind I like is apple-tart"?'

This time they did not call me a typical Frenchman or a telly-viewer. Their attitude was one of solemnity and restrained fervour. I read in their expressions, or thought I did, how touched they were by the simple humanity of this midnight avowal. It was just like Porteur. The only kind of pastry he liked was apple-tart. And said with such simplicity—Jocelyne's eyes were moist at the thought! It went without saying that Lormier had never so much as heard the name of Porteur. I could imagine the contempt with which he would have brushed aside this nonsense, and, imagining it, there were moments when I came near to sharing the enthusiasm of Jocelyne and the others.

The senior members of the staff with whom I ordinarily came in contact were very different from Faramon. They were men well aware of their own importance who did not take at all kindly to the intrusion of a newcomer into their affairs, on the pretext that he was learning the business. Lormier had to intervene personally more than once on my behalf. But despite the difficulties, I managed to work my way in and, guided by Jocelyne's experience, to find out the things it was essential for me to know. I found that Lormier was right in suspecting Hermelin of manoeuvring for the support of certain of the larger shareholders by making concessions which were extremely costly to the company. But I also discovered that Lormier made no bones about doing the same, which was the reason why he could not openly accuse his rival. After comparing certain figures I came to the conclusion, without being absolutely positive about it, that the Chairman was running an export swindle for his personal profit. A Swedish shadow-company, probably his own creation, was buying electronic equipment under export licence from S.B.H. at a 25 per cent reduction on the French price, and re-selling it in France without its having ever left French territory. The 25 per cent went into the account of the Swedish company, that is to say, into Lormier's pocket. I merely surmised this from a study of documents and correspondence in various departments, but it seemed to me more likely than not. The turnover was very considerable, and Lormier's private gain, if I was right, ran into tens of millions of francs a year. I do not think Lormier was actuated by mere greed in the matter, or a fondness for risky transactions. Being the man he was, he was more likely to consider himself justified in using fraudulent means to get what he held to be his due, and very possibly he also considered them no more dishonest than other methods countenanced by law. I wondered whether to tell Odette and Jocelyne what I suspected but in the end decided not to do so. If I told them I should either have to leave S.B.H., which would make life very difficult for me, or else I should have to connive with them in covering up the Chairman's sharp practice. I must confess that I did not have much trouble with my conscience. Moral certainty was no substitute for concrete proof when it came to making a charge of this kind, even in confidence. When I asked Tatiana what she thought she shrugged her shoulders and replied:

'You're crazy. Why on earth should you interfere and get yourself into trouble? So Lormier's robbing some of his fellow shareholders, all of them probably millionaires. When the rich pick each other's pockets all the poor have to do is let them get on with it.'

Acting on Sonia's advice I had made my peace with Tatiana, who was still passionately interested in the mystery of the unknown writer. She had dropped the Bijoux family and was following another trail, that of a family called Camassar. He was a big banker, a protestant, married, with two sons, Philippe and Jean-Jacques, aged eighteen and thirteen. We wondered whether Jean-Jacques was to be regarded as a 'corny' name, like Flora, and concluded after much discussion that it depended on how you looked at these things. Madame Camassar fitted into the picture more or less, a fashionable society woman but with high principles and inclined to severity in her behaviour. Philippe, the older boy, was ostensibly a boarder at a school in Switzerland, but according to Paulette, one of the fitters in the Orsini establishment, his mother became evasive and seemed upset when questioned about him, and this was confirmed by Jean-Etienne, who dressed the lady's hair at least twice a week. There was evidently a mystery here of some sort. On the other hand, it seemed that the banker was not a homosexual; all our sources of information were agreed upon this. 'But then, with protestants you never can tell,' said Tatiana. 'They'll give their wives eight children just to keep up appearances.' It was a matter on which I held no views, since the only protestant whom I could remember knowing at all well was a twelve-year-old boy I had been at school with, a nice-looking, bright-eyed youngster with whom I had been on quite friendly terms. One day as we were coming out of school together he had suddenly asked, 'How long's your cock?,' a question which, in my view, betrayed no particular tendency but merely pointed to a certain uneasiness of mind. Taken aback I replied, very much at random, that it was about a foot long, or perhaps ten inches. He repeated these statistics in a voice of awe while his eyes grew heavy with disquiet, and during the next few days he was filled with a melancholy which I did not understand. He did not come back to school next term and I never heard of him again. Anyway, in the end we dropped the banker because Tatiana discovered, by a curious conjunction of circumstances, that the boy Philippe, whom we had thought might be our unknown writer, was exceptionally good at grammar, spelling and punctuation.

I was now in the habit of visiting Tatiana twice a week; and it happened on one occasion that I fell asleep so soundly that I did not wake until six in the morning. I started to get up but she stopped me, and when I said something about her mother she laughed.

'How silly you are! Do you really think mother doesn't know? Go back to sleep again.'

Nor did Sonia show any surprise when later I emerged from her daughter's bedroom. She was lying on her stomach on the floor, reading a life of Saint-Just that she had bought at a stall on the quai. 'Your revolutionaries, from Louis XV to Louise Michel, are real-life heroes of fiction,' she remarked. I replied that this was very true, and without inquiring into her reasons for considering Louis XV a revolutionary I asked her, on Tatiana's recommendation, if she could lend me a razor. I have a dark, heavy beard which I have to shave every day if I am not to go round looking like a tramp.

'I've still got Adrien's things,' she said. 'There's a safety razor and a brush and shaving-soap and a thing for if you cut yourself. Come, Volodia.'

I followed her into her bedroom which, although it was sparsely furnished with a narrow iron bed and an oak wardrobe, was in a state of remarkable disorder. After shifting a large number of clothes, books, boxes, packages and miscellaneous objects she turned to me with an expression of concern.

'I can't think what I've done with it. I know I've seen it somewhere. It's a book with a blue paper cover.'

'Dear Sonia, we haven't come to look for a book but a razor. The book in the blue cover is the one you're reading at this moment.'

Sonia blushed. Diving under the bed she brought out a big suitcase from which she extracted a rolled-up shirt, a camembert cheese-box containing an old steel watch, and, wrapped in newspaper, the razor, the shaving-soap, the brush and the thing-for-if-you-cut-yourself. 'But please don't say anything about me looking for the book. She gets so cross with me for being muddle-headed. She was scolding me only yesterday. She says she's sick of it.' There had been no need for Sonia to ask. While I was shaving in the kitchen Tatiana came in, and standing naked at the sink, with her hair in a net, washed in cold water. When I had finished and was wrapping up the shaving-tackle again in its newspaper she said:

'Put it on the shelf. You'll be stopping the night next time you come. I was happy while I was asleep and when I woke, just to feel that you were there, so safe and solid. I so long to be everything to you. Promise that you'll stay other nights.'

I promised, meaning it, but perhaps not with all the enthusiasm she had hoped for. For a moment we were silent, and suddenly I saw that she was crying, her big eyes brimming with tears that ran down the cheeks she had just dried. I did not try to stop her. The tears that women shed over their destiny in the early morning are tears of clear-sighted grief that no soft words can charm away, and I knew in my heart that it was not really I who loomed so large in the destiny of Tatiana. When she had washed away their traces with more cold water I took her hand and promised that I would always do for her what she truly thought best, and her frank, almost gay, answering smile was like the dropping of the curtain on a little tragedy of which she had afforded me a glimpse. 'I must run now or I shall be late,' she said.

Lormier kept me in his room at the office until well after twelve telling me how lucky 'people of my kind' were in not having to bear the burden of riches with all its attendant vexations. He even talked of the joy of travelling by métro and meeting (I quote his words) 'One of those little midinettes whose favours you can buy with a bunch of violets.' When I got home I found Porteur up and dressed, to my great surprise. I asked him if he was ill, but he assured me that he was not. Contrary to his general routine, in which he was a model of regularity, he had slept elsewhere and had only just come in. He was rather worried at not finding Valérie at home. I had to confess that I too had not slept in my own bed, which made it seem that she might be meaning to punish us both by not coming home for lunch. We were still in the lobby discussing this possibility when Valérie entered with a distraught countenance. At the sight of us she stood motionless in the doorway, then gave a long sigh of relief and burst into tears. She came slowly towards us, moving deliberately and never taking her eyes off us, as though she expected us suddenly to vanish; and grasping a hand of each of us she drew them together and bore them to her lips. Only then was she able to speak, in a trembling voice.

'It gave me a shock when I woke up this morning and found that neither of you was here, but I thought to myself, I know what it is, they've done it on purpose, but I'll show them. And then when I got back at twelve there still wasn't anyone here. I waited and waited and you didn't come. It just didn't seem natural, so in the end I got in a panic and when it was half-past and you still hadn't come I rushed out like a mad thing. I thought I'd try to find that friend of Michel's, the one in the green shirt. I've seen him once or twice in the street at lunchtime, talking to a tart in the Rue Saint-Denis. I went to the hotel and I found her all right, but green-shirt wasn't there. Then I rang up S.B.H., but some fool of a woman answered who didn't know anything about anything. I thought to myself . . . But never mind. You must be hungry, seeing how late it is. I'll do you an omelette. Lay the table, Martin.'

Our meal was a happy one. Valérie gazed at us with eyes brimming with tenderness. Michel, when she questioned him, accounted in the simplest terms for his absence.

'The party broke up, and at about two I found myself alone with an Italian girl, a film starlet, long and slim with rather startling breasts, like water-melons under a white woollen jersey. Well, of course, I might have dated her to come here this afternoon, but the mood came over me and so I went with her to her hotel. Her thighs were a bit skinny but the bosom was quite something.'

'An Italian,' said Valérie. 'Foreigners as usual. And you, Martin. I suppose you spent the night with your Yid, that great Russian mare. Those bitches, they're all Moscow agents the whole lot of them, Judeo-Marxist whores recruiting for the Party. It's enough to make one vomit. I just can't wait for Pinay to come into power. The first thing he'll do is to clear all that riff-raff out.'

I think even Michel was touched by the distress which our absence had caused her. I went with her into the kitchen to make the coffee, and when she laid her head against my shoulder I kissed her with tenderness and gratitude, conscious of the warmth and cohesion that her presence, often acrimonious but always regardful, brought to our odd little household. A minute later when I went back into the living-room I found her in Michel's arms with her mouth pressed to his. This family tableau did no more than illustrate a state of affairs which I had already accepted, yet I could not help being somewhat disconcerted by it, unlike Michel, who was in no way put out, and still less Valérie herself, who challenged us both to deny that her charms and allure were in a different class altogether from those of our Yids and foreigners.

The same afternoon, when I got back to the office, I had a violent flare-up with Hermelin. Lormier was not there. He had business interests outside S.B.H. to which he devoted a part of two afternoons a week. Hermelin, knowing that he ran no risk of encountering him, had come to talk to Odette about a requirement he had received from the management of a factory belonging to the S.B.H. group arising out of a recent change in their production policy.

'I know nothing about this change,' he said. 'I take it the

matter was agreed between the Chairman and the factory manager without anyone troubling to let me know, a thing that happens more and more frequently. It's extremely annoying to me to get the information in this roundabout way.'

'I can assure you,' said Odette, 'that we know nothing about it either.'

While she was reading the letter he had brought to show her Hermelin opened the newspaper he also had in his hand.

'Things are looking up!' he exclaimed. 'The police have arrested an escaped convict who murdered an old man to rob him of five thousand francs.'

I was seated at my desk arranging some notes I had made that morning. I watched Odette put down the letter, while Hermelin turned to me and said with the most bland of smiles:

'It seems that after all crime doesn't pay.'

'Neither does boorishness,' said Odette sharply. 'Please take back your letter, Monsieur Hermelin. I don't want to read it.'

'Dear Odette,' I said, 'you mustn't be cross with the Managing Director. He's only teasing me about my police record, and with such wit and charm that no one could resent it. In any case we murderers—it is one of our weaknesses—adore being reminded of our crimes by God-fearing citizens. I remember when I was sixteen and had only committed my second murder—it was a woman I strangled in her bed so as to be able to rape her more conveniently—one of my uncles, who was an inspector of police and looked remarkably like the Managing Director, besides having the same neat turn of phrase, remarked that——'

But I got no further. Odette, Jocelyne and Angelina were all gazing at Hermelin, and their sudden burst of laughter caused his fleshy ears to redden. Beside himself with rage he came at me shouting abuse and slapped my face so that the sound echoed through the room. It was a contingency which I had long foreseen, and knowing that with my record I should be in serious trouble if I attempted to hit back, I simply got to my feet so as to be better able to parry another blow. But I had no need. The three women flung themselves on Hermelin. Odette, who was decidedly muscular, twisted one of his arms behind his back while Jocelyne and Angelina, seizing hold of the other, tried to drag him to the door. He stood his ground, calling them fools and idiots and shouting to them to let go. The temptation to kick him was very strong, but I resisted it. I opened the door and summoned the messenger, calling in a loud voice, 'Hurry! The Managing Director has gone off his head.' He came running in and Hermelin, who had broken away from Jocelyne and Angelina, met him with a punch on the nose which started it bleeding. Odette was still hanging on to his left arm. Jocelyne ran out into the main corridor and shouted for help, saying that the Managing Director had gone mad. A dozen people came rushing in and held Hermelin while he struggled and cursed, but by degrees he grew calmer and eventually consented to leave the room. Odette promptly telephoned to Lormier and went so far as to use the words 'delirium tremens,' which was why when Lormier returned to the office, and, summoning Hermelin, cross-examined him in the presence of Odette and myself, he started by asking him if he was an habitually heavy drinker or if this outburst of drunkenness was accidental. Every detail of the business, into which the Chairman inquired with the most meticulous care, was a source of cruel humiliation to the Managing Director. I displayed my magnanimity by promising not to bring a charge for assault or even to report the matter to my union.

The next day, when I told Tatiana about it, she besought me not to go too far in exasperating Hermelin, because, she said, I could only keep my job with S.B.H. by the grace of Lormier, and should there be a reconciliation between the two men it might prove disastrous for me if I had made myself intolerable to either. There was a worldly wisdom in this which I had not expected of her, and when I said as much she replied that she was learning to live.

'I'm not contradicting you,' I said, 'but I've known you to study in better schools than that of Raphaëlo.'

'How do you know? In the old days all that mattered was not starving to death. When things are easier, and you're able to look at yourself and your job with some detachment, you begin to think, and that's when you start learning.'

'I don't quite follow. Did you take up modelling so as to have time for thought?'

'The questions you ask! You want to know absolutely every-thing. I find it so boring.'

It is true that I have always been disposed to believe that everything can be explained. I stayed silent while I brooded on the fact that Tatiana found me a bore, and seeing that she had wounded me she pressed her cheek to mine. We were lying together in her bed, and the time was eleven o'clock at night. She kissed me ardently. But a moment later her eyes became remote; she turned her head away and I knew that she was thinking of something else. It had been the same all that even-ing. She had been abstracted both during and after dinner. I switched off the light and tried to go to sleep. In a drowsy voice Tatiana said, 'Darling, I can count on you, can't I, no matter what happens?' I said yes and fell asleep a minute later. When we parted the next morning we arranged that I should come to supper on Sunday and stay the night. I spent the afternoon of that Sunday in the Rue Saint-Martin. Valérie, rather bored, suggested that we should play a game of draughts in the bedroom so as not to disturb Michel, who was working on his play. We sat playing on the big bed, my bed, and after winning several games she pushed aside the board and talked to me about Tatiana.

'She's a lovely girl but she's too big for you. I don't know if you realise, but when you're together she makes you look rather comical. And I can just imagine you in bed together, that great wench not knowing what to do with her body, too violent in her movements. I'm sure she must sometimes irritate you.'

There was a great deal of perception or intuition in that remark. Quite often, in manifestation of an ardour which she did not truly feel, Tatiana would grapple and pinch and cling to me with a clumsy violence that I found exasperating.

'Anyway,' said Valérie, 'I hope you won't marry her, for her sake as much as for yours. A beautiful girl who chooses to become a model when she's well enough educated for a dozen other careers isn't going to settle down happily with an under-strapper in an office. You might as well get that into your head.'

'There's no question of marriage between Tatiana and me. No one wants to marry an ex-convict.'

'That may be her idea but it isn't mine. I'm ready to marry you.'

'It's very sweet of you, but what about Michel? I might be jealous of him if we were married. To say nothing of your friend Gilbert.'

Valérie was ruffled by this mention of Gilbert, whom she declared she no longer saw and who in any case had never been important to her. We went back into the living-room. The youth in the green shirt was seated in his usual place with his back against the wall. Michel, who had been re-reading his work, tore a sheaf of pages out of his exercise book exclaiming, 'The whole thing stinks. I've a good mind to scrap it and write a song with three verses instead. It would be a lot simpler.'

When I arrived at the Rue Eugène-Carrière that evening I found Sonia in conversation with a lady of her own age. They were talking Russian, and it was in Russian that Sonia introduced me and addressed me as she handed me a letter. The envelope was inscribed with my name in Tatiana's handwriting. 'Darling Martin, I'm flying to Berlin in an hour or two with some of the other girls to show the Spring collection. I'm so terribly sorry not to have been able to say good-bye. I'm afraid we shan't be seeing very much of one another these next few months. Raphaëlo is sending me on a tour of Europe and America. I shall have a chance to travel and earn a little money. We'll meet whenever we can. You mustn't be sad. I think of you always and I embrace you with all my heart. Tatiana.' There was also a postscript. 'I read this just now in yesterday's newspaper: "Monsieur and Madame Souffard and their daughter Floriane, confronted with the young man suffering from loss of memory who was found wandering in the Gare de Vendôme, stated that despite a certain resemblance he is not their son Léopold who, it will be recalled, mysteriously disappeared on the evening of the 23rd September last."'

Despite the insistence of Sonia, who had rediscovered the use of the French language, I hurriedly took leave of her and returned to the Rue Saint-Martin. Valérie and Porteur had both gone their separate ways. I found a box of sardines and ate it standing up with a hunk of bread. It was too early for bed. I went into the living-room and sat in Michel's chair. I tried to think about the disappearance of Léopold Souffard and of his sister, Floriane, whose name was deserving of attention; but, as I realised, I was growing less and less interested in this business of the unknown writer, and all I could think of was Tatiana and her sudden departure, which had brought me near to despair. I reached idly for the exercise book out of which Michel had torn the pages, and began to read.

XIV

CONTENTS OF YELLOW EXERCISE BOOK
(NO TITLE)

Act I

The audience, a sparse one, is composed of women under thirty and men under forty, all wearing brightly coloured clothes. Voices are suddenly raised, 'Algérie française!' to which other voices reply, 'Algérie libre!' The spectators fall upon one another. A brief but violent battle. The three knocks are heard denoting the rise of the curtain and the spectators return to their seats. A dead man is carried out on a stretcher. The curtain rises. Scene: on the left a table and chair, on the right a chair and down-stage, with its back to the audience, a wicker armchair. No backdrop. The cowl of the prompter's box, mid-stage, is turned towards the public, not towards the actors.

Jean-Pierre Donadieu is seated at the table examining a folder of papers. The head and shoulders of Bordeur, the prompter, appear beneath the cowl. Célestin enters up-stage right and comes down-stage stepping over ropes and planks while Bordeur plays a drinking-song on a mouth organ.

CÉLESTIN: (*standing by the armchair*) May I come in?
JEAN-PIERRE: Come in. Ah, it's you, Célestin. How are you?
CÉLESTIN: I'm all right. And you? You sent for me.
JEAN-PIERRE: Yes, but wait a minute. Sit down.
BORDEUR: (*addressing the audience*) Jean-Pierre Donadieu, the handsome, well-dressed young man, is the owner of the factory and Célestin is a member of his staff. Célestin's father was the night-watchman, so the two young men have known

176

each other a long time. Old Monsieur Donadieu, Jean-Pierre's father, who was stowed away in the family mausoleum three years ago, insisted that Célestin should receive the same education as his son. Unfortunately Jean-Pierre was always bottom of the class and Célestin was always top, in which he displayed a lack of lifemanship. So when he was fourteen years old Donadieu gave him a job in the factory. Thirty thousand a month. His parents were delighted. He has now been raised to fifty thousand—nice money for a bachelor in a small town.

JEAN-PIERRE: Well, that's done. It seems a devil of a long time since I've seen you. Of course your office is in another building, and then, I'm always so busy. You don't know how lucky you are—nothing to do but down tools when the whistle blows. Well. . . . And how's Ernestine? Still in Paris?

CÉLESTIN: I think so. My sister doesn't write to me very often.

JEAN-PIERRE: Curious notion, to go to Paris to be a meccanograph operator. She could have had the same job here at the factory. Do you remember how you and she used to come and play with us on Thursdays when we were all at school?

CÉLESTIN: Yes.

JEAN-PIERRE: (laughs) One time, I remember, Yolande pulled Ernestine's knickers off and we tickled her behind.

CÉLESTIN: *You* tickled her behind. I didn't.

JEAN-PIERRE: Well, perhaps it was only me. Anyway, it's fun to look back on. But you don't seem to think so.

CÉLESTIN: Look at it from my point of view. Suppose when I was twelve I'd tickled your sister's behind, and that now——

JEAN-PIERRE: (curtly) That'll do.

BORDEUR: You see, it's not the same thing at all. Célestin ought to realise that.

JEAN-PIERRE: You're wondering why I sent for you. Well, listen. I've been hearing stories about you, that you're an absolute Don Juan, playing merry hell in the factory. You needn't try to deny it. I have excellent sources of information. And anyway I'm not going to preach. I'm as broad-minded as anyone, and I'd be the last to scold you for sleeping with the factory girls. Some of them are very pretty.

CÉLESTIN: But as I work in the office building I scarcely ever see them.

JEAN-PIERRE: In other words, you're cutting loose with the ladies of the office-staff. Well, that's just it, old boy—that's why I've got to try and calm you down a bit. In these days more and more girls of good family go out to work. They become professors, editors, private secretaries, anything you like. It's perfectly understandable, they're simply following the trend of the times. You see what I mean?

CÉLESTIN: No.

JEAN-PIERRE: Well, never mind. It's my duty to keep an eye on these well-bred girls coming from respectable homes and see that they don't do anything to discredit themselves or their families. I hear you're making a play for Olga Couturier?

CÉLESTIN: You've been misinformed. But even if I were, I don't see what harm I should be doing her. Everyone knows that she used to be your mistress.

BORDEUR: Well there again Célestin just isn't with it. He ought to realise that a girl of good family doesn't suffer in the eyes of the world because she has slept with a wealthy young industrialist. Far from it.

JEAN-PIERRE: You've got to remember that you have a position to keep up in this business. You are one of the people who are expected to set an example. I don't know why you've suddenly taken it into your head to go chasing after girls. You used to write poetry. Why you even published a little book called—what was it?——

CÉLESTIN: 'Platform'.

JEAN-PIERRE: Eh?

CÉLESTIN: The title you couldn't remember is 'Platform'.

JEAN-PIERRE: That's it—'Platform'. And a very good title too. It says exactly what it means. Well, why don't you go on writing poetry? It's much more sensible than womanising, and I'll bet it wastes a lot less time.

CÉLESTIN: I'm not so sure about that. I do a lot of crossing out. But anyway, it's different.

JEAN-PIERRE: You know what, Célestin? The sensible thing would be for you to get married. Why don't you find yourself a nice girl and——

CÉLESTIN: Sorry. I'm not interested.

BORDEUR: This young man is hiding something from us.

JEAN-PIERRE: Well, it's up to you, of course. But what matters to me—(*he lowers his voice*)—what matters to me is that you should lay off Olga Couturier. It's true she isn't my mistress any longer, but I wouldn't want her to be yours. I'm just telling you that between ourselves—in strict confidence.

(*Yolande, Jean-Pierre's sister, appears up-stage. While she comes towards them Bordeur plays a love-song on the mouth-organ. Jean-Pierre starts as she passes behind the wicker-chair.*)

JEAN-PIERRE: (*angrily*) Yolande, I wish you wouldn't slam the door. It gets on my nerves.

YOLANDE: A very good reason for doing it. Why, Célestin, this is a surprise! How nice to see you.

CÉLESTIN: Me too. Are you well?

YOLANDE: No, not at all. Sit down. Have you heard from your sister? Is she still in Paris? Still a meccanograph operator? Poor Ernestine. What exactly is a meccanograph operator?

CÉLESTIN: She operates a machine that punches holes in a strip of paper.

YOLANDE: It can't be very exciting. Poor dear. Do you remember how you used to come and play with us in the garden on Thursdays?

179

CÉLESTIN: I remember it as though it were yesterday. Mother always dressed us in our best clothes.

YOLANDE: And we did our best to get them dirty and torn. Poor Ernestine, I shall never forget that time we got her down on her stomach on the gravel path. I held her legs and Jean-Pierre tickled her behind. I'm sure you both remember.

JEAN-PIERRE: Of course we do. We were talking about it only a minute ago.

YOLANDE: (*to Jean-Pierre*) You were disgusting. (*Jean-Pierre starts.*) Yes, you were—disgusting. The sight of you bending over her with your beastly hot dirty little boy's face gave me a sort of—a sort of electric shock that went right through me. Even now, when I think of it. . . . (*She falls silent, staring fixedly at him.*)

JEAN-PIERRE: Did you go to the tennis party?

YOLANDE: Yes, I went but I very soon came away. Do you think I'm crazy? (*to Célestin, who has made a move to withdraw*) Don't go, Célestin. I want you to stay. (*to her brother*) After all, we've known Célestin since we were children, and he's devoted to us both, and just for once I'd like to talk to somebody who isn't a block of wood. (*to Célestin*) You know how it is with me. I've been a widow for eighteen months, after two years of marriage. My idiot brother saw fit to marry me off to a man of forty-two.

JEAN-PIERRE: Wait a minute. I introduced you to Victor, that's all.

YOLANDE: A man of forty-two, and used up, worn out, even if he still looked like a man. Victor had always lived in Paris, with nothing to interest him but horses, whisky and women. It's incredible the number of women a man can have in his life by the time he's forty-two. When he inherited his uncle's château and came to live down here he decided that one woman would be less exhausting than a few dozen. His idea was that we were to have separate rooms—but I had my own ideas.

JEAN-PIERRE: Yolande, Célestin doesn't want to hear all this. Neither do I.

YOLANDE: But I want to say it. It's time it came out. The confessional's no use when it comes to relieving my feelings. Victor was my lawful husband. We weren't sinning. On our wedding night, after he had taken me——

JEAN-PIERRE: This is revolting.

YOLANDE: I forced him to tell me about his love affairs. He was tired and he tried to put me off, but I sat astride him on his stomach. (*She sits astride the chair, with her arms on the back.*) You remember what he was like, hairy all the way up to his neck. I clutched the hair on his chest and I said, 'Tell me! Tell me!'

BORDEUR: (*putting his head out through the cowl*) But, darling, what do you want me to tell you? (*yawns*) Those stories are always much the same.

YOLANDE: Tell me. . . . Tell me about a maidservant. I'm sure you've had maidservants.

BORDEUR: Of course. Well, one time when I was driving back from Deauville the car broke down and I had to stop the night at a little country inn. The *patron* and his wife had gone to a wedding and I was alone there with the waitress. A great mare of a girl built like a Normandy wardrobe, with curves in front and behind—terrific! . . . While I was having dinner I asked her, 'What does one do in the evenings in these parts?' 'Well me,' she said in her Normandy accent, 'well me, if there's nothing wanted I go to bed.' So I said, 'How about coming along to my room for a chat?' (*yawns.*)

YOLANDE: Well?

BORDEUR: But when I got up to my room, what with thinking about the car and one thing and another I forgot all about her. But then I heard a board creak outside the door and a voice asked, 'Was there anything Monsieur wanted?' The voice sounded extraordinary.

181

YOLANDE: How—extraordinary?

BORDEUR: It was shy, and husky with a kind of anguish—yes, the anguish of delight—or perhaps of sin. . . . So I went and opened the door. That's all.

YOLANDE: Oh, no. You aren't going to leave out the best of it. I want to know everything.

BORDEUR: For God's sake, what more do you want to know? (*Sighs in exasperation, then speaks furiously*) She asked me to switch off the light. She undressed and got into bed, and I sorted her out.

YOLANDE: Sort me out!

BORDEUR: I know you by heart already. (*He yawns and withdraws into his box.*)

YOLANDE: (*getting up from the chair and speaking to Célestin*) Believe me, the stories I heard—some of them unspeakable! One every day for two years.

JEAN-PIERRE: He must have repeated himself.

YOLANDE: Never. I wouldn't have allowed it. I wrote them all down. I have eight notebooks full. Women of all sorts and shapes and sizes, not counting the ones in brothels. He took to getting up early in the morning, just to escape from me. He'd go off on his horse for hours, but I was always there when he got back. . . . Victor, where have you been?

BORDEUR: (*emerging*) I've had a wonderful ride! Spring in the forest! The song of birds! . . .

YOLANDE: You can tell me about the Spring afterwards. Hurry up.

BORDEUR: Yolande, I beseech you to have pity on me, at least for today. I'm exhausted.

YOLANDE: Don't be absurd. It's your duty. You must and therefore you can.

BORDEUR: You're an ogress!

YOLANDE: It's no good calling me names. You know you'll have to give in.

BORDEUR: (*sighing*) All right. I'll go and wash my hands.

YOLANDE: Poor Victor. I could feel that he was having a hard time of it towards the end, but I thought that men were the same as women. I never thought the male creature was so fragile. One morning Victor died in my arms. His heart suddenly stopped beating. But after all, that was eighteen months ago. I can't go on living alone.

CÉLESTIN: There must be plenty of men who would be happy to marry you. You're free. You have only to choose.

YOLANDE: You're wrong. My life belongs here, my friends, my interests, my family. I wouldn't leave this town for anything in the world. In any case, I loathe Paris. So what am I to do?

CÉLESTIN: Even so, in a town with fifteen thousand inhabitants there are men to choose from.

YOLANDE: I'm the daughter of the Donadieu family. I'm rich. I can't marry a nobody. The two other factory-owning families, the Lamberts and the Chabrus, have only daughters, that is to say, rivals. I might at a pinch settle for a lawyer, but they're all married. Their sons are still at school. Still, it's true, there must be a few possible men. If my brother would help me.

JEAN-PIERRE: There you go again. But only today——

YOLANDE: Very well, I'll tell you about it. The other day my brother mentioned a young doctor who has just come to live in the town. It's not a particularly exciting prospect, the thought of being married to a small country doctor. Even a surgeon would be better. They work with their hands, and generally speaking they're stronger and tougher. However I went to the Lamberts' tennis party this afternoon to meet this doctor. He's about thirty, and weedy and pale-faced, no shoulders and no nothing. I like a man to have shoulders and buttocks, I like him to fill his clothes. That's what I want in my bed—a man, not a human tapeworm. And to cap everything this little nonentity, this frippet, he looked at me without so much as a gleam in his eye, the way he might have looked at a rabbit. He didn't even know I was a woman. I'm not as badly shaped as all that!

CÉLESTIN: You're marvellously shaped. Your legs, your— your— You're wonderful!

YOLANDE: Do you think so? But that's the kind of creature Jean-Pierre is ready to unload me on—a man who's tired before he has even served, and who takes no more interest in women than my dog does in mathematics. (*to Jean-Pierre*) Your selfishness is unbelievable!

JEAN-PIERRE: This is the first time I've heard you express a preference for any particular type of man. I thought you preferred intellectuals.

YOLANDE: I'm not joking, you idiot. But it doesn't matter a damn to you. You can have all the women you want, in the office or wherever you choose. In fact, it's your main occupation, and I'm blessed if I know what else you'd be any good at. When Olga Couturier was your mistress you were having affairs with at least two other women. Perhaps sometimes you had all three together! Oh, why should religion and morality prevent me from having three men—or four—or half-a-dozen? (*her voice rising*) I'd devour them. I'd wring them dry, all six of them! . . . But why am I talking like this? I haven't even one man, and it's killing me. I lie awake at night tossing and turning in my memories. I take tranquillisers, but they're no use. Last night I took two, and lay burning. Even in the daytime when I'm alone a memory will come to me suddenly, a picture that thrusts its way into my mind, and then a pain grips me by the throat, a sense of anguish that works down through my breasts and my loins like pincers torturing my whole body!

JEAN-PIERRE: Really, you know, this sounds serious. You must be very unhappy. But while you're looking round for a husband why don't you take a lover?

184

YOLANDE: Jean-Pierre, will you please not be disgusting. Ever since you turned Radical-Socialist you have had the most revolting ideas.

JEAN-PIERRE: But I haven't turned Radical-Socialist. I simply supported the Radical candidate as a matter of business, because in this constituency it is sound policy to do so. And I'm thankful I did. It saved me from a strike.

YOLANDE: He who panders to the devil surrenders to the devil. But I won't compromise. I have been able to keep my dignity as a widow and my honour as a woman because I have never yielded anything to the devil, not an inch. There are moments when I'm like a besieged fortress, no more ammunition, no more food, no more water. My throat is literally parched. But still I go on fighting, I fight tirelessly against temptation with the aid of God and my confessor. I pray, I confess, I take the sacrament—and then it has to be done all over again. When I was married I had the Abbé Fouchard for my confessor. You know him, a sturdy, vigorous man with warmth in his eyes. But after Victor died I was afraid to have him any more. I was afraid of myself. So I took the old priest, Père Mouchet.

(*She kneels on the chair at the side of the stage. Jean-Pierre and Célestin go out.*)

Father, I am more than ever afflicted with horror at my own abomination. For three days I have been visited with a tempest of desire which has robbed me of my sleep. It is like a tide rising from loathsome depths that sweeps in waves through my burning flesh, allowing me no peace or rest. I am tormented by monstrous visions of the sin of the flesh, visions which I myself evoke and in which I take an infamous delight.

BORDEUR: (*scarcely visible in his box*) And what precisely are these visions? Describe them, my child.

YOLANDE: I am ashamed to do so. There are naked men. There

are men unbuttoning their trousers. They come to me and they take me.

BORDEUR: And what is your posture at these moments?

YOLANDE: My posture? Why—I'm lying on my back. But are there others?

BORDEUR: That is the only approved position. My dear child, God is subjecting you to a severe ordeal over which you will triumph only by turning to Him. It is by prayer that you will save yourself, and by good works. In this connection I may mention that some of our congregation are distressed at the shabby condition of our sacerdotal robes. Certainly it is a great shame that our stoles and chasubles should be worn threadbare and of a dingy colouring that does no honour to Our Saviour. A committee is being formed to look into the matter, and it has been suggested that you should become its chairman.

YOLANDE: I accept, Father. Another chairmanship which will come expensive. There's no end to them. However, priests must certainly have chasubles.

BORDEUR: The Lord will value your generosity and so will the parish. Are you still anxious to marry again?

YOLANDE: Most certainly, Father. I think of nothing else. My brother has suggested the young doctor who has recently set up in practice in the town.

BORDEUR: I should be very sorry to see you marry that young man. According to our information he is a Socialist, and moreover a dissident Socialist, the worst kind we get in France.

YOLANDE: Socialist or no, there's no guts in him.

BORDEUR: You are quite right. It had occurred to me. . . . Well, there is Monsieur Hermangaut, the dealer in real estate, who had the misfortune to lose his wife last year. A wealthy man. An exemplary Catholic. A rare spirit.

YOLANDE: But, Father, he's hideously ugly!

186

BORDEUR: It is he who carries the banner of St. Anastasia at the Parish Festival.

YOLANDE: He's strong, certainly. I have heard that he is much addicted to women.

BORDEUR: As it happens, I am his confessor. He has never said anything about affairs with women. On the contrary, he has confessed to undergoing the same torments as yourself. Only recently, when we were talking together in the Sacristy, he said to me, 'I don't mind telling you, Father, the day I get married again the balloon will go up. My wife will have no cause to complain.'

YOLANDE: (*breathing heavily*) Did he really say the balloon would go up?

BORDEUR: Those were his very words. An exemplary Catholic as I said, but there—he's as strong as a bull. Dear child, do not attempt to answer me today. Think it over. His christian name is Léonard.

YOLANDE: Léonard ... Léonard. ... I'll think about it. What penance do you order, Father?

BORDEUR: A *Confiteor* in bed the last thing at night, followed by a *Pater* spoken aloud to relax your nerves. Do you enjoy dishes such as *boeuf bourguignon* and *poule au riz*?

YOLANDE: Yes, Father.

BORDEUR: Very well then, no spiced meats for a week. And now repeat your *Confiteor*.

(*Unintelligible murmur from Yolande, accompanied by mumble from Bordeur.*)

Now go, my child.

(*Liturgical music on the mouth-organ. Yolande rises and goes up-stage. Upon reaching the back of the stage she turns to face the audience, makes a genuflexion and goes out. Célestin enters from the left.*)

187

BORDEUR: Célestin has just entered his bed-sitter, a small room, modestly furnished. It contains a bed, a wardrobe, an armchair and a wash-stand. The closet is on the landing. That is why we can't see it. A water-colour by his friend Mortier hangs on the wall. It depicts the tower of the Church of St. Anastasia. Quite pretty. (*speaking in a woman's voice*) Knock, knock. Can I come in?

CÉLESTIN: (*moodily*) Yes, come in.

BORDEUR: Darling—Darling. . . . But what's the matter? Why are you looking so angry?

CÉLESTIN: I'm not angry. I'm just not feeling very bright this evening.

BORDEUR: And I know why. You were sent for by the boss, weren't you? I know you were. I saw you cross the yard. And the boss said, 'Listen, old boy, I'm very fond of you, but I'm asking you as a personal favour to stay away from Olga Couturier.'

CÉLESTIN: Almost exactly that. And that was his only reason for sending for me.

BORDEUR: I thought as much. It's wonderful, isn't it? I had him on top of me every night for more than a year, and then one day he laid me off like a redundant workman and gave me a silver-gilt evening bag in compensation. And now he thinks he's going to stand guard over me. He doesn't want me any more, but he doesn't want anyone else to have me. Isn't it wonderful?

CÉLESTIN: (*sitting down*) Open the window a little. It's hot in here.

BORDEUR: An evening bag. What am I supposed to do with it—take it when I go to the movies on Friday? And silver-gilt, at that—peanuts! What will you give me, darling? Plastic, I expect.

CÉLESTIN: Now what are you getting at? I've always told you I'm not in love with you, but I've no intention of walking out on you.

BORDEUR: Darling! You're always on the level, aren't you? Don't you want me to kiss you? Why not? Because of Jean-Pierre? Well, because of his sister? She went to see him while you were there. Célestin look at me. No, look me in the eyes. I can see what it is. You're in love with the beautiful Yolande.

CÉLESTIN: I don't know.

BORDEUR: You always were, probably. That bitch! Any time she found me in Jean-Pierre's office she'd try everything she knew to humiliate me. I could have strangled her. You know, although I'd almost die of jealousy I'd give everything I've got for you to sleep with her. The glorious Yolande Donadieu sleeping with the son of the night-watchman! Well, why don't you?

CÉLESTIN: Shut up. You're crazy.

BORDEUR: (*speaking in his own voice*) Which does not alter the fact that the next night Célestin comes down from his attic to try his luck.

(*Célestin leaves the stage by the steps leading down to the stalls, Yolande enters from the wings.*)

BORDEUR: Yolande is in her bedroom, furnished with taste and simplicity. The Louis XVI commode, the big troubadour bed, the dressing-table of the same period, the writing-desk of veined lignum vitae and the Armagnac arm-chairs. A photograph of poor Victor on the chest of drawers and on the wall a handsome oil-painting by Banquier, the great regional painter, representing the belfry of the church of Saint-Anastasia, in a period frame. (*He changes his voice*) Has Madame got everything she wants? May I go to bed now?

YOLANDE: Yes, go to bed, Mélina. Oh, tell me—do you know Monsieur Léonard Hermangaut?

BORDEUR: That ugly man? I certainly do. The other evening when I was out taking the air in the Chestnut Walk he caught up with me and he put his hand Madame can guess where.

YOLANDE: He put his hand. . . . But what did you do?

BORDEUR: I will be quite frank with Madame. I was in a romantic mood that evening and at first I didn't try to stop him, but then when he wanted to bring matters to a head I just couldn't make up my mind to it. He really is too ugly. Madame knows how quickly one thinks at such moments. I said to myself, Well, Mélina, I said, if you should get in the family way, in the first place Monsieur Léonard is too good a Catholic to acknowledge the child, and in the second place it might take after him.

YOLANDE: That's true. It's a risk one has to consider. Thank you, Mélina. You may go now.

BORDEUR: Good night, Madame. The tranquillisers are on the bed-table.

YOLANDE: Good night, Mélina.

BORDEUR: (*in his own voice*) Yolande is now alone in her bedroom. Lascivious images rise in her mind. She tries to think of her old priest but can't manage it. She goes out on to the balcony hoping that the fresh night air will soothe her. Célestin is hiding behind a clump of rhododendrons. He gazes up at the beautiful Yolande as she leans over the balcony and, it must be said, she knocks him for a loop. Her sex-appeal is terrific. A moonbeam irradiates the cleavage of her ivory bosom. Another moonbeam lights upon the curve of a thigh emerging from her peignoir. Yes, indeed, she's quite a dish, the daughter of the Donadieu factory. When finally he has overcome his agitation and his shyness Célestin picks up his accordion and causes the notes of a Chopin melody to soar throbbing into the profound silence of the night.

(*Plays 'Il était une bergère. . . .' on the mouth-organ.*)

And now that he has got her into a receptive frame of mind he is going to recite poetry to her.

CÉLESTIN: Nocturne.

BORDEUR: Blank verse at that!

CÉLESTIN: Nocturne. (*Recites*)

 I looked for old, old words to say to you

 Words of hard and supple love

 Let fall in the morning of the world

 By a hunter of aurochs

 Clasping a ravished girl to his bearskin

 I found two only . . .

YOLANDE: Who's there?

CÉLESTIN: It's me.

YOLANDE: Who's me?

CÉLESTIN: Célestin.

YOLANDE: Célestin? (*Bursts out laughing*) What are you doing here, you fool? The maids' rooms are at the back of the house.

CÉLESTIN: Oh, I see. I'm sorry.

YOLANDE: Célestin, wait a minute. I'm responsible for the girls who live in my house. Come up here for a moment, but take care no one sees you.

CÉLESTIN: Perhaps it would be safer if you put the light out.

YOLANDE: Yes. (*Goes through the motions of switching off the light, which remains unaltered.*) I am now in complete darkness. You can come up. (*Célestin climbs on to the stage.*) Célestin, I want to know the truth. Are you after Mélina?

CÉLESTIN: No, Yolande, I came for you. I love you.

YOLANDE: What! You mean—(*Célestin takes her in his arms and kisses her. A prolonged embrace. Then she pushes him away and smacks his face*) Célestin, have you gone mad?

CÉLESTIN: (*moving away*) It's true. I must be mad. (*He goes out through the wings.*)

YOLANDE: I'm not cross with you. I won't tell Jean-Pierre.

BORDEUR: Yolande paces nervously up and down the

balcony, pressing her clasped hands to her wildly beating heart; and suddenly she stops dead, confronted by a discovery she had never suspected.

YOLANDE: He's a man! The son of the night-watchman is a man! What is the world coming to? But that kiss. . . . (*her voice rises to a cry*) that kiss! . . .

Curtain

Act II

The same set as Act I. Ernestine, clad in a gold-lamé gown, the skirt split high up the thigh, is seated on the chair on the right.

BORDEUR: We are in Paris, in that celebrated nightery on the Champs-Elysées called 'The Firmament', which is patronised by the high aristocracy of money and by a rabble in evening dress picking up the crumbs. Beneath the gilding and the changing lights you may recognise Prince Cordoban, the banker Jacobstein, the arms-manufacturer Dumont-Leroi, Deborah Warner, the most expensive film-star on earth, Tex MacFinnegan, the oil-magnate, and in the background, kicking up her legs at the foot of the great staircase, the famous Diamantine, the hermaphrodite with the dazzling bosom, one of the least contested glories of Paris. It is one o'clock in the morning. The gaiety is at its height. Champagne is flowing like water. Everyone is having a wonderful time. Prince Cardoban asks the glamorous Deborah Warner for a dance. Perhaps, who knows, a great romance is beginning. The gossip-columnists take feverish notes. Camera-flashes dazzle the dancers. The coloured orchestra plays a demonic cha-cha.

(*Bordeur plays* 'Malbrouck s'en va-t-en guerre' *on the mouth-organ, and while he is doing so Jean-Pierre enters up-stage and comes slowly down-stage as though working his way through the*

192

*jostling crowd, now stepping back a pace, now apologising with
a smile, and looking about him as he comes.)*

BORDEUR: The orchestra is making such a racket that we
can't hear what anyone is saying. The beautiful girl whom
Jean-Pierre rediscovers by accident is none other than Ernestine,
the sister of Célestin. In the small town of her birth she is
supposed to be a meccanograph operator in Paris. But don't
you believe it! That gold-lamé gown split right up the thigh
—you understand, do you not? Yes, ladies and gentlemen,
she is a harlot. Ah, now they're playing a tango. That is less
noisy.

ERNESTINE: *(dancing a tango with Jean-Pierre)* You know, you
haven't changed. How fortunate that you should have come
here tonight.

JEAN-PIERRE: But you're changed, Ernestine. You have
become unbelievably beautiful.

ERNESTINE: I'd rather you didn't call me Ernestine. It's a
little embarrassing. I'm known here as Gloria.

BORDEUR: There are two vacant places over there if the lady
and gentleman would care to sit down.

ERNESTINE: Thank you, Etienne. *(to Jean-Pierre)* You sit on
the banquette. No, really, I prefer it. *(Jean-Pierre sits down at
the table. Ernestine fetches the chair on the right and sits facing him.)*
To think that it's ten years since we last met. Yes, it's ten years
since I left home.

JEAN-PIERRE: How quickly time passes. Do you remember
those Thursdays when you and Célestin used to come and play
in our garden?

ERNESTINE: Poor Célestin! I can never tell you how good he
was to me. He loved me very much. But now. . . .

JEAN-PIERRE: *(with relish)* Do you remember the time when
Yolande held your legs while I tickled your behind?

ERNESTINE: I do. And also the time when you had my

virginity in the tool-shed, with Yolande keeping watch outside the door. Do you ever think of that?

JEAN-PIERRE: Of course I do.

ERNESTINE: I wasn't even fifteen.

JEAN-PIERRE: Still, it had to happen sooner or later, so it might as well have been me.

ERNESTINE: And did Yolande lose her virginity before she got married?

JEAN-PIERRE: Of course she didn't. I should think not indeed!

ERNESTINE: Yes, indeed! There's some point in virginity if you're rich. Did she make a good marriage?

JEAN-PIERRE: Yes. But she's a widow now.

ERNESTINE: That's even better. Money, respectability and peace—the perfect life. (*sighs*) What did you think when you saw me in this place?

JEAN-PIERRE: Oh, well, you know, I've seen enough of the world not to be surprised at anything.

ERNESTINE: You're more hard-boiled than I am. There are times, even now, when I'm astonished at finding myself here, just for a second. . . . Deborah Warner's leaving, do you see?

JEAN-PIERRE: The film-star? Where? Which is she?

ERNESTINE: The tall red-head standing by the stairs. She looks like a lamp-post, and a real vulture's face. All the same, I wouldn't mind having the dough she's got. I could even make do with less, just seven or eight millions. I'd go straight back home. I'd buy a shop in the Rue du Général-Trochu, and have a sales-girl that I'd bawl out whenever I felt like it. I'd knit things for the curé's jumble sales. But it isn't going to happen tomorrow, or the day after either.

JEAN-PIERRE: Shall we dance?

(*Ernestine puts her chair beside the wicker armchair. She dances*

194

with Jean-Pierre. They vanish up-stage, and Yolande enters and sits in the armchair).

BORDEUR: While her brother dances with Ernestine at 'The Firmament' Yolande lies sleeping in her big troubadour bed, but her slumbers are restless despite the tranquillisers. At this moment she is dreaming that she is walking over an empty plain, nothing to see whichever way she looks, but sparse grey grass. Then, suddenly turning her head, she sees a doorway standing on the plain. She runs to it and opens the door and finds herself face to face with Léonard Hermangaut. She shuts the door and turns back, but now Célestin is standing in front of her. She opens the door again, goes through the doorway, then returns and so goes back and forth between the two men. Exhausted by this toing and froing her strength fails her. Listen to her groan!

YOLANDE: No, no, no!

BORDEUR: Suddenly the doorway falls flat on the plain which is again deserted. Célestin and Léonard have disappeared. Yolande lies on the ground. She dreams that she is lying in her coffin before the grand altar in the church of St. Anastasia. She sees everything that goes on around her, she hears the saying of the Mass, the singing, the organ. (*The mouth-organ plays a few bars of the* 'Dies Irae'.) Seated in the front row of the congregation she sees Jean-Pierre with tears in his eyes and a pang goes through her heart. When the family gathers to receive the condolences of their friends she leaves her coffin and stands beside her brother. People are shaking his hand with words of sympathy, and Mélina says, sobbing, 'I grieve so dreadfully for Madame!' A man wearing a black mask and black gloves pushes Yolande away from her relatives and out through a side-door giving on to the Rue du Chapitre. He takes her hand and they run together along the Rue des Tonneliers. If she is to be saved she must be outside the town before the bells begin to ring. The man drags her along, half-carrying her, but she feels that she has not the strength to go fast enough. They are still in the Rue des Lavandières. She can go no further. Her breath has failed her. She stops. No, she starts to run again. At last they reach the meadows. She is saved. The bells of St. Anastasia begin to peal. She has fallen on her knees in the long grass. Then the man takes off his mask and gloves. Do you see?—he has a death's-head and skeleton hands. He bursts out laughing. And Yolande says: 'I knew.'

End of Contents of Yellow Exercise Book

XV

I HAD heard no news of Tatiana for three weeks when one Thursday, at lunch-time, I found her waiting for me at the main entrance of the S.B.H. building. She was wearing her coat with the rabbit-skin collar. We went along to a café on the Avenue de Friedland.

'It's lucky I was able to get away at twelve,' I said. 'Lormier generally keeps me late. But he phoned this morning to say he's laid up and probably won't be in for several days.'

'Darling, I'm so glad to see you,' said Tatiana. 'I got back from Stockholm last night, but it's only a flying visit. They're sending me to Rio de Janeiro on Friday.'

She then asked me to kiss her, which I did reluctantly and hurriedly, for there were other customers in the café. I have never been able to ignore the opinion of strangers in public places. My natural tendency is to presume them all to be persons of refined sensibility who will be outraged by any display of bad taste. But as I drew back my head Tatiana seized it with both hands and kissed me again, thrusting her tongue an inch into my mouth. I was so angry that I could have hit her, and sensing my annoyance she uttered an unnatural-sounding laugh and suddenly burst into tears. I closed up even more. Everyone in the place was staring, and since she was beautiful I felt that I was in the wrong. After first looking like a stuffed shirt I had become a coarse brute making odious demands.

'If you don't stop crying I shall clear out,' I said firmly.

Tatiana's face at once brightened in a smile, and the rest of our conversation was pursued with dignity and calm on both sides. We arranged that I should go to supper the following evening and stay the night. But as we parted her expression became unhappy again, and I seemed to discern in it so much distress, even apprehension, that I clasped her to me regardless of onlookers.

Halfway through the afternoon Lormier summoned me to his house in Neuilly to report on the day's proceedings at the office. I sat at his bedside with my brief-case on my knee reading out the letters, while at the same time I observed him from the corner of my eye as he lay listening without looking at me, his eyelids heavy with fever and fatigue. I had never before seen him in this aspect, all his gross flabbiness on display, relaxed against the pillows. In his office, combed and scrubbed and harnessed, with his neck clamped in a stiff collar, Lormier had a weighty impressiveness: but now he lay in the big ornate bed spread out like a sow. Whenever he moved his head a wave passed over the sagging folds of his face and the double chins seemed to overflow on to his chest, causing a sluggish tremor of flesh that rippled away under his pyjama jacket. I was slightly sickened by the acrid smell of sweat coming from the sheets, and still more by the sight of a glass utensil, a wide-necked bottle, lying on the bedside-table and containing a drain of urine.

Occasionally he motioned to me to be silent while he took time to think over some particular point; and during these pauses I tried to consider him apart from the luxury of the room in which he lay, wondering why it was that this sick man, who made me think of a grey sea-monster, should still contrive to look like one of the rich. I thought for a moment that it might be accounted for by the thick neck, like that of a Roman Emperor, and the lips pouting like those of a pampered child; but these were mere externals, too commonly met with to have any particular significance. On second thoughts it seemed to me that the reason lay in a particular kind of arrogance, the habit of taking oneself for granted in all circumstances, regardless of the presence of any other person, with a cool, unconsidered assurance that was slightly more than human. And as though in witness of this he cut me short abruptly while I was in the middle of explaining a rather intricate matter, which meant that when we returned to it I should have to go over the whole thing again.

'I want to pee,' he said. 'Give me that bottle.'

I hesitated for an instant, and then said in an ill-assured voice: 'No. No—I'm sorry.'

I still cannot be sure whether I regretted those words the moment they were uttered, but I certainly realised their folly. I had refused him a service which he was entitled to ask of anyone. It was true that he had asked in a very peremptory fashion, with no attempt at courtesy. Since then, and particularly during the hours immediately following the incident, I have thought about it a great deal, and I am sure that if he had said, 'Would you mind. . . .' I should have done it without a thought. For that matter, he might have mentioned his need in a way that would have caused me to pass the thing without waiting to be asked. But what offended me most, I think, was that he had had no intention of offending. He had spoken as he did without giving the matter a thought, as though it went without saying that he should treat me in this way.

The bottle was near enough to the bed for him to be able to reach it himself with a little difficulty. I felt hot all over. I felt that I was in the wrong, I expected the worst. Lormier turned his head to look at me. His eyes dwelt briefly on my face, and then he looked away. He said slowly, in a cool, deliberate voice:

'Do I understand, Martin, that you refuse to do what I ask?'

I replied yes, while my heart sank to my boots. I could not possibly have said anything else.

'You might at least address me as "sir".'

'Yes, sir.'

With a heaving movement, which may well have cost him more effort than reaching for the bottle would have done, he groped for the bell-push hanging over the bed.

'Shall I go on?' I asked.

'No.'

While we waited for someone to come he ignored me entirely and lay gazing through the two windows at the almost leafless trees outside, those in his own garden and those, more distant, in the Bois de Boulogne. For the first time, as I sat contemplating this fifty-seven-year-old man whose age and insistence upon living were to me as a rule a matter for resentment, I was abashed by the sense of my own youth. At some more favourable moment I might even have been inclined to apologise for it.

Either the bell had not rung or there was no one there to answer it. With his expression darkening, his eyes fixed on the window, Lormier lay vainly waiting, and I thought with a vexed compassion that he must be increasingly tormented by his need. I felt odious and absurd, but the thought of being misunderstood still kept me motionless. Nevertheless I was just about to get up and do what he wanted when, with a second convulsive effort, he pressed the bell again. This time I heard it ring, and almost instantly the door from the corridor opened, admitting a nurse and a valet, and a moment later Madame Lormier appeared through the communicating door from the next room.

'The urine-bottle,' was all that Lormier said.

The nurse and the valet both made a rush for it. I had risen in deference to the mistress of the house, and I moved aside to get out of their way. Lormier snatched the bottle and as he thrust it under the bedclothes I followed its progress to its destination. There was a sound of splashing waters. An expression of profound relief came over the Chairman's face, but his eyes remained cold.

'How do you feel?' asked Madame Lormier.

He replied with a grimace and a gesture of his hand indicating that he had more important matters than his health to think about. The nurse reminded him that it was nearly time for his medicine, and the valet made a move to straighten his pillows, but he ordered them curtly out of the room. When we were alone with his wife he looked at me and said:

'Martin, who do you think you are?'

'I don't understand the question, sir,' I replied.

'I think you understand it very well, and that's why you don't want to answer. So I'll answer it for you, my ex-convict!'

Despite his wife's attempt to quieten him he then began to shout abuse at me in his high-pitched, slightly feminine voice.

'Gaolbird! Gallows-bird! Nasty little crook! Will you or will you not answer me? Without me where would you be at this moment? What gutter would you be in? But you're not grateful, are you?'

'No, sir, I am not.'

I could only stick to my guns. I had no wish to enrage him still further, but under that flood of insults I could not bring myself to lie. I tried to explain why I was not grateful, despite all he had done for me, but he cut me short.

'I don't want any more insolence. Is there any reason why I shouldn't throw you out? And have you stowed back in prison, for that matter, where you belong? I've been too good to you altogether. What the devil am I doing with a murderer on my staff!'

'You mustn't get so excited,' said Madame Lormier from the other side of the bed. 'You so badly need to rest.'

She had evidently known nothing of my murderous past. At the mention of the word she looked quickly at me, but without any undue display of horror. I had seen her once before, in the Chairman's office. She was a woman in her

201

middle forties, quite without beauty or charm, who seemed to find life endurable without expecting it to be anything more. Her grey eyes had a look of striking melancholy. It was generally known that her marriage to Lormier (which I always thought of as though it had taken place in 1900, although it had actually occurred in 1935) had been simply an alliance between two large fortunes. This mention of my crime in the presence of a third party drove me to fury and desperation.

'You can sack me if you like,' I shouted at Lormier. 'I shan't be sorry to go. It's not pleasant, even for a killer, to have to stand by and watch the frauds you perpetrate in your office.'

Lormier started at this, and his eyes flickered as they met mine. I went on without taking breath:

'You see, Lormier, when I came out of prison I had a great desire to go on living. If I've made myself your accomplice by keeping quiet about the things you do, it's because I might have starved if I hadn't. That made it all right with my conscience. But now I'm not so keen on living as I was.'

I broke off here with a lump in my throat and a sudden pricking in my eyes at the thought of my own desperate straits. I saw myself leaving S.B.H. and going from one employment agency to another, carrying my police record like a millstone round my neck. Lormier must have seen the tears and my frantic effort to restrain them.

'Youth, youth!' he exclaimed in a changed and positively amiable voice. 'Always rushing to extremes!' And he uttered a little, breathless, almost paternal laugh.

Feeling peace and security return I could not prevent one or two defeated tears from rolling down my cheeks. With awkward movements, which he watched with evident pleasure, I deposited my papers and brief-case on the chair and got out my handkerchief. He let the appeasing silence last as long as he judged fit, and then said indulgently:

'My dear boy, you're too touchy altogether. You must be on

your guard against the weakness, which is liable to be aggravated by your circumstances. Well, let's get on with our work. Mathilde, would you mind leaving us?'

Madame Lormier left the room and I returned to the affairs of S.B.H.; but the episode of the urine-bottle had tired Lormier, and a series of coughing fits exhausted him still more. He was less and less able to concentrate, and finally, after a particularly violent spasm, he gave up and said weakly:

'I shall have to rest. Come back in an hour. I've something more to say to you.'

I went out into the passage, and here Madame Lormier, who had been talking to the nurse, took charge of me. She took me into a small drawing-room handsomely furnished with Louis XVI pieces which looked genuine to me, although I know nothing about these things. But then my attention was caught by a writing desk of plain yellow wood, similar to those used at the office, which was markedly out of keeping with the rest of the room. Indeed, with its six drawers it seemed in all respects identical with the one at which I had sat in that empty room during my first days at S.B.H. We went over to the window and stood gazing out at the rain that had begun to fall on the trees in the garden. It was nearly five and growing dark. I could not feel that we had much to say to one another, but when, for the sake of conversation, I said something about her husband's illness, Madame Lormier abruptly turned her sallow face to confront me, and gazed long and fixedly at me with her sombre eyes.

'So', she said, very calmly, 'my husband commits frauds?'

'Certainly not,' I said. 'I lost my temper just now and talked a great deal of nonsense. There was no truth in it.'

'I am quite sure it was all true,' she answered without raising her voice.

I made another attempt to deny it, but she checked me with a motion of her head which clearly indicated that her husband's dishonesty was for her something that might be taken for granted. To my astonishment I heard her say in a quite expressionless tone, as though she were reciting a lesson:

'The concentration of capital in private hands creates a will to power which seeks to fulfil itself by every means, and primarily by the exploitation of the proletariat.'

I stared at her wide-eyed. She went on to talk of the growing awareness of the proletariat, and asked me finally, in a voice containing a hint of exaltation:

'This crime for which you were imprisoned, you committed it as an act of revolt against the social injustice by which your class is oppressed? You needn't be afraid to tell me!'

I was about to undeceive her, but at this moment we were interrupted by the entry of Lormier's brother, the former Minister, Lucien Lormier, who had caught sight of us through the half-open doorway. I had a feeling that his sister-in-law viewed his arrival with some apprehension.

'Well, and how is he?' he asked.

'The influenza is running its normal course,' said Madame Lormier. 'Tell me, Lucien, did you know that Gabriel is a swindler?'

'My dear Mathilde, of course I knew. I've told you so a dozen times in his presence, but you would never believe me. People regard me as a trifler, unable to take anything seriously. I'm one of those absurd people who can't make money. Even my own family have no respect for me. But I can't help it. To me money is just something you spend, which is why I no longer have any.'

Lucien Lormier had indeed squandered his share of the paternal inheritance at the gambling tables and in every kind of childish frivolity. But his most unforgiveable crime in his brother's eyes was that at a time when he was hard pressed he had sold his S.B.H. shares outside the family. The elder Lormier would probably never have spoken to him again had it not been for the fact that, after the Liberation, he had needed his help, as a leading member of the Resistance, in overcoming certain prejudices which the management of S.B.H. had incurred during the Occupation by trading with the enemy. Lucien Lormier was complaining about his brother's meanness, to which he ascribed his present state of penury, when the sound of youthful voices outside caused Madame Lormier to look up and quickly leave the room. I asked him if he was still writing poetry.

'I've tried to start again,' he said, 'but one can't be in politics for fifteen years without paying for it. An unbroken round of political meetings and speeches is more deadly to a poet than an incurable disease. Anyway I seem to have lost my erotic vein. And it must be said that the times are not propitious. We live in a squalid era, my dear Monsieur Martin, an era of glut and satiety.'

Madame Lormier returned with a worried look which caused him to exclaim:

'Is anything wrong, Mathilde? Has Lormier the Great got suddenly worse?'

'No, but it's very trying. Valentine can't do her Latin translation. She worked at it all this morning and she's been trying again this afternoon, but she still can't do it. And the girl we got in as a tutor doesn't seem to be any use. Lucien, couldn't you——'

'No, my dear, I could not. The last time I helped Valentine with her Latin she got three out of twenty and we were both severely scolded by her father.'

'But what is she to do? It has to be handed in tomorrow.'

'That's tiresome, certainly. Monsieur Martin, are you any good at Latin? It is a matter of rescuing the martyred young.'

'I dare say I could manage, if it's not too difficult.'

Having said as much I was inclined to regret having put myself forward, but Madame Lormier at once took me by the hand and led me upstairs, talking in an agitated fashion as she did so.

'Oh, I'm sure you can help. We shall be so grateful. Poor Valentine is always bottom in everything. It's such a worry to us. My husband gets furious and no wonder. The children have got to be in a position to earn their living. No fortune is secure in these days and the richest children are the most in danger. Last year Valentine had to give up Greek and we've never heard the last of it. It's quite right that privilege should be abolished and that only merit should be rewarded, but it's terribly hard on the parents. The poor child has no aptitude at all for school work, just like her brothers and sisters.'

By now we had reached the children's domain on the second floor, with Lucien Lormier following behind us. Madame Lormier paused on the threshold of the schoolroom and tried to persuade him that his presence was undesirable, but he came in with us nevertheless. It was a big room lighted by two attic windows facing the same way as those of the paternal bed-chamber. A little girl of ten and two boys of fourteen and sixteen respectively were seated at plain deal tables each surmounted by a shelf containing their school books. All three were good-looking, with bright, candid faces, which was remarkable when one considered their parents. Valentine, seated at the other end of the room with her Latin, was partly hidden from us by the tutor, who was bending over her. Her brothers and sister all bowed their heads over their lesson-books as we entered. The tutor, a girl-student of about twenty, short and full-figured, turned to gaze at us with a face pink with intellectual stress and anxiety.

'Lucette,' said Madame Lormier, 'go and help Jean-Jacques with his sums. Monsieur Martin is going to help Valentine with her Latin.'

Valentine, a tall, robust and very good-looking girl of nineteen, with a sensitive face framed between shining coils of chestnut hair, rose deferentially to greet us. We sat down side by side and I picked up the Latin text while her mother gazed hopefully at me. Having read it through without finding anything very difficult in it, I turned to Valentine's rendering, which was a sort of word-for-word approximation having little to do with the original and so clumsily put together that it scarcely contained a grammatical sentence of French. The handwriting, which might have been that of a child of ten, moved me to pity. I started to revise the first sentence, and as I did so there was a burst of laughter from behind us. Looking round I saw the former Minister lying flat on the carpet entangled with his two nephews, who were having a mock battle with him, while the little girl, Beatrice, sat jigging up and down in delight and the tutor watched them with embarrassed but sympathetic eyes.

'Lucien!' exclaimed Madame Lormier. 'You ought to be ashamed of yourself. Will you please leave the room at once. And you boys go back to your work. Really, Lucien, I think you do it on purpose. You deliberately ignore the trouble we have with these children.'

The boys went back to their seats, and Lucien picked himself up with a half-hearted apology.

'My dear Mathilde, they were only saying good-afternoon. A natural thing to do, surely. After all, I'm their uncle.'

'Please go away.'

He started to obey her, but suddenly changed his mind and turned back, his face flushed with anger.

'Mathilde, I think that to keep these children working at their books all through Thursday, their weekly school holiday, is nothing less than abominable. You're ill-treating them and dulling their wits. It is gross tyranny. They have a father who earns a prodigious amount of money, but they'd be far better off if they were orphans living on public assistance.'

Madame Lormier, no less indignant, took him by the arm

and tried to thrust him towards the door, but he shook her off and went over to his eldest niece.

'Valentine, you'll be of age in eighteen months. When it happens I hope you will have the sense to kiss your gaolers good-bye and come and live with me. You'll get up in time for luncheon, you'll go for outings, you'll buy clothes, you'll dine out every night and afterwards I'll take you to night clubs. And once a year, no more, you will send your parents a post-card trusting that they are in the best of health. In the meantime, my dear, tell yourself that the hour of deliverance is not far off.'

He kissed her on both cheeks and went out whistling. After the door had closed behind him Madame Lormier, controlling herself, said in a cold voice:

'Your uncle is a madman who does not understand the times we live in. The truth is that our world is crumbling. Heaven help those who have not the education and training to fend for themselves.'

I picked up Valentine's pen and proceeded to translate the passage of Latin, explaining the grammar and syntax as I went along. It was a task I was well accustomed to, for before my arrest I had regularly earned extra money by giving lessons in Latin and French. Valentine, when she did not understand, looked up shyly at me without venturing to interrupt, and I paused and went over the passage again. We were seated side by side, so close that we brushed against one another when we moved, and I was troubled by the thought of her girl's body still unaroused in its limbo of school-going. The last sentence of the Latin contained a slight double-meaning which despite my efforts I could not get her to grasp. Gazing at me with admiration, and blushing slightly, she said:

'I'd better put something else in any case. Our Latin teacher would be bound to know I hadn't thought of it for myself.'

I was touched by the candour of the avowal and the humility

with which this glowing, lovely creature accepted her wretched status as the classroom dunce. When we had finished the translation I thought of making her go through it all again without the help of my rendering, to make sure that she had grasped it, but from sheer pity I refrained. It seemed to me monstrous that her parents should force her to undertake studies for which she had no aptitude, when in their hearts they must surely know it, and when she was certainly capable of shining in other fields. Madame Lormier had by now left the room, leaving us together. It was while she was copying out the draft that I fell in love with Valentine. I could not take my eyes off her. Beautiful and modest, she had that tender flush of youth which Tatiana no longer possessed. I am not saying that Tatiana was old, but still she was twenty-six, which is not the first flush. Valentine was a miracle of purity, grace and everything else. By ten minutes past five I was profoundly in love. It went without saying that Lormier's daughter, be my intentions honourable or otherwise, was utterly beyond my reach. So far as that went, I thought nothing precise. I was simply intoxicated with Valentine, I breathed her, I devoured her with one eye and with both. I let a pencil fall under the table, bent down to retrieve it and as though by accident touched her legs with my hands, and sight and touch and heart and loins all were ravished. When I emerged again into the light of her eyes I bent over her, pretending to examine her work, with my cheek touching her hair and one of my hands at the edge of the table brushing her breast through the woollen jersey she wore. Lormier's daughter. To avoid losing my head entirely I broke the rather prolonged silence.

'Have you ever heard of Porteur?'

'Oh, yes. The more intelligent girls in my class often talk about him, particularly a girl called Claire de Popineuil, who's a great friend of mine. She knows a university student who has met Porteur and actually talked to him. Claire's very sweet. She said yesterday that she likes me as much as Porteur.'

I was in the act of asking what Porteur meant to her when Madame Lormier returned to say that her husband wished to see me again.

I found the Chairman in conversation with his brother. As I crossed the big bedroom he surveyed me with half-closed eyes, his gaze curious and mistrustful, as though he were seeing me in a new light.

'Well, Martin,' he said, 'it seems that you're a Latin scholar?'

I uttered a modest disavowal, and he lowered his head with his nose to the sheet, seemingly plunged in thought. I could see the flesh quivering round his small mouth, as though his reflections were of an agitated kind, and suddenly he turned to his brother and exclaimed furiously:

'It's a very extraordinary thing! The son of the concierge at S.B.H. goes to high-school and is top in everything, and my four blockheads can't even keep up!'

He uttered a bitter laugh and cast a venomous look in my direction, brooding with evident resentment over a fundamental inequality which outraged his sense of justice. To Lucien's remark that his children had no need of diplomas to be assured of a comfortable future he retorted with a gesture of impatience:

'We have less than ten years to go. In ten years France will be finished, and as for us—well! . . .'

When Lucien had departed I again got out my papers and resumed where we had left off. But Lormier, besides being exhausted—he still had a high temperature—was now pre-occupied with other matters. At the conclusion of our business he said:

'That girl my wife has got as a tutor for the children is a perfect fool. I'm getting rid of her. See if you can find me someone like yourself, who knows something about it.'

I promised to do my best, gazing almost with affection at

the father of Valentine. If he had wanted it, I would have passed him the urine-bottle in a flash.

On my way home in the métro I thought of the years of happiness that lay ahead of me—the rapture of loving Valentine, no more, but it was all I wanted. By my selfless devotion I would preserve her from the squalid commerce of love, the disillusion, the disenchantments, the sordid pangs of jealousy. Upon arriving I found Valérie in the kitchen, and I joyously embraced her, saying that I had never known her so pretty as she looked that evening. She smiled at me with tenderness and I am sure she was touched. Michel was seated on a corner of the table in the living-room, gazing up at the ceiling. I said jovially:

'Well, how's it going? Been working at your play? It gets off to a wonderful start.'

'My play?' said Michel. 'I couldn't care less about it. I'm in love.'

I then looked more closely at him. There was, I swear it, a look of radiance, of rapture, on Porteur's face.

'You remember the first afternoon you were here? A girl called Lena had dropped in. It was the first time she'd been here and I wasn't really paying much attention—too busy with that play. But she came again this afternoon, and this time. . . . Well anyway, she's coming to live here. And so I've got to find a job.'

'A job? Do you mean you're going back to the stage?'

'No, I mean work. Something boring. I want to be able to say to myself—it's for her! Surely you can understand?'

'Well, in that case,' I said, 'I may be able to help you. I'm not certain. I'll let you know tomorrow.'

Porteur embraced me, his eyes moist with gratitude. There was not much conversation at supper but we laughed a great deal, nearly always for no reason. When I went to bed I found Valérie there before me with her arms outstretched, and I was

211

so happy, I loved Valentine so much, that I was ready to oblige anyone. After telling me how handsome and utterly delightful I was, she handed me her watch, which she had forgotten to take off her wrist, and said:

'Be an angel and put it in the drawer.'

And this made me think of the office-desk which I had seen that afternoon standing incongruously amid the Louis XVI furniture in the small drawing-room in Lormier's house. I fell asleep thinking of it, and of Valentine.

XVI

THE first thing I did, when I reached the office next morning, was to go down to the room where I had spent my first two days at S.B.H. The desk was gone, and nothing had been put in its place. I closed the door behind me while I thought the matter over. Obviously the desk was the one I had seen in Lormier's house. As to how it had got there, Tatiana, in order to ingratiate herself with Lormier, must have told him the secret. I could think of no other explanation. Since Keller had been rebuked for putting me in quarantine on my arrival, new members of the staff had, as I knew, been posted immediately to one or other of the departments. I was the last person to have occupied that small room. Seated on the single chair which was all it now contained, I again thought for a little while about the mystery of the unknown writer, which I had almost lost sight of since I had been out of touch with Tatiana.

I went along to Faramon's abode in the basement, to see if I could find out anything about the removal of the desk. Faramon in his glass cage was already busy at his typewriter. Since my first visit to him I had been to see him several times, not on business but simply to have a breathing-spell away from the Chairman's office.

'I see the desk has been taken out of room 23,' I said. 'Did you have it moved?'

'Yes. The Chairman sent for me about ten days ago and said that his gardener was waiting in room 23 and I was to send my man along to help him carry it out to the van. That was all. No explanation. It was done in five minutes.'

So that was that. The desk was now in Lormier's small drawing-room. It remained for my other surmise to be confirmed, and I asked if I might use Faramon's telephone. He left me alone in his box and I looked up the number of Orsini's dress establishment.

'I wish to speak to Monsieur Raphaëlo. This is Professor Martin.'

I had to wait some time, and while I was doing so I glanced mechanically at the sheet in Faramon's typewriter. I read: '. . . as he walked past the platform he slowed his pace and Forquier, the representative of S.F.I.O., handed him a letter which he slipped into his pocket. . . .'

'Professor Martin? My dear Professor, I am so delighted that you have rung me up. Such a nice surprise and on such a fine morning!'

'Monsieur Raphaëlo, I have to read a paper to the Académie des Sciences, and there's a point I want to discuss with Tatiana. May I be allowed to speak to her?'

'Really? A paper for the Académie des Sciences? How fascinating, and how important! But, Professor, didn't you know? Our beautiful and beloved Tatiana left us a month ago. Alas, yes. The bird of the steppes took flight. We were all very sad about it.'

So there had been no foreign tour for the purpose of showing the Orsini collection. And then, while Raphaëlo and I were exchanging the final courtesies, I suddenly started. My eyes were again wandering over Faramon's desk and I noticed beside the typewriter a sheet of shorthand with longhand corrections in a sloping handwriting. But one word was in a straight, up-and-down hand, presumably because the position of Faramon's arm when he was writing it had obliged him to write in this way. It was the word 'normally', written in the margin, and the sight of it brought a visual memory of unusual vividness to my mind. I saw that word 'normally' as it had appeared in a sentence written by the anonymous writer on the last of the six drawers. 'If nothing happens to me, if I

214

leave this room normally to go somewhere else, I'll make a cross on the underside of the desk. . . .' The sentence was one which I had so often re-read, because of its importance to the story, that not only the words but the very look was engraved upon my memory.

Leaving the glass case I went over to Faramon, who was straying about the room amid the rows of office equipment.

'Faramon', I said, 'you never told me you were an author.'

'Now and then I amuse myself by scribbling, when I've nothing else to do. Writing is a way of travelling.'

'Yes. As it happens I've read an excellent story of yours, although the manuscript was awkward to handle. I've another fault to find with it. You don't disguise your handwriting very well. If that set of drawers had fallen into the hands of the Managing Director, instead of those of the Chairman, you'd be in serious trouble.'

Utterly disconcerted, Faramon did not even attempt a denial. He looked unhappily at me, awkwardly huddled in his long, thin body.

'For God's sake, Faramon, what got into you? You're accusing Hermelin of the most abominable things. Why did you do it?'

'It's not easy to explain,' said Faramon. 'I have a great love of literature, and yet, despite the pleasure it has given me, I find it unsatisfactory. Writers such as Marx and Freud have made history, but pure literature has no direct impact on life. You repeat a poem by Baudelaire in the way you take an aspirin, and you read a novel to lose yourself in a world that is already over, a sort of artificial paradise. So I have been thinking in terms of applied literature—literature that only begins when I have finished writing it.'

'I couldn't care less about literary theories. What's clear to me is that you have grossly libelled Hermelin, and for no reason.'

'I don't think I've libelled him. I've had dealings with him and I'm beginning to know him.'

'Are you telling me that this story of yours is true?'

'Certainly not. It's invented from beginning to end. But I think it is a true picture of Hermelin.'

Faramon then asked me how I had discovered the story and the hidden door-key. It had all happened just as he intended and he was delighted. I left him at about half-past nine to make a tour of the building, and at a little after eleven I was in the department which handled the 'Electronica' apparatus, looking through the morning's correspondence. A letter caught my eye which, as I saw at a glance, was from the Chairman's point of view nothing less than disastrous. It was from S.S.A., the fictitious company created by Lormier for the ostensible purpose of exporting electronic equipment to Sweden. Addressed to the Chairman of 'Electronica' it ran as follows:

'Stockholm, 23-11-58. Dear Sir, We enclose a cheque for 57,000 Swedish crowns, representing your share of the company's profits for the month of October.'

The letter was as uncalled-for as the cheque which had presumably accompanied it, since for all practical purposes Lormier was himself the S.S.A. company, and its profits were no doubt transferred in the ordinary way to a private bank-account kept by him in Sweden. In short, it was an error, only to be explained by a series of blunders and mishaps in which possibly some newly joined member of the staff had been involved. But however this might be, the letter and the cheque together constituted clear and damning evidence of Lormier's defalcations. I pretended not to have noticed anything, and chatting to one of the men in the room I ascertained that Hermelin had already looked in that morning and had taken Anjubé, the head of the department, off to his own office. This looked ominous. Hermelin would certainly have had the cheque passed on to the Accounts Department, whence I could not recover it. The only thing I could do, which would at least gain a little time, was to arrange for a telegram to be sent from Stockholm saying that a mistake had been made and asking for the cheque to be returned. Not wanting the phone-call to go through the company switchboard, where it would be noted, I went out and telephoned from the public call-box in the Rue Balzac. It took me a long time to get the connection and then I found myself talking to a Swedish secretary who didn't understand what I said and finally hung up on me. I made a second attempt, but when at last I got through again there was no reply. The time was then five minutes past twelve. I would have liked to talk the thing over with Odette and Jocelyne, but when I got back to the office they had gone out to lunch. As I was leaving Hermelin emerged from his room and asked me to step inside. He was alone.

'Monsieur Martin,' he said, 'you have been out of the build-ing for nearly an hour. Would you care to tell me where you've been?'

'I was doing something for the Chairman.'

'You went to the call-box in the Rue Balzac, did you not? And there, if I am not mistaken, you telephoned to Stockholm.'

'Are you spying on me?'

'Don't talk to me like that! Bluff won't get you anywhere, my lad, now I've caught you in the act.'

'In the act of what, Monsieur le Directeur Général?'

'That call to Stockholm proves definitely that you're involved in the S.S.A. set-up. And now you're going to talk and tell me the whole story.'

'With all respect, Monsieur, I don't have to do any talking between midday and one-thirty. This is my lunch hour.'

'Today you're going without lunch. It won't be the first time, will it? The only reason you're here at all is that a trollop introduced you to the Chairman, but we can go into that later. At present I want you to talk.'

217

'I've nothing to say. I'm going.'

I turned towards the door, and Hermelin caught me with a muscular grip on my arm.

'Let me go,' I said. 'Or are you proposing to keep me here by force?'

He certainly wanted to. He would have liked to hit me, but he thought better of it.

'All right, clear out and tell Lormier I don't give a damn. Van der Helst, the chairman of the Dutch syndicate, will be here this afternoon. We shall file an injunction, and there's nothing to prevent the other shareholders doing the same.'

I took a taxi to Neuilly and tried to sort things out on the way. This time Lormier was in real trouble. The worst of it, so it seemed to me, was that with the story on the desk-drawers in his possession he must think himself in a very strong position for dealing with Hermelin. But Faramon had been quite definite about that—'an invention from beginning to end'. And for my part, I could not tell Lormier what I knew, since it would have meant Faramon's instant dismissal.

I hurried into the house without seeing anyone but a man-servant to whom I did not stop to give my name. Running up to the first floor I tapped on the Chairman's door and, getting no reply, went in to find him asleep with his mouth open. The countenance which the relaxed muscles no longer held in place seemed strangely deformed, the blubbery flesh falling away to pile up between the chin and the pyjama top in a series of thick, livid folds. Beholding that big, formless mask one had the feeling that the man was drained of all his strength, that there was nothing left in him but a diminished life with slackened springs, capable of little reaction in the face of danger. I had the sudden conviction that Lormier was done for, finished, and would never again be able to rise to meet a crisis in his affairs. The urine-bottle, now within easy reach of his hand, was half-filled with pinkish liquid, and I had a moment of genuine remorse at the thought of my refusal to help a sick man who was already defeated. I tapped him lightly on the shoulder and at length his eyes opened and he looked up at me with a vague and troubled gaze. He contemplated me for a moment in that state of hazy rumination which fever induces, then shut his eyes again. But then he started up convulsively and again looked at me, this time with lucid eyes. Realising that only a matter of extreme urgency could have brought me thus to his bedside, he asked me sharply what it was.

I told him about the letter and the cheque, my fruitless attempts to telephone S.S.A. and my enforced interview with Hermelin. Without realising it, while he lay intently listening, I told the story entirely from his point of view, wholly accepting my own allegiance and complicity in the matter. It was not the desire to be revenged on Hermelin which made me do so. I was simply following my natural course as a dutiful subordinate.

'Martin,' said Lormier, 'you have done very well.' And the words of praise gave me an acute, almost voluptuous pleasure in which there was just the needful element of shame to render it keener still.

'I must remind you,' I said, 'that Monsieur Van der Helst will be arriving at three-thirty.'

'Don't worry,' said Lormier. 'I'll be there.' And he pressed the bell.

'There's another thing, sir. Yesterday I noticed an office-desk in your Louis XVI salon. If I'm not mistaken it is the one with the writing on it which was in Room 23 at the office. I think I should tell you that I'm convinced that story is a fake.'

Lormier gave an ironical nod of his head and I knew that he did not believe me. His valet entered, followed a moment later by Madame Lormier. He gave orders for a bath to be run, clean linen to be prepared and the chauffeur to have his car in readiness.

'Your temperature was over a hundred this morning,' Madame Lormier said.

He answered only with a slight frown. I left the room with Madame Lormier and after she had closed the door she said in a resigned voice:

'My husband's been caught out, hasn't he?'

'Caught in what, Madame?'

'He wouldn't be going out today, weak as he is, if something very serious hadn't happened. Well, it was bound to come sooner or later.'

I tried to persuade her that it was only a normal business matter, but she was not to be convinced. Yet she said nothing that betrayed any hint of resentment where her husband was concerned, seeming rather to feel that she too deserved that justice should be done.

'Things are coming to a climax. I had hoped that it might be delayed a few more years, for the sake of the children, but we have no reason to complain and you are being too kind when you sympathise with us in our misfortune. No, Monsieur Martin, do not say any more. I know very well that the bourgeoisie is utterly corrupt. I was reading about it only yesterday in a newspaper which the gardener had left in the tool-shed.'

'What newspaper does your gardener read?'

We had reached the head of the stairs. Before we started to walk down Madame Lormier turned to me and I seemed to catch in her unhappy eyes something like a gleam of desire as she said in a low voice:

'He reads the Communist paper, *l'Humanité*. But you must not tell my husband. He is naturally on the side of corruption and he wouldn't understand. And now that everything is lost what good would it do to upset him?'

I might have replied that the Chairman's private fortune amounted to something between fifty and a hundred milliard francs, and that in all likelihood nothing was lost, but this, I think, would have disappointed her. We went into the dining-room and she sat me in Lormier's chair, facing her. The four children had already taken their places at the table. Valentine responded to my greeting with a smile of gratitude for the Latin translation which bathed me in felicity. Madame Lormier apologised for the fact that there were no *hors d'oeuvres* and that we were starting with the main dish.

'Their father wants them to be accustomed to a modest diet. They may soon have nothing except what they earn for themselves.'

I saw a shadow pass over the children's faces, and they looked round at me, the proletarian, with expressions of respectful unease. That sense of guilt, particularly on the part of the little girl, Béatrice, who was only just ten, was the more touching to me since I remembered having experienced it myself at the same age, but for the reason that I was a child of the poor. A few minutes later Madame Lormier left the table to see how her husband was getting on. Not wanting to talk to Valentine about her work I asked her if she often went to the theatre or the cinema. She smiled at the question, foreseeing the astonishment her reply would cause me.

'I never go to either. My father won't hear of it, and neither will mother.'

'But there are plays and films that are suitable for the young.'

'I expect there are, but that isn't what matters to my parents. We aren't allowed to go out at all, because it wastes time when we ought to be working. But however hard I work, and Heaven knows I try, I'm always behind. The only thing I get top marks for is good conduct.'

There was no affectation in the words, no playing for sympathy, and none of the smugness that one sees often enough in the children of the rich when they blandly concede that they are 'no earthly good at school work'. While she was speaking I studied her beautiful face, its purity of form and healthy firmness of flesh and colour. It was clear to me that she possessed the kind of intelligence that can be applied only to everyday reality and which draws no sustenance from the discourses of a Bossuet or a geometrical proposition. I was suddenly furious with Lormier for his pig-headed resolve to make a university graduate of her.

'I'm only speaking of myself, but it's the same with my brothers and sister. They haven't reached higher level yet, but there are all the intermediate examinations. Nothing but exams, and such a dreadful lot of upsets.'

Madame Lormier returned looking more than ever distressed.

'My husband will be down in a quarter of an hour,' she said to me. 'But for him to be going to the office in his present state is sheer madness. I'm afraid it will kill him.'

No one suggested that he should be restrained from going, since they all knew the uselessness of attempting to oppose the master's will. When the main dish had been taken away Madame Lormier ordered cheese to be brought, and I saw expressions of surprise and delight appear on the faces of the children. Valentine's eyes shone with greed as it was set on the table. The cheese was followed by tangerines, and from the remarks that were passed I gathered that so much luxury was quite at variance with the custom of the house. A positive gaiety spread round the table, and despite his mother's remonstrances the younger son, Renaud, exploded in a fit of laughing which infected little Béatrice. But when Lormier entered the room, followed by the valet, who seemed to expect him to collapse at any minute, a silence of dismay fell upon them all. He was crimson and terrible to behold, his eyes shining and wild, the corners of his mouth dragged down with the physical effort he was making, his breathing loud and hurried, his whole aspect very similar to what it had been when I went into the bedroom. He sat down heavily beside me at the head of the table and while he struggled for breath contemplated his children with a feverish glare.

'Well, Valentine,' he demanded, 'and how many marks did you get for your Latin?'

This was not the Latin translation I had done the day before but an earlier piece handed in the previous week and returned with corrections that morning.

'Five', murmured Valentine, bowing her lovely head beneath her father's gaze so that her rounded shoulders and young breasts seemed to shrink within her jersey.

'Five!' gasped Lormier in a tone of the utmost scorn. 'Five out of twenty! My poor, idiot girl, what chance do you think you will have in June when——'

A fit of coughing cut him short, and, still coughing, he pointed a finger at his younger son.

'Renaud', asked Madame Lormier on his behalf, 'what did you get for your French composition?'

'Five and a half', muttered the unhappy Renaud, deeply conscious of his shame.

That extra half-mark must have seemed to Lormier like an irony of chance, a jest flung in his face. He burst into a mocking laugh which caused the folds of his neck to bulge terrifyingly over his stiff collar. Aching with sympathy for the four dunces as they sat trembling beneath the explosion, I wished with all my heart that it would stifle him.

'Five and a half! Ha ha! Five and a half! Numskulls, the whole lot of you—blockheads—idlers! And what do you think you're going to do in the world? Are you going to be shop-assistants? Not even that! Casual labourers is all you'll be—errand boys—domestic helps—even. . . .'

But here he was forced to give up. With a gesture he warned them that the occasion was only postponed and that he would return to the subject some other day, as soon as he had recovered the strength to browbeat and humiliate them to his heart's content. There ensued a long silence broken only by the gasps and whistles of his breathing. The children sat erect and motionless with their eyes on their plates. Lormier touched me on the knee.

'Martin, have you found what I asked for these four wretches?'

'Yes, sir, I think I have. My brother, Michel, is getting married and he needs to earn some money quickly.'

'Well, he's to come every day from four to eight. And on Thursdays and Sundays he'll come all day, from eight in the morning to eight at night.'

It was now time for them to return to school. The four wretches stood up and I was able to admire the grace and elegance of Valentine, the outline of stomach and buttock, the curve of her thigh and the long line running to the nape of her neck. Each in turn went to embrace their father, and in the tenderness with which he pressed them to him, the fond gaze which he bestowed on each, there was so much despair and anxiety to hope for the best that I was truly touched, and for the moment filled with compassion for this enormously rich man who, no longer believing in the future of wealth or his own social class, and torn with paternal anguish, nevertheless hoped that something of his millionaire's luxuries and privileges might yet be retained by his diploma'd posterity.

We reached S.B.H. at a quarter-past two. Despite the heat of the office Lormier was shivering, but he insisted on taking off his overcoat and scarf. Odette telephoned Hermelin to say that the Chairman wished to see him immediately and I asked leave to withdraw, but he ordered us both to stay. He looked to me in even worse shape than when we had left Neuilly, and I was afraid his strength would fail him in the coming battle.

Suddenly his eyes rolled, he clapped a hand to his mouth and made a dash for the toilet, reaching it only just in time to rid himself of the infusion of herbs he had drunk before leaving the house. He came back shaking, and a moment later Hermelin entered, vindictiveness and assurance written all over him. Seeing Lormier's lamentable state his smile of approaching triumph became blander still.

'Why, Monsieur le Président,' he said smoothly, 'I hadn't expected to see you here today. I'm delighted that you should have made so rapid a recovery.'

'Thank you. I've come to discuss this matter of a cheque connected with Swedish deliveries. Sit down.'

Hermelin seated himself in the visitor's armchair facing the desk. Odette and I took up positions facing one another at either end. I got the impression that she already knew all about the S.S.A. business.

'I didn't dare hope that you would be able to come,' said Hermelin. 'It will enable us to clear up one or two points that remain a little puzzling, in spite of what Martin has told me.'

I started to protest at this but the Chairman silenced me with a glance.

'The facts,' Hermelin proceeded, 'are as follows.'

He went on to give a long and detailed account of what he called the S.S.A. affair, citing figures and dates, pointing out discrepancies in the statements of different departments which appeared to substantiate one another, and finally drawing his conclusions. Lormier, huddled in his chair, made no response, and the sight of that gross sagging figure, apparently quivering with apprehension, must have been singularly encouraging to the Managing Director.

'Well, and what are you proposing to do about it?' asked Lormier when he had finished.

'I intend to bring the whole thing out into the open,' said

Hermelin aggressively. 'Van der Helst will be arriving shortly. We shall naturally inform him.'

'My dear fellow, I think you would really be wiser to forget about it. It would be bound to make things awkward for certain people.'

'But that can't be helped, can it, Monsieur le Président?'

'Hermelin, I strongly urge you not to try to be more malicious than you really are.'

'You needn't think that anything is going to stop me. I'm going through with it.'

Hermelin's tone was harsh and decided, as was the gesture with which he accompanied the words. Lormier sighed, moved slowly in his chair and said in a tired voice:

'Have you forgotten that it was owing to me that you were appointed Managing Director?'

'I was particularly well qualified for the position, as this affair proves.'

'And do you know why I had you appointed? No, you'd never guess. It was because it suited me that my Managing Director should be a half-wit.'

'In view of what I've discovered today,' said Hermelin, 'your opinion of me doesn't much matter. But still, I must ask you to be polite.'

Lormier was passing to the attack, evidently counting on his secret weapon, the story on the desk. I wanted to warn him again, but before I could do so he sat upright and said in an icy voice:

'Listen, Hermelin. When Martin first came here and was put in Room 23 he had the notion of examining the drawers in the desk. He found a story on their underside, written by a youth who had occupied the room before him.'

It was just as I had feared, and moreover Lormier was bringing me into it. Again I nearly told him that he was hopelessly mistaken.

'I have the desk, with its curious narrative, at my house. After reading the story I caused a thorough investigation to be made, and I now know all I need to know about a certain young man called Raoul Dudevant. Hermelin, I can have you arrested in ten minutes. I need only telephone.'

Hermelin made a stifled sound. His whole aspect had changed. He was staring open-mouthed, his face as haggard as Lormier's own.

'You will kindly apologise, Hermelin, for your insolence. You will do so on your knees.'

Hermelin started to his feet, and clearly his first instinct was to refuse. But then he thought again, and I fancy it was only the presence of Odette and myself which prevented him from submitting to the intolerable demand. He moved towards the table, stammering as he did so, evidently with some idea of bargaining and obtaining remission on less outrageous terms, but he met with a stony refusal.

'Go down on your knees, Hermelin, and say: "Monsieur le Président, I beseech you to forgive me for my insolence."'

Hermelin continued to protest, talking of his age, his high position, the services he had rendered, his dignities, his Légion d'Honneur. He pleaded in anguish, wringing his hands.

'It's just as you please,' said Lormier and reached for the telephone.

So then Hermelin went on his knees on the carpet. His hands clasped in supplication rendered the spectacle indescribably painful. Lormier rose from his chair the better to observe him across the desk.

'Monsieur le Président, I beseech you to forgive me for my insolence.'

'Very well. Now get up and get out, you revolting animal.'

I turned away my head so as not to witness Hermelin's departure, but I saw Lormier's smile of horrid triumph at the thought that he had settled with his adversary for ever.

His chauffeur helped him down to his car, and after he was gone I went out for a breath of air. A few flakes of snow were falling, to melt when they reached the pavement. Five minutes walking was enough to settle my stomach, but I was still bewildered by the extraordinary turn the interview had taken. Who was this Raoul Dudevant, the mere mention of whose name had defeated Hermelin? It seemed to me astounding and indeed inconceivable that so crafty a man should have behaved so carelessly as to lay himself open to a hasty investigation conducted, presumably, by a private inquiry agency. The likelihood was that the agency had unearthed very little more than the actual name, which Lormier had then used as a bluff; but clearly Hermelin must have something weighty on his conscience, a serious misdemeanour if not an actual crime; and it was remarkable that Faramon in his work of fiction should have contrived, knowing nothing of the matter, to persuade the reader that this was the case. The concept of 'applied literature', it must be said, had got off to a wonderful start. Faramon had told me a little about the story he was now working on, the one of which I had read a line or two while I was telephoning Raphaëlo. It was about an explosive device intended to destroy a Ministry. Someone left it at midnight on the banquette in the Brasserie Lipp, beside a prominent politician. Unfortunately the events of the 13th of May had rendered the operation impossible, and Faramon was only going on with his story for the sake of practice; but there was always a chance that it might come in handy later on. I was thinking about this as I walked along the crowded pavement of the Rue de la Boétie when I happened to notice a long, low car, almond-green in colour, which had just pulled up at the curb about forty yards ahead of me. It was a sports model of some kind, possibly a Jaguar—I know nothing about cars— but anyway something lavish and remarkable. The door opened and Tatiana wriggled out from behind the wheel. She crossed the pavement and went into an art-gallery, and I turned down a side street.

I went to the Rue Eugène-Carrière that evening as we had arranged and found the almond-green car parked outside the house. Tatiana opened the door to me, wearing a long, holland working-smock. She embraced me with all her usual warmth, and I submitted passively.

She gave me a quick glance to see if I knew, but asked no questions, evidently preferring to avoid the subject of her new way of life. Leading me into the kitchen, where the scent of roasting meat filled me with melancholy, she pulled off her pants and then opened the oven door to see how the joint was getting on. After which she tucked up her skirts round her waist, kissed me passionately saying 'I love you' in a hoarse voice and then said, 'Hurry, darling.' It was all very fine, but I too was wearing a pair of pants, one of those labyrinthine affairs created by Anglo-Saxon genius for the conquest of the world and the supersession of the plain shorts of my youth, which had offered little or no obstruction in moments of urgency. Tatiana grew impatient. I asked her if her mother was in. Yes, that was just it, she was in the living-room talking to Jules Bouvillon, and either of them might come into the kitchen at any moment. I was tempted to say that there was no desperate hurry and that I would stay to supper and afterwards we would repair to the bedroom. In short, I was on the verge of giving way all along the line; but then I changed my mind and kept my distance. It cost me a pang, nevertheless, when Tatiana's ravishing legs vanished under the petticoat, the skirt and the holland smock.

'Dear Volodia', said Sonia, 'it's so long since I've seen you. You've nothing to bring you here when Tatiana's away in America. I think of you so often. I've been wanting to tell you about the Russia of my childhood, and about poor Illyinka who lived in our house and killed himself because he had fallen

229

in love with the daughter of a rich horse-dealer. Her name was Mashenka.'

'Mother, you mustn't keep Martin,' said Tatiana. 'He's in a hurry to leave. His fiancée's ill.'

She had stressed the word fiancée, and she glanced coldly, almost contemptuously at me as she did so. The news seemed to surprise Sonia. I did not deny it.

'And so, my dear boy, you are getting married?' said Jules Bouvillon. 'I am glad to hear it. We should all experience the extremity of human suffering. My own wife left me after six months for a *garde municipal*. I tried to suffer but I couldn't. I trust you are more gifted in that respect than I. But before you enter the married state I should like you to read my book. I lent it to my friend Moncornet, and he took three weeks to read it and didn't understand a word. I fear he will not be the only one, for it is very abstruse. But you, I am sure, will be able to follow it. Do come and see me in the Impasse de la Baleine. Ask for Jules Bouvillon.'

'I'll come one Saturday afternoon, I promise.'

I made my farewells and went home, where I was not expected. As I entered the lobby I heard sounds of heated argument in the living-room, where Valérie, Michel and Lena were discussing where Lena was to sleep—she had arrived that afternoon to take up her abode in our two-room apartment. Porteur was refusing to give up his narrow divan in the living-room, saying that he couldn't sleep a wink with anyone beside him.

'Martin can take Valérie into the big bed,' he said, 'if he doesn't dislike it too much. Or else he can take Lena.'

'You're abominable!' cried Valérie. 'You really mean you'd let your wife sleep with your brother? I've never known anyone as immoral as you are. You ought to be ashamed!'

'You think that Martin and Lena. . . . Well, but what if they do? Lena and I love one another, and that's all that matters. What do you say, Lena?'

'Oh, I'll agree to anything provided it suits everyone,' said Lena with a charming German accent.

'Well, upon my word, I ask you, talk about a free for all! Pure Judeo-Marxism, that's what it is. No principles and no anything else, just a permanent foursome—conjugal Communism! But there's me, don't forget, and I'm not a Yid or a foreigner. I'm French and I believe in French morals and French traditions. No, but honestly!'

At this point I offered a simple solution which had the merit of not disturbing anyone or offending against French morals. I proposed that Valérie and Lena should share the big bed while I slept in the iron one. Valérie refused point-blank. She could not, she said, stand the smell of another woman. I had to give way, and the only other solution was that I should occupy the big bed with Valérie. But I was touched that Michel should have been so ready to let me sleep with the woman he loved. Although I was far from understanding it, his attitude in the matter caused me to forget the slight mistrust I had felt for him ever since the beginning of his affair with Valérie, before the death of Chazard.

Lying at Valérie's side that night I sought to evoke the image of Valentine, but was compelled to accept the fact that the enchantment was gone. The grand passion of the day before had evaporated.

XVII

Aᴛᴇʀ his victory over Hermelin the Chairman's frame of mind greatly improved. There were even moments, in the course of those chats between us which he generally reserved for the end of the day's work, when he went so far as to be optimistic. He saw in the coming of de Gaulle a hope that we might take the socialist rabble in hand, fortify the sense of property and generally toughen the ego. The General, as he saw it, would come to terms with the F.L.N. and bring a few hundred thousand soldiers back to France, where they would fall upon the Communist Party and scatter it like chaff. The paratroops and the Foreign Legion would work wonders. An enlightened class of employers, their boards staffed with retired generals, would reduce wages and cut salaries by half, thus bringing about a prodigious boom in exports. High finance and heavy industry would work together to solve the agricultural problem; they would buy and merge and re-equip and rationalise until, having acquired all the land, they would be able to flood the continent with meat and corn and fruit at unbelievably low prices. Strikes would be made illegal ('Just like behind the Iron Curtain,' said Lormier happily) and the children of the poor would be brought up in the love of religion, in consequence of which France would enter a new Golden Age of affluence and grandeur.

But, even more than the defeat of Hermelin, what so heartened Lormier was the change that had come over his children. It seemed that Porteur, that incomparable peda-gogue, had tapped new springs in them, and especially in Valentine, of whom no one now doubted that she would pass her finals in June. The Chairman was unwearying in his praise of my brother, whose salary he raised every week.

'Do you think,' he said to me one evening, 'that he would like me to get him a Légion d'Honneur?'

I persuaded him not to, saying how modest Michel was. So instead, in his overflowing gratitude, he gave him a bonus of a hundred and fifty thousand francs, which Michel divided between Lena and Valérie, keeping none of it for himself. Valérie bought, among other things, a suit, a pair of shoes with stiletto-heels and another for everyday use, a wooden spoon for stirring stews, which she had long coveted, and for me she bought a puce-coloured tie which I had to wear occasionally in order not to offend her. I asked Michel more than once how he had contrived to transform his four dunces, but he only said, 'Oh, I just amuse them' or 'I get them to relax.' One Thursday afternoon I had to take a document out to Lormier who was on his way to see a lawyer in Saint-Germain-en-Laye. I caught him just as he was hoisting himself into his car, and he suggested that I might like to go up to the schoolroom. Madame Lormier went with me as far as the foot of the stairs, explaining that neither she nor her husband was allowed to intrude when lessons were in progress.

'My brother-in-law is the only one whom Monsieur Michel allows in,' she said, 'and he goes very often. Your brother says he has a great gift for teaching, which I am bound to say I had never suspected. You'll be able to see for yourself. He's up there now.'

The four pupils, when I entered, were sitting on the floor with their backs to the door, watching their uncle and Michel do a circus turn. The ex-minister was wearing a clown's hat and a pink suspender-belt round his waist, no doubt to enliven the sober grey of his jacket. He still managed to look elegant. Michel, who was flapping about in a vast jacket and pair of shoes belonging to Lormier, also wore a false nose and a ginger wig. I had arrived near the end of the act.

233

'Monsieur Auguste,' Lucien Lormier was saying, 'you have flat feet.'

'I have flat feet, Monsieur Félix?'

It did indeed seem, in Lormier's enormous shoes, that Monsieur Auguste had flat feet.

'Yes, Monsieur Auguste, you have flat feet.'

'But you haven't got flat feet, Monsieur Félix?'

'No, Monsieur Auguste, I have arched feet. And what is more, I have a kick like a mule.'

'And I haven't a kick like a mule, Monsieur Félix?'

'No, Monsieur Auguste, you haven't a kick like a mule.'

'Really? I haven't a kick like a mule? Well now, Monsieur Félix, would you mind placing yourself just there?'

Monsieur Auguste then arranged Monsieur Félix to his liking, stepped back a pace, took aim, and saying, 'Well, I say I *have* got a kick like a mule,' launched a kick at his bottom which caused him to fall flat on his face. He then stood on his back saying, 'So I haven't got a kick like a mule?' The children laughed till they shook, but silently, with their handkerchiefs stuffed in their mouths. The two men got rid of their stage-effects and sat down, and the children at once clustered round Michel chattering about the performance. The younger ones, Béatrice and Renaud, sat on his knees and hugged him, while Jean-Jacques and Valentine stood leaning on his shoulders. No one paid any attention to me except Lucien Lormier, who glanced at me and said:

'He's the only one they're interested in. I ought to be jealous, but it's such a miracle that I'm as delighted as they are. What a remarkable person your brother is!' He turned to Michel and asked: 'Now what are we going to do? A little dancing?'

'No,' said Michel, looking at his watch. 'It's time for history. The Revolution and the Legislative Assembly.'

To my surprise those forbidding words, far from causing

dismay, were received by his charges with as much pleasure as if a new game had been proposed. Michel worked on the principle that the younger ones could gain something from the lessons intended for their elders, and *vice versa*, and so all four followed all the courses and seemed to profit by them. For my part, history was the one I would have chosen to follow. Besides setting forth the facts with great clarity Michel dramatised them as though he were twenty actors rolled into one. Until then I had never thought of history in general, and the Revolution in particular, except in two-dimensional terms; now I encountered them brought to life and thrown into relief. After writing a date on the blackboard Michel entered the Legislative Assembly, where he improvised a speech in the character of Vergniaud; he then moved on to the Club des Feuillants, debated with La Fayette, replied to himself, moved on again to the Tuileries, where he became in turn the King, the Queen and the Dauphin, crossed the river to the Club des Cordeliers, was applauded by Lucien Lormier, and once again crossed the Seine to take the air in the Palais-Royal. His four pupils, playing the part of the crowd, the Garde Nationale or the Assembly, had no difficulty in understanding that when he moved to the left he was entering the Club de Jacobins, and when he advanced a few paces he was in the Hôtel de Ville. He carried them with him all the way, and I was sorry to have to leave before the lesson ended. When Madame Lormier tactfully asked me what I thought I could not refrain from showering praises on Michel and her brother-in-law.

At the office I was now on terms of such intimacy with Odette, Jocelyne and Angelina that I might have been another woman where they were concerned, despite my crime and my prison-sentence, which lent me an added virility in their eyes and also a sort of seniority, accepted even by Odette. I think they were proud of me and proud of putting so much trust in an ex-convict. They talked in my presence of their love-affairs as freely as they might have done among themselves, and, without actually asking for it, often looked to me for advice. Jocelyne was less forthcoming in this respect than the others, but one day when we were alone together she confided to me that she had fallen in love with a twenty-nine-year-old chemist who lived in the same house. They travelled to work on the same bus and had long conversations on a variety of subjects, everything except love, which Jocelyne did not dare to hope for, conscious as she was of her physical unattractiveness. I assured her that beauty was of no importance, scarcely even an adornment flattering to the vanity of men and by no means an essential ingredient of sex-appeal. And for the rest I referred her to the teachings of Porteur: she should take the initiative with authority, get her chemist into bed and then persuade him that he had achieved something remarkable. She might not have taken me very seriously if I had put forward these views as my own, but the mention of Porteur greatly impressed her.

One evening as I was leaving the office I encountered Tatiana in the corridor, wearing the suit she had worn five months earlier when I had run into her in the Rue de Castiglione, the day I came out of prison. She kissed me, hugged me to her bosom, and since we were relatively speaking alone— that is to say, people were not actually standing round us—she proceeded to announce, in a ringing voice that dominated the clatter of homegoing feet:

'I'm fed up with being kept by that character! You needn't think it's because of his weight. I've never given a damn about that, or about being a tart either. I'm not suffering from a guilty conscience and I don't lie awake all night brooding. It's nothing like that. It's just that he and I don't belong to the same species or even the same universe. Every time I speak to the great boob I want to cut him down to size. So I've put in for a school-teaching job and now I'm on my way to hand back the keys of the car and the apartment, where he'll find the furs and the diamonds and all the rest of the junk.'

She laughed and said more quietly:

'I promise you, it's nothing to do with principles or noble gestures. For the last three months I've been living the mink-and-super-sports life, and this morning I caught sight of myself in the glass and I looked as big an idiot as Christine de Rézé. I was scared. That's how it is. Good-bye.'

I was delighted by this news, which was what I had always hoped for. But the next morning I arrived at the office a few minutes earlier than usual to find Odette there already. She came to meet me with a look of great distress, and taking my hand held it clasped in her own.

'Martin, I've got to do something which I find hateful. The Chairman rang me up at home last night to say that you're dismissed from S.B.H. and that he wants you out of the place by half-past nine this morning. Also, you're to tell your brother that he doesn't want to see him any more at Neuilly. I asked why, but he wouldn't tell me. I simply couldn't believe it. I've just rung him up at Neuilly and said that you're indispensable, but he won't change his mind.'

Jocelyne and Angelina came in a few minutes later and had to be told. As to the reasons for my dismissal, I could make no reply to their dismayed questions or even offer a theory. The truth had to be concealed. This embarrassed me and I cut short our leave-taking.

'I'll write soon,' said Odette. 'It may not be easy for you to get another job, but I'll find one for you.'

'I'll look round for one too,' said Jocelyne.

We parted with kisses all round, and I went to the personnel department. Here Keller ignored me, and it was one of his underlings who handed me my work-certificate and a chit to the Accounts Department for my past fortnight's salary and an extra week in lieu of notice. Hermelin was in the room, as though he had dropped in by accident, but in contrast to his former arrogance his manner was amiable, even obsequious. He believed, of course, that I shared with Lormier a secret that might be dangerous to himself.

'So you're leaving us, Monsieur Martin? I'm very sorry to hear it, for I have always had a high opinion of you.'

'Don't worry,' I said. 'By sacking me the Chairman has shown that he trusts me to keep my mouth shut. You can do the same.'

His ears turned bright red and he went off wishing me good luck. That morning, for the first time in my life, I went for a walk in the Bois de Boulogne on a week-day. It was misty and there were not many people about. Although I contrived to lose myself more than once the time passed slowly.

The country, after all, is rather disappointing. Trees are all very much the same, and there is nothing more like a stretch of grass than another stretch of grass. I was putting off the moment for going home, where Porteur would be sound asleep and I should be as much alone as I was here, since Lena was following a course at the Sorbonne. On my way back I went into an art-gallery in the Faubourg Saint-Honoré, which was another thing I had never done before. There was a lady seated at a table to whom I said good morning but who ignored me. It was an interesting place. The painter whose works were being displayed was named Marcel Pinglard, and a printed placard intended for the enlightenment of the public began as follows: 'The great Marcel Pinglard is unquestion-ably the most original and valid painter of a period which will be for ever distinguished by the fulguration of his oneirical genius.' These arresting words, so helpful for the layman like myself, instantly heightened my sensibilities and enabled me to perceive without effort the oneirical fulguration in the canvases on display: especially in the one entitled, 'Bike in the Desert', in which a pedal, a pair of handlebars and a bicycle-pump were scattered like skeleton remains over a rectangle of sand, reflecting in cones of variously coloured light the rays of a candle planted in the earth at one corner. An audacious concept. But not all this wealth of beauty could distract my mind from the thought of Tatiana. It was because of her that I had entered the gallery, in memory of the day when I had seen her get out of her sports-car to enter a similar establishment in the Rue de la Boétie. I reflected very sadly that she would almost certainly get a teaching job in the provinces and I should never see her again. I had no thought of going to see her now. It would have been as impossible for me to hide the fact that I had been sacked from S.B.H. as it would have been for me to tell her. The fact that her break with Lormier had led to my instant dismissal would have filled her head with notions of debts and obligations where I was concerned.

I got home at half-past twelve, my usual time, and met Lena in the street outside the house, on her way back from the Sorbonne. As we went upstairs together she talked about her course and her studies in general. After spending a year in France she was to return to Bonn University, where she had already done two years. The things she said about her past life and her future plans never bore much resemblance to the things she had said the day before. She was a sweet girl, full of kindness, gentleness and lies. We found Valérie and Michel in the kitchen. Since Lena had come to join us Michel no longer had luncheon in bed.

'You've got a queer look about you,' said Valérie. 'What's happened?'

'I've got the sack from S.B.H., and Michel's got the sack too. It's no use asking me why. I've no idea.'

Seeing that I was hiding something Valérie gave me a sharp look and was about to cross-examine me when Porteur stopped her.

'Don't bother. It's my fault. Yesterday afternoon Madame

Lormier caught me in bed with Valentine. She was very cross, of course, but she didn't scream the place down. I tried to get her to see that I was doing it for Valentine's own good, for the sake of her artistic and intellectual development, which was partly true. She seemed to understand, but she kept saying, "No doubt you are right, but it is a matter which I cannot possibly keep from my husband." All the same, after we'd argued for a couple of hours she promised not to say anything. But as you see. . . .'

For my part I was by no means convinced that Madame Lormier had said anything. It was at least equally possible that Lormier had been stung to vindictiveness by the candour of Tatiana's parting words. Lena burst out laughing and with her arms round Porteur's neck said that he was her dearest love. Valérie shrugged her shoulders.

'It sounds fine but just the same thanks to your filthy behaviour you're out on your ear. You might at least have had the sense to realise that there's something to be said for parsons' morals when you've got a living to earn. Also that judeo-libertarian ideas about emancipation and off with the petticoats and sleeping around right, left and centre are all right when father's there to foot the bill. People who haven't got a bean are only entitled to be virtuous—one wife, one love and the forty-hour week. And what's more it's a very good thing and you can thank Pinay's government that it still goes on.'

Lunch was a dismal affair. Porteur, more melancholy than I had ever known him, was evidently thinking of the four pupils he should have been visiting that afternoon. When Valérie had gone back to work and Lena was in the kitchen he said to me:

'It's rather awkward. I thought I was in love with Lena, but I find I'm not. I wish you'd go and tell her. Of course I'm not turning her out.'

Lena received the news sadly but with calm.

'It's a shame,' she said. 'I love him so much that I'd stay with him for ever, but still, I've kept on my room in the Rue des Ecoles. I'll finish the washing-up and then I'll leave. I've kept two other lovers as well, one young and one not so young, he's thirty-nine. So I hope I won't be too unhappy.'

Two tears welled up from her soft blue eyes as she spoke, and she wiped them away quickly with an apologetic smile. When I returned to the living-room Michel was whistling, his face serene. He did not ask me how the interview with Lena had gone and I think he had forgotten about her. He sat down at his writing-table and said:

'I'd like to do a scenario on love.'

I said politely, 'Why not?' and went out. I had been thinking of the promise I had made to Jules Bouvillon to call on him one afternoon in the Impasse de la Baleine. I could not allow myself to go to the Rue Eugène-Carrière and trouble Tatiana's conscience, so I cheated my own with the hope that I might have the luck to find her at her cousin's. The Impasse de la Baleine, contrary to what I had expected, was in no way remarkable. Because of its odd name I had thought of it as a narrow, twisted alleyway between overhanging roofs, swarming with tattered children and loud-mouthed matrons. In fact this 'Blind-alley of the Whale' is straight and spacious and relatively deserted. Nor did Jules Bouvillon's dwelling turn out to be the scene of picturesque disorder I had imagined. The old clock-maker lived in a meticulously clean and tidy apartment. He was engaged, when I arrived, in repairing a clockwork Donald Duck. Tatiana, I need hardly say, was not there. Nor did I have a chance to ask him if he had seen her. He at once thrust his manuscript into my hands, with its illuminated cover bearing the title 'God', and sat me down near him, where he could observe my reactions while he went on with his work. I had to read the thing whether I wanted to or not, and I started to do so in some exasperation at the folly which had let me in for this tedious business. But by the time I had read the first few pages my ill-humour was forgotten; I was enthralled. In the first third of the work Jules Bouvillon proved in plain black and white, not by any kind of sentimental reasoning but by the use of hard-boiled, logical arguments, brilliantly developed, meticulous in their precision, overwhelmingly convincing, without a weak link anywhere or a trace of ambiguity (and when I say 'proved' I do so with a proper sense of language, not being one of those artistic souls aspiring to the illimitable and the infinite who let themselves be carried away by words, and accept as authentic proof affirmations and aggregations of human testimony only good enough to convince a Court of Law)—he proved, in short, for irrefutable reasons that God exists, that He created the world and that He watches over the outcome of His Creation. From that day on I have believed in God (no option); but Jules Bouvillon's masterly exposition, although it caused me to marvel, brought me no nearer to God than I had been before I believed in Him, and so it had no particular effect on me. By the time I had finished the first part of the book Donald Duck was mended and lurching about the table. Jules Bouvillon, who had kept an eye on me the whole time, knew exactly where I had got to.

'Well, my boy,' he said, 'and what do you think now?'

'Obviously God exists. There can't be any argument about it. But if I were you I'd put this manuscript on the fire.'

'You too? That's what Moncornet said. He said that to publish it would be to bring disaster on humanity, that the priests would get completely out of hand and in the end they'd become rulers of the earth.'

I strongly supported this view, and to such effect that after an hour of argument I persuaded Jules Bouvillon to put the whole thing in the stove. I myself blew on the coals and I had the satisfaction of watching it go up in flames. The poor man was rather depressed, but I think I consoled him a little by pointing out that for its believers religion must always be an adventure, and that an absolute, demonstrated certainty tends to dispel faith and hope, cardinal virtues of which the prime nourishment is doubt.

I returned to the Rue Saint-Martin at about five and was surprised to find Tatiana there, having arrived a few minutes before me. I embraced her tenderly, and she seemed touched by my very apparent delight at seeing her. Michel had already told her of our dismissal, and she was furiously indignant at Lormier's behaviour. 'I thought he was more of a sportsman,' she said, words of which the true meaning was known only to me. In order not to burden her conscience I resolved as soon as we were alone to tell her of the part Madame Lormier might have played in our tribulations. But we had done no more than exchange a few words when Lucien Lormier appeared. Since Tatiana and he had not met I introduced them. He was civil but displayed no interest in her and turned at once to Michel, who had got up to receive him.

'I've just come from Neuilly. The children are in tears. I don't understand what has happened. I asked my sister-in-law but she wouldn't say a damned thing. I wanted to go along to S.B.H. to see my brother, but the children all begged me to come here first. I've brought a letter for you.'

He held out an envelope to Michel on which I detected Valentine's handwriting.

'It's nice of you,' Michel muttered, and I saw his hand tremble as he took it. Lucien Lormier then brought out of his pocket a very small bear of grey plush, the only toy little Béatrice possessed. 'She asked me to give it to you for you to keep.' At this Michel shed tears which were doubled when Lucien patted him on the shoulder. Tatiana, after looking at her watch, signed to me to come with her into the other room. I had made up my mind. I was resolved never again to be separated from Tatiana and to marry her if she asked me. I locked the door and putting my arms round her passed a hand under her skirt to re-discover the smooth curve of her thigh. As she slipped into the big bed she looked again at her watch and murmured: 'I've a date at six. There's only just time.'

When it was over I stayed lying in bed, breathless and happy. Tatiana was hurriedly pulling on her stockings.

'Martin, I've got some wonderful news. I'm getting married at the end of the month. There wasn't time to tell you when we met at S.B.H. yesterday, and anyway perhaps I was afraid.'

I too got up and began to dress. I felt no anger. I simply thought to myself, 'So God really exists. I have just had proof of it.'

'He's an engineer, twenty-seven. He's just back from Algeria. He's quite special—very intelligent, very sensitive, and with the sort of humour you don't often find. I think Porteur, if there really is such a person, must be rather like Alain. His name's Alain.'

There was a pause. Tatiana straightened her hair and I buttoned my waistcoat.

'It's queer, the first time I saw him I didn't like him. And now I'm crazy about him, literally crazy. He's only got to raise his little finger. . . . Heavens, it's a quarter to and he's expecting me at six!'

I don't think I said anything. I just stood there in the middle of the room. Before hurrying out she found time to say:

'I'm not very consistent, am I?'

She smiled and raised her hand in a gesture of farewell. While I was re-making the bed, to avoid questions when Valérie returned, the thought occurred to me that the day was Friday. If she had not known of my dismissal Tatiana could not have called here at five in the afternoon with any idea of finding me. How had she found out? I concluded that, Lormier having threatened reprisals, she had telephoned S.B.H. to ask, and then had come here to give herself to me in consolation, or in payment of her debts.

Michel, when I went back to the living-room, was talking to Lucien Lormier about his plans for continuing the education of the Lormier children. He proposed to write a series of courses which their uncle would read to them, miming the parts according to his stage-directions. But at this point the youth in the green shirt dropped in. Instead of sitting down on the floor in his usual place he came over to Michel and laid an open magazine on the table in front of him. A headline streamed across the page—'Who is Porteur?' and beneath it were two photographs, one full-face. Lucien Lormier stared blankly at them and then at Michel, looking as though he could not believe his eyes.

'The swine, they have to balls up everything,' said green-shirt, and went and sat on the floor.

Lucien and I were both reading the article, leaning over the table. 'Who is Porteur? How many are there under the age of thirty, young people of both sexes, who pronounce that name with a strange fervour? Two thousand?—ten?—perhaps even more. It is too soon to attempt to give even an approximate figure, while myth and reality still do battle around this curious personage. Let us at least try to discover the significance of the new-born legend. It is not an easy matter. Hearing that there was a Porteur group at the university college in the Rue d'Ulm I went there to interview them, but the young gentlemen turned their backs on me with disdain. One of them, however, was so kind as to remark over his shoulder that I could take my notebook, my camera and my stinking carcass elsewhere because I'd never find out anything about Porteur. . . .'

I had reached this point in my reading when Porteur got up and left the room. I heard the outer door of the apartment open and shut. But there was nothing unusual in this. He was in the habit of going off abruptly, without a word to anyone. Valérie and I thought nothing of it when he had still not returned at eleven, when we went to bed. It was not until six o'clock the next morning that I heard the news of Porteur's death. His body had been found in a street in the Saint-James quarter of Neuilly, beneath the surrounding wall of a house which was that of Lormier. He had received a charge of shot in the back which, according to the police doctor, must have killed him instantly. The inquiry produced no evidence and was soon dropped. We heard nothing from the ex-minister.

Michel had always been indifferent to matters of religion, but having received proof of the existence of God I thought it well that he should be buried according to the rites of the Church. After the ceremony Valérie and I returned home in company with the youth in the green shirt. When we entered the living-room he went to the writing-table and laid his hand on the blotting-pad where Porteur's hand had so often rested. I read aloud, before giving it to him, the scenario on love which my brother had begun to write.

*   *   *

PAGES WRITTEN BY PORTEUR ON THE AFTERNOON
PRECEDING HIS DEATH

View of a rectilinear corridor with no end. The doors on the left-hand side bear odd numbers, those on the right-hand side even numbers. Now and then one of the left-hand doors opens and a young woman appears and with her eyes turned upwards plays a tune on a mouth-organ. A door opposite opens and a man emerges. They exchange smiles and go into her room. In the foreground Porphyre, aged 23, comes out of room 127, that of a young woman. His own room is No. 14. He is naked to the waist, wearing jeans that come halfway down his calves and carrying his sandals and tie in his hand. His room, separated from that of his neighbour by a low partition, has no wall on the street side. He sits on his bed, adjusts his tie—a bow, which he fixes round his neck with elastic—and puts on his sandals. Across the street is the bedroom of the Norberts. He observes the couple asleep and watches with interest as the wife awakes. His next-door neighbour, Sylvestre, puts his head over the partition and asks Porphyre if he wants to get married. What attracts Porphyre about marriage is the thought of only working every other day. The three hours five days a week which he spends at the office seem to him interminable. Meanwhile Madame Norbert has got up and is taking a shower while her husband still lies asleep. A bus pulls up at the curb, three feet from Porphyre's room. He gets in at the same time as Madame Norbert who has crossed the street in a short skirt and a brassière. They sit facing one another. Both open the food locker under their seats. He eats a sausage and she a bunch of radishes. They begin to chat. 'You have a nice behind,' he says. 'You think so? You're not so bad yourself.' 'I'd like to go to bed with you.' 'I'd like it too, but it would be wrong. As you know, I'm married.' 'So you are, I'd forgotten. Where do you work?' 'In the Ministry of Literature.' 'Well, I get out before you, I'm in the Office of Architecture, but I've got to look in at the Truth Centre.' 'That's a good idea. I'll come with you.'

The Truth Centre is a large, glass-paned rotunda in the centre of which is a raised dais with steps leading to it. Two men and three women are ahead of the new arrivals. A woman goes on to the dais, stays there a few seconds and then returns pursing her lips. A man follows her. He at once rises six feet into the air and sinks back to earth. The woman after him rises eighteen feet into the air amid murmurs of applause. The next one stays on the ground. Porphyre, when it is his turn, rises nine feet in the air. But Madame Norbert, although she flaps her elbows in an effort to take off, remains firmly earthbound.

'I don't understand,' she says as they go out. 'I'm absolutely faithful to my husband.'

'Well, you see what comes of it. We'll go into the matter some time if you like.'

Porphyre sits down in his office, puts a helmet on his head, plugs it in and starts up a machine which traces a graph on a roll of paper. A girl of twenty-two comes in. 'I'm the new secretary. My name is Norma and I live in the unmarried corridor, No. 3833.' 'Glad to meet you, Norma. Just let me finish this graph and I'll be with you. You can be getting undressed.' Norma starts undressing. Porphyre stops the machine, takes off the helmet and unrolls the graph. A man of forty enters, also stripped to the waist but wearing a black bow tie and a decoration tattooed on his left breast. He looks at the graph and exclaims: 'But that's wonderful! That's terrific!' Norma, who still has her brassière on, turns round with a smile which rapidly fades. 'My dear Porphyre, you're making remarkable progress.' 'You think so, chief?' 'I think your sub-conscious has a great future. Won't you come to lunch tomorrow, Porphyre, at my house in Monbel?' 'I'd be delighted, chief, but I'm doing my military service every afternoon this week.' 'Well we'll have to make it next week.' The director goes out. Porphyre takes off his bow-tie and says to Norma, who is now stripped: 'You impress me very favourably. Come into the next room and I'll give you a test.'

The same afternoon—military exercises. Porphyre is dressed as he was in the morning except that he wears a high, conical forage-cap with stripes. He is in command of eight soldiers, boys and girls of twenty, all clad in civilian clothes and wearing forage-caps. The scene is a bare room undecorated except for a portrait of the Chief of State, bare-chested with forage-cap. The eight soldiers are sitting in two rows of leather armchairs each with a metal arm across it from which a dark-coloured knob projects. He puts a question: 'Soldier

Theodore, what should the projectile's trajectory be?' 'Orbital, colonel.' 'An excellent reply. We will now carry out the exercises. Get ready. Five—four—three—two—one—press! Splendid! You can all have an hour and a half's rest.' The soldiers get up and move towards the door, but Porphyre calls: 'Soldier Gertrude!' A tall girl with ample curves turns back and stands to attention in front of him. 'Soldier Gertrude, I have been most favourably impressed by your tactical ability.' To which Porphyre adds, taking off his bow. . . .

End of sketch of scenario by Porteur

★   ★   ★

It was during the week following my marriage to Valérie that I ran into Odette and heard from her that Valentine had got her degree.

I asked if she had seemed sad, if delight at her success had not been tinged with a veil of melancholy or a dampness in her eyes. Odette found the question surprising.

'Why should she be sad? There was certainly no sign of it when I saw her. She and her uncle came to her father's office the day the results were posted up, to tell him the news. I was there. She was in the highest spirits. The Minister and she danced a cha-cha all round the room. No, I'm sure she wasn't sad.'

Presumably it was natural that Lormier should not consider the death of the magician too high a price to pay for the transformation of his daughter. But Valentine? No doubt she had too much sense to burden herself with the memory. I walked a little way with Odette, who asked how I liked the job she had found for me. It was far less important than the one I had had with Lormier, but it satisfied my modest ambitions. I missed Jocelyne most of all, her tender and generous heart.

I think if I had stayed with S.B.H. I should have ended by falling in love with her, despite her plainness.

'Tell Jocelyne I often think of her.'

'She'll be glad. She's very fond of you. I'm so happy for her. She's getting married soon to a young chemist who lives in the same house.'

We parted by the church of Saint-Augustin. When I got home I found my wife talking to Sonia Bouvillon, who had come to supper with us. I had not seen her for more than three months. Seeing her now in a summer dress, her face warm and tranquil, her arms dimpled, I thought without displeasure of that evening when I had taken her in my arms.

'Tatiana has gone off in the car with her husband,' she said. 'Alain has three weeks leave. He picked her up in Tonnerre, the little town where we've been living for three months, and took her on into Italy. So I came back to Paris. They've been gone a week now, and I'm worried for the future. On the day they left, while he was in the lavatory, Tatiana said to me, "I must say, I'm afraid he's a bit of a square." Oh, I know what she meant. He's handsome and always well turned out and all correct and in good order and sticks to everything he says and proud too, Volodia, so proud that you'd think he had a corset for his figure and another for his voice and another for his mind. And I look at him and I listen and it reminds me of my poor Adrien—may he forgive me if he can hear what I'm saying!—but Adrien with a college education, and you can't think how much worse that makes it. You'd think he rode on horseback through life and always liable to spit in the faces of the people who go on foot. Since they were married Tatiana has only been seeing him once a week, when he came to Tonnerre on Saturdays. It makes me tremble to think that they'll be living together for the next three months, three weeks in Italy and the rest in Paris. But what reassures me a little is that he has eyes, well I don't know how to describe them, hot eyes, the sort that bring warmth to a woman's face when he looks at her, and when I say face that isn't exactly what I'm thinking. And you know, eyes like that, they make me think of a man who used to live in Kharkov, a shy little schoolteacher with a high, stiff collar, and he——'

'The one who engaged Mariushka to do his house work?'

'Oh, have I told you?'

'No. You started to several times, but then you went on to something else.'

'Well, I'll tell you now. His name was Panteley Kolyshkin and he had eyes like that. And Mariushka, well she wasn't so bad-looking but she never smiled, always a scowl on her face, and so big and strong that the men were afraid to say a word to her, which may have been the reason for the scowl. I remember that time when Kolyshkin met her in my father's shop to make arrangements with her. Mariushka had been doing our washing in the yard and she came in with her arms hanging and her hands all red and wet. That little schoolteacher, he was smaller than she was, he looked at her and a flame darted in his eyes and he flushed all over his face, and there was Mariushka standing with her eyes lowered and he asked her if she would come at five every evening to clean up for him. She said she would. And now listen. Mariushka's husband was a prisoner-of-war in Austria and he never wrote to her because he didn't know how to write. And they had a boy of twelve whose name was Volodia, and he was simple-minded. Well one night when he was hungry Volodia the simple-minded went up to the schoolteacher's rooms and called to his mother through the door. And Mariushka came out and—her own child, mark you!—she threw him downstairs saying, "Clear out, son of a pig!" The next day when she came to do our washing my mother asked her what she was up to with the schoolteacher, and she turned away her head and without looking at her she said, "Maria Stepanovna, you don't want me to do the washing and scrub floors any more and I'm leaving." Four days running Mariushka went to clean up for the schoolteacher at five o'clock, and the neighbours watched and saw her leave at ten o'clock at night and they said it was a disgrace to a respectable street. And now listen, the fifth day Mariushka arrived just as usual. The summer had come suddenly and I remember it was very hot. Alexandra Gavrilovna, the baker's old aunt, had gone upstairs to lie down, but first she went and leaned on the window-sill to get a breath of air. And suddenly she uttered a great cry. The schoolmaster appeared at the window of his room on the second floor across the street, and he was waving his arms and Mariushka came up behind him and took his neck in her two great hands and strangled him. He fought and struggled, but then his tongue stuck out and it was over. And Mariushka, I oughtn't to tell you this but I must, she undid her blouse and pressed his head with its tongue sticking out against her big, naked breasts, as big as its fashionable for them to be in these days. So that is how he died, Panteley Kolyshkin, the shy little schoolteacher with a high, stiff collar.'

'Talk about cinema!' said Valérie. 'But why did she have to strangle him?'

'Because she'd found out that he was friendly with another woman.'

Valérie got up saying that that was taking things bloody seriously. While she was in the kitchen Sonia said to me in a lowered voice:

'Oh, Volodia, I'm so ashamed. Tatiana particularly asked me to tell you that she'll be back in a fortnight. She wants you to come and see her.'

'Of course. I should love to.'

Sonia gazed hard at me for some moments, wondering if I had grasped the true purport of the message. Being reassured she heaved a deep sigh.

'Tatiana will be the death of me. Oh, and there's another

thing. I've just been to see poor Jules Bouvillon and he told me about his manuscript being burnt. He's so sad. All those years of work. He gave me his word of honour that he had proved the existence of God. Volodia, is that possible?'

'Well yes, it's true. God does exist.'

'Oh, I've always been afraid of it, but I hoped for the best. One can't help hoping.'

Anxious for her daughter, anxious for herself, Sonia broke down and wept. But fortunately God soon vanished from her thoughts. She settled down to tell me the story of Rodion the ne'er-do-well who reduced his mother to beggary and ended by making a very rich marriage through stealing an ikon and a pot of jam.

MARCEL AYMÉ

Marcel Aymé was born in the town of Joigny, France, in 1902. He completed his first novel, *Brûlebois*, before he was twenty. *Table aux Crevés*, published in 1929, won the Théophraste Renaudot award as the best novel of the year. For forty years M. Aymé has been writing novels, plays, essays, literary criticism and short stories, as well as books for children. Among his works translated into English and published in America are *Across Paris*, *The Green Mare*, *The Magic Pictures*, *The Transient Hour*, *The Wonderful Farm* and, most recently, *The Proverb and Other Stories*.